SINISTER
SISTERHOOD

JANE BADROCK

Cover art by dave@hmdesigners.com

Cover design by BAD PRESS iNK

ISBN: 978-1-9160845-2-0

published by www.badpress.ink

Dedicated to my late sister Gillian Walker,
who in her youth, picketed a fairground stall
which was giving out goldfish for prizes

CHAPTER ONE

Beautiful Beginnings and Badass Bookkeeping

Many years ago, somewhere in the garden of England, a sweet little ten-year-old boy called David Swallow was spending a glorious summer's day in a terribly English way in the company of the little girl he had just fallen in love with. To him, she looked like a little angel with tumbling blonde locks and bright blue eyes; the prettiest thing he had ever seen. And so he called her Angel and it stuck because it fitted her so well.

David was a true nature boy and delighted in showing his six-year-old companion the exquisite sights to be found in the woodlands in summer. And she, from her city background in smoky old London, watched him adoringly and followed his every move. First, they paddled in a little brook and caught sticklebacks in jam jars; just to look at, mind – David insisted they be returned to the stream. Then they stalked butterflies and David taught her the names of every one they saw. He pointed out mushrooms and berries, telling her which ones they could eat and which they couldn't. He shushed her, and they saw a little faun scampering off to find its mother. Over there a rabbit, here a squirrel, up there – songbirds and buzzards. The little girl took it all in with wonder and never forgot a moment of that special day.

Finally, exhausted and knowing that they had to be home very soon (lest their parents, who were having tea together, be

cross), David made his pledge. He picked some daisies and made a garland to go around Angel's neck, and wove a crown of buttercups for her head. He swore that he loved her and would marry her as soon as he was old enough, and they would live together in the woods forever. He kissed her shyly on the cheek, and she told him she loved him too.

They heard calling. Only then it wasn't a voice calling; it was a shrill ringing sound and the little girl was torn from her idyll; pulled from the grass, out of the woods, round the corner, over the hill, dragged through many years and finally back up Memory Lane to the ringing of a telephone.

'Good afternoon,' she shook her head awake. 'Damned right we will.'

In another place, but not so far away, Beryl sat at her home office desk filing her nails and waiting for a call. She had recently parted company with an agency due to a complaint about her behaviour but, obviously, she couldn't tell the new agency that. She had found this agency from a strangely placed advert in the paper. They had readily accepted her story about her poor mother's recent demise which had freed her up for work again after a long spell of being a carer. In fact, they had set up a short assignment for her almost immediately and, naturally, she excelled. After that, she had been called in to the head office for a full and thorough assessment with the head of the agency herself; a formidable lady called Ms Elle Scarlett. Strangely, the assessment had been done with Ms Scarlett sitting behind a screen. Beryl guessed that it was a two-way screen but she couldn't be sure.

The psychometric tests she had been given surprised her. She was clever enough to know that there was an agenda behind the questions, but not quite proficient enough to spot all the pitfalls. Nonetheless, she had seemingly passed with flying colours

and had been promised a very exciting and rewarding contract. Now, looking at the telephone, as if by magic, it rang. She listened carefully and nodded enthusiastically.

'Monday. Nine o'clock? Ask for Mr Porcine. Right you are. And you'll email me...' After the undercoat to her nails had been applied and dried, she looked at her emails. 'A pork packing company,' she recited. 'This is going to be very meaty indeed.' She began to read through the details with relish, now and then making notes in her tiny red leather-bound notebook. Being exceptionally efficient, she also searched the internet and studied everything she found on one Ernest Porcine, before squashing his digitised face under the lid of her laptop and smiling contentedly to herself.

It was Friday evening and Beryl began to prepare, leaving nothing to chance. She swept open her double-doored wardrobe, exposing a perfectly colour-coordinated assemblage of blouses, jumpers, cardigans, skirts, and dresses, coupled with a collection of shoes which would have made Imelda Marcos partly swoon, partly vomit. Item after item was scrutinised and checked. A blouse discarded; a skirt moved a couple of places along; a dress extracted for hand washing; a pair of shoes pulled out for polishing. This will do for now, she decided confidently. There's always time for shopping whether it's necessary or not.

The remainder of Beryl's weekend was spent working out; not her body – that was already rounded to perfection. She needed to practise her facial expressions, her postures and her appearance. All were filmed with her appropriately-placed camera then examined and retaken until at last, she believed she could even fool herself. The final touches were a new hair colour, bleached teeth and some major depilation, all pulled together with a light spray tan.

Monday morning Beryl was up and dressed ready for action.

3

Turning to look at herself in the mirror, she smiled and wiggled her bosom against her crisp white blouse with the slightly dodgy middle button. Then she put on her thickest framed glasses and left her bedroom, pausing to flick the light switch before stepping flinchingly into her sensible lace-ups. At 8:55 precisely she was outside the office of Porkers Packing Plc. She rang the bell and cooed into the answering buzz. 'Cheryl Smythe, bookkeeper, here for Mr Porcine.' As the door bleeped, she pushed at it, taking care to whip off her glasses and smile winningly at the camera as she went in. She walked smartly up to the young receptionist's desk and spoke charmingly to her. 'Good morning. Pleased to meet you.' The receptionist looked up, disinterested.

'Cheryl Smythe?' Beryl nodded. 'Take a seat and I'll ring him.'

'But before you do,' Beryl began earnestly, 'Could you tell me something about Mr Porcine please? I've found that often it's best to talk to other staff members just to get an idea of what the boss is like.' The receptionist gave her a strange look.

'I'm sorry, my dear.' Beryl looked away, ashamed. 'I didn't mean to talk out of turn. Heavens! What will you think of me?'

'It's all right,' the girl whispered to her. 'Call me Caroline.'

Beryl turned back, just seeming to blink the faintest tear from her eye. Caroline was smiling sheepishly. 'I'm sure you'll be all right, Cheryl,' she whispered. 'He's a bit of a ladies' man if you know what I mean. If there's a chance later on I'll...'

Before Caroline had finished the sentence, the big door at the end of the corridor flung open and an impatient-looking rotund man with red cheeks and a comb-over strode up the corridor towards them both. He took one almost-scowling look at Beryl and without any introduction, he snarled, 'I hope you're better than that last woman they sent. Right sourpuss she was.'

Beryl gave him her best simpering smile. 'I do my best, sir.'

'This way then.'

Beryl followed him back to his office, flashing a quick, nervous

glance back at Caroline. She crossed her fingers, waved them in the air for Beryl to see and smiled sweetly at her.

Ernest sank into his big pink leather-cushioned chair, nodding at Beryl to sit opposite. He stared at her for a moment, giving Beryl time to wonder if, should he disrobe, she would be able to tell where the chair ended and he began.

'Now see here,' he began with authority. 'That last woman, she, well, let's just say she had a vivid imagination. She had ideas that I had designs upon her. Now let me tell you...' He searched on his desk for the paperwork. 'Let me tell you, Miss Smythe, I am a happily married man and I'm well fed at home thank you very much. I don't need to stray.' And in that moment, he was being totally sincere; Beryl seemingly had nothing to offer him.

'Gracious me, of course!' she exclaimed. 'I wouldn't dream...' she soothed. 'Let's get on to the matter in hand then. Now, about these books...' Beryl reached for her handbag and took out her ordinary black notebook and pen, but unfortunately, she dropped the pen. As she bent down, she accidentally popped that mischievous button and as she blushingly did it up again, she just caught Ernest's eyes staring at her cleavage and smiled to herself. Now she knew she could save the cow eyes and hair flick for later.

As it turned out, Ernest was away on business for the rest of the week but he gave Beryl access to his intranet work diary so that she could contact him if needed. He'd also shown her round her office which was linked to his by a communicating door. It was small but well equipped and most importantly, completely private. Beryl was delighted; much better to have her own space, although she did pride herself on being able to manage with whatever resources she was given. Better still, she no longer had to wear the glasses or the sensible shoes while Ernest was away and she was itching to look around the place. Her very first reconnoitre was to survey the external premises in their entirety. She had absolutely no doubts about her abilities to do the job, but she did need to

ingratiate herself with as many staff members as possible for her plan to work.

Tuesday morning, she made a point of taking a short but productive walk around the plant in her lunch hour. As she went out of the front door, she heard a wail above her.

'Oi, you down there. I need a P!'

'Gracious,' Beryl replied to the man in overalls up the ladder. It was pretty obvious what he meant when she realised he was trying to replace a couple of the letters above the factory entrance, but having an extraordinary ability to blush at will, she was very soon a delicate shade of puce. The man scuttled down the ladder, taking his cap off as he reached the bottom, and almost bowed.

'Err, so sorry, miss. I thought that little scamp John was down here. I was talking letters you know.'

Beryl smiled sweetly. 'I know now,' she whispered. 'It was just a bit of a surprise.'

'No offence?' The man asked.

'Absolutely not,' replied Beryl. 'May I introduce myself?' She paused for his nod.

'My name is Cheryl. I'm the new bookkeeper. Temporary, for now anyway.'

Half an hour later, Beryl knew almost everything there was to know about Kevin the head of maintenance, including his bank account details. But more importantly, she had also learned a little more about Ernest Porcine.

Beryl worked late that evening and saw Bert the security guard as he came by on his rounds. 'I remember you from the camera,' he exclaimed. All it took was a coy smile from Beryl and in a jiffy, she knew all about Bert's troubles at home with his wife. 'My missus likes to eat early,' Bert began. 'But this blimmin' shift means I don't get home till nine. If only I could nip home, have my

tea and come back... well that would be perfect.' Beryl listened sympathetically.

'I'm sure something could be worked out,' she mused. 'Maybe when I get to know Mr Porcine a little better...' Bert was rattled.

'Don't you go to that man on my account. Don't say I said, but he's a wrong'un and no mistake.' Beryl nodded wisely.

'Well maybe I can help anyway,' she said, smiling sweetly.

While Ernest was away exercising his wallet to keep him in female company, Beryl was pleased with her progress. She had dealt efficiently with all the business demands and most especially meeting the key staff members. Tom Higginbottom was next on her list and the most important. He was the supervisor of the processing plant. Beryl spied him sitting on a bench outside the factory that lunchtime and introduced herself.

'I'm Cheryl, the new bookkeeper.'

'Clever lady,' Tom replied. 'Never one much for figures meself. I'm more handy with me hands.'

'And that is something I've never been,' Beryl mused, holding out her hands expressively. 'I'd love to be able to do more with my hands than just type and add up. I've always wanted to be able to mould things with my hands.' Tom's eyes widened at her gestures.

'I'm sure you could do anything you put your mind to.'

Before long they were chatting like old friends – or at least, Beryl was listening intently to him; especially the bits about the cutting machinery. Tom, who had continued without interruption, was very impressed and somewhat taken with Cheryl.

'It's not all women that are interested in my job. Normally it's a turn off, I'm told.'

'I find it fascinating,' Beryl gushed honestly. 'How a whole carcass can be turned into all the cuts with such precision. And then you use all the other bits to automatically make sausages. So

perfect, everything is used almost without any intervention at all.'

'Aye. We do have the latest technology. I'll give Mr Porcine that; he does know how to spend his money to make money. In his father's day, there'd have been lines of men and women chopping away...'

'Very impressive,' Beryl replied. 'I do like big plants and machinery.' She smiled sweetly at him. 'And a jumbo sausage.'

At that, various organs were activated, especially Tom's pounding heart. Respite came courtesy of Beryl's ringing mobile; one of her preprogramed precision calls to herself. 'I'm so sorry Tom, I must take this,' Beryl smiled and got up to move away. Tom nodded with relief and crossed his legs firmly, trying to stop his face from going beetroot; it was a long time since any woman had affected him quite like this Cheryl one. She didn't look particularly sexy, he noted, but by God, she could get his juices going. Beryl, the very picture of innocence, merely walked to the end of the path with a slow, knowing sway of her ample buttocks, then went back into her office and sat at her desk.

She looked around furtively as if someone was watching her, and she wasn't wrong.

Somewhere else, a thin hard-faced woman was watching a screen. 'How's she coming along, Elle?' said a voice behind her. 'Any good?'

'She's doing quite nicely,' Elle replied. 'I think she might be an asset. Maybe even one of the best.'

Beryl had been invited to the pub for girls-only drinks that evening. It was Caroline's birthday and Beryl went along happy to join in but held her tongue while waiting for the Snakebites to loosen the others'. She was not disappointed. After pleasantries had been

exchanged, all the conversation revolved around Ernest Porcine and his foibles.

'Gracious! I'm sure he can't be that bad. He was perfectly polite to me,' Beryl exclaimed.

'I bet he ogled your boobs,' someone said.

'Don't ever bend over, or he'll accidentally brush past you with his fun-sized Mars bar,' another added. Caroline herself was more circumspect.

'This is why I've only invited us girls,' she stated. 'He's tried it on with all of us, one way or another, and that poor Mavis...' Before long, Beryl had found out all about poor Mavis; how Ernest had sacked her when she refused to play with his porker and how he'd stitched her up, accusing her of stealing from the company.

'Why on earth do you still work for him?' Beryl asked, genuinely perplexed.

'There's not many employers around here,' another girl piped up. 'It's all right for them that's got qualifications, like yourself, but for us locals, there's not much of a choice.'

'That's awful,' said Beryl sincerely. She went home that night and typed up her notes. She always tried to ignore superfluous office gossip and maintain a professional distance, but this man was clearly a pig in every sense of the word. She reviewed her plan and decided to raise it to level three.

Friday afternoon brought Beryl her first real crisis. One of the biggest suppliers, and he really was big, hadn't been paid on time and he was very angry. Caroline rang Beryl to warn her that Farmer Styes was on the warpath.

'I've told him Mr Porcine's not here but he wouldn't...' Beryl heard Caroline's pleas at the other end of the phone. 'No Farmer Styes, you can't go in there...' Sure enough, just as the conversation tailed off, Beryl heard a loud thudding noise followed by her door bursting open so hard it popped a hinge. She held back her shock very well as she turned round and looked the

intruder over. This was a monster of a man; ruddy-faced, bald on top with ginormous orange sideburns and dressed in a checked suit big enough to play giant chess on. He made Ernest look like a chipolata in comparison.

'My goodness!' Beryl clutched her chest like a maiden about to be ravished.

'Eh?'

'Can I help you, sir? I am Cheryl Smythe, the new bookkeeper.' Felled by her voice, the farmer stopped in his tracks and took in the loveliness of Beryl, sans spectacles and with heaving ample bosom. King Kong morphed into a lovesick puppy in an instant.

'Oh, my dear,' he slimed, 'I do beg your pardon. I was looking for that bas— was looking for Mr Porcine. Is he in?'

'Please sit down,' said Beryl, pointing to the visitor's chair and hoping he would fit in it. 'Mr Porcine is away on business. He won't be back until Monday. Can I be of any assistance?' Farmer Styes was so taken aback he was quite unable to speak. 'Shall I check your account with us?' Beryl asked helpfully. There was still silence as the poor man went from pink to purple. When he began puffing, Beryl walked a very slow jiggly sort of walk to the water fountain just outside her office and came back with a glass of ice-cold water. If she had thrown it all over him, Farmer Styes wouldn't have minded one bit. Instead, he took the cup from her and knocked it back in one.

'Never you mind, miss,' he spluttered when some of his senses had returned. 'It can wait till Monday.'

'Are you sure?'

'Will you still be here?' he simpered.

'I will,' she nodded. Farmer Styes got up and without another word left the office a good deal slower than he had arrived. Beryl, when she was sure he had gone, gave a tiny sigh of relief. But only a very small one. Big suppliers – and he was one of the biggest – were invaluable.

Beryl was still working at knocking off time when Bert the security guard came round. 'I'm so sorry,' she explained when she saw him. 'Farmer Styes came in and made me a little behind.'

I wouldn't call it little, Bert thought to himself, *nice and rounded!* 'He can be a bit tricky. I hope he didn't upset you?'

'No,' Beryl smiled. 'I'm fine, but I wanted to make sure I locked up properly. I know the factory is open tomorrow, but the office is closed isn't it?'

'Don't you worry Miss Cheryl, I'll sort it,' Bert assured her.

'I was just thinking,' Beryl pondered. 'Perhaps you should show me what to do. Then, if you like, you can nip off for your tea. I don't mind working late.' Before Bert could say *Security* he was giving Beryl a guided tour of the whole site including, thanks to her photographic memory, all the code numbers to the safe and access points to the factory. Then, dashing off home, he left Beryl to savour the experience.

Bert was very apologetic when he returned an hour later. 'I'm sorry Miss Cheryl. I should have let you get home. I'm sure you've got lots to do. Husband? Kids?' He began to inquire, but Beryl put him right.

'My personal life never, ever,' she looked at him almost sternly, 'gets in the way of my professional life. So never you mind about that.'

'Right you are,' replied Bert, a little dumbfounded. He had never met anyone quite like her before.

Beryl said a charming, 'Goodnight,' and dropped the spare set of keys he had so adoringly handed her, carefully into her handbag. Then she headed off to The White Horse where she had a very important appointment of her own with someone from the agency for her first week's debriefing.

That someone had taken great delight in reading the results of

Beryl's psychometric tests. 'Devious, conniving, untruthful and loyal only when absolutely necessary,' was the conclusion, and this was looking very promising.

At seven o'clock precisely, Beryl walked into the pub and looked around. She had no idea what Ms Scarlett even looked like; all the face to face stuff had been done with an underling. Going further in she saw a strange-looking, impossibly thin figure dressed in black. Her face was stern and she had the sort of eyes that could burn right through you. She nodded at Beryl, who tentatively walked over to join her at the table.

'Good evening, Cheryl Smythe,' the woman said. 'Or should I say, Beryl Braithwaite?' Beryl gulped and sat down.

Later that night, a shell-shocked and dazed Beryl arrived home to kick off her shoes and reach for the gin. She knew there was something odd about the agency, but never in her wildest dreams would she have thought... Now she had two choices. She could leave now, making her excuses to Mr Porcine and try another, rather more normal agency. However, she had been told very clearly that there would be serious *Implications* if she did. By that, Beryl assumed that she would not get a reference. Well, she'd been there umpteen times. New alias, new fake passport – not really a problem; except that she'd done it a little too often and was now treading a very thin line.

The other choice was to stick with the agency, but she had no idea what this meant either; it was all far too vague. She was expected to carry on as if nothing had happened. She would get her wages as usual, but then there would be a deal to be struck. This felt a little like protection money to Beryl. On the other hand, they did apparently offer a great deal of protection. What had upset her most was that they seemed to know not only everything she'd done at Porker's, and everybody she'd spoken to, but they'd hinted at some of her earlier escapades as well. They had even mentioned Billy. So spooked was Beryl by this that she stripped

off, pausing briefly to admire her generous proportions in the mirror, before checking every single piece of clothing for bugs. But no, there was nothing to be found; even under her special microscope. Slipping into something genuinely more comfortable, she found temporary solace eating a pizza in front of the TV before slowly nodding off on a gentle haze of alcohol, just waking in time to crawl into bed. Beryl never slept on sofas.

Elle Scarlett was also having an unsettling evening sitting in her flat. It wasn't Beryl she was worried about; that situation looked very promising indeed. Instead, she was embarking on her Five-Year Plan revision, but this year it happened to correspond to her fortieth birthday. This wasn't any common old mid-life crisis; this was major stuff. She was the owner and manager of one of the most successful employment agencies in London – well, it was if you counted all the black-market money, but that wasn't the point. Her business goals were meant to be her life goals and, once again, she'd gone off track. It was time to move things forward and hit forty running.

CHAPTER TWO

Billy 'Big Nose' Brannigan Butts In

Beryl had not yet come to her own conclusions; Saturdays were too busy to allow time for worry. Years of practise allowed her to always switch off at weekends subject to overtime (legitimate or otherwise). Sundays too were precious and devoted entirely to chores, but as the evening drew on, Beryl knew decision time had arrived. Gazing in the mirror, her forty plus years were showing and took longer and longer to disguise. She reckoned she didn't have that long before she would have to become, well, a bookkeeper, and she wanted so much more than that. Just one more con, but a really big one would do it. She turned round and spoke to her favourite person.

'My dear woman,' she said to the Beryl in the mirror. 'You're too young to be frumpy. Live a little. Give the agency a whirl. What can go wrong? It can't be worse than...' she gave a little shudder, then toasted herself in the mirror.

'Cheers,' her reflection responded. 'We'll take a punt and see where it takes us.'

'I agree,' Beryl replied. 'You only live once.'

Monday morning, Beryl was back to full confidence. She had rung the agency at the appointed hour and had been given an

enthusiastic response.

'Welcome on board, Beryl, and well done. This could be the most exciting move of your life. There is something really big coming up and you will receive a reward greater than anything you could imagine anywhere else.'

It required a great deal of skill for Beryl to return to the boring, dowdy bookkeeper in time for Ernest's return to the office. The bottle-bottomed glasses usually helped her get in the mood, and they certainly worked for Ernest. When he put his head round the door to check she was there, he took one look and scuttled back to his office. *No bad thing*, he decided, having had his full wallet's worth of fun the previous week. *But not sure I can put up with that for long*, he thought.

Beryl knuckled down for the week and this time began to implement some changes.

She made the invoicing easier and more efficient, changed some long-standing errors on the payroll system and even paid off Farmer Styes. Her telephone call to him in her deep, throaty voice almost sent him into orbit. By the end of her second week, the whole factory was talking about her and how good she was, and Ernest was hearing all of it. He looked in on her on Friday afternoon, but couldn't bring himself to lavish praise on her. Instead, he remembered that he needed to go through the budgets and would have to deal with her then.

'Miss Smythe?' he asked, hardly bringing himself to face her. 'We need to look at budgets next week.'

'Yes, Mr Porcine,' Beryl replied. 'All in hand. My predecessor left a diary.'

'Very good,' said Ernest. 'Have a good weekend.'

Beryl packed up her things and tidied her desk. The glow she felt from throwing her lot in with the agency was beginning to dim. Why should she share her ill, but hard-gotten gains? She was also wondering how the agency knew so much about her. As she left

at her usual time, Caroline's cheery goodbye made her nose twitch just a little. Sadly, it didn't twitch quite enough to guess what was going on. It did, however, pick up the whiff of a filthy, smelly old tramp; probably hanging around the gate in the hope of leftover pies. She shuddered as she brushed past him and quickened her pace to get away as speedily as she could. This was probably a rare mistake on Beryl's part; had she looked a little more closely she would have spotted under the beardy growth and grime, the unmistakeable beak of Billy 'Big Nose' Brannigan.

Beryl thought Billy was well and truly consigned to her past. It never occurred to her that he was about to resurface in her life. She had met him in the days before he lost his fortune and his wife slung him out. His name was forever ruined and he became homeless, destitute, pathetic, dirty, and so smelly that people had been known to pass out in his presence. In fact, she had been responsible for that downfall, she remembered with a strong sense of pride. One of her best jobs ever. And he'd deserved it, the stinking rat. He had cheated on his wife, underpaid and overworked all his employees and he'd spilt coffee on her best Gucci suede shoes.

Billy had made it his only mission in life to find her; that terrible woman who had brought about his monumental crash from the dizzy heights of chairman of the board of Exploits Plc; the company which made a fortune out of mining huge mineral deposits from African tribal lands for a pittance. Once he'd had a private jet, loose women, stayed in the best hotels, gone on safaris; now he slept outdoors, travelled on foot, and the only game he saw were the rats and mice that gnawed at his toes. It was hard at first; she moved around a great deal and was careful to change her travel routes often, but Billy soon discovered that there was no cloak of invisibility better than the guise of a tramp. He was never challenged for tickets or asked for fares whether he was on the bus, underground or overground. Everybody simply gave him

room. Lots of room. In some ways, he had more freedom now than he'd ever had as a top executive and he used this newfound freedom to tail Beryl. It had taken him months to piece all the bits of the journey together, but now he had sussed her route from town to the factory. He knew where she worked – all he had to do was think through what he was going to do about it.

'I've got you now, Meryl Cuttleswaite,' he waved his fist at her as she walked away with her smartest wiggle-free walk. 'You and your posh ways and proper speaking. Oh yes. You and me have unfinished business. Er, I mean you and I. No I don't, you bitch, you've no hold on me now...' Billy watched Beryl until she was almost out of sight, and very slowly he began to smile to himself, cracking the crud around his mouth in a very unappetising way.

Beryl's weekend whizzed by uneventfully. There had been no further contact from the agency, which only strengthened her resolve to short-change them. Ernest's finances promised to be more lucrative than she'd first thought, but they wouldn't know that, how could they? She was doing all the hard work, so why should she give up half?

On Monday morning she prepared as usual; pleated grey skirt, white high-necked blouse, thick glasses and dumpy lace-up shoes. But then she added a little extra touch. Just a spray, but *what* a spray! Checking herself in the mirror, she smiled at herself before heading off to the office where she was about to receive a double surprise.

Beryl approached the front gates as usual, swiping her pass at the front door with a smile and a warm hello for everyone. She went straight to her office and sat down, but when she opened her personally-locked and sealed desk drawer she was shocked to see a bright yellow Post-it sticky with a note written in anonymous print. It was a timely warning message, but she was shocked that

her personal security been breached and she had to cover her surprise quickly – she was already catching the unmistakable waft of Ernest's aftershave in the building. Quick as a flash she pulled out her budget papers and assumed an air of complete efficiency.

'Good morning, Mr Porcine,' she said, as Ernest walked through her office door. Ernest stopped momentarily; something was different. He looked at Beryl, the same frumpy old witch he'd seen before, but there was an exotic fragrance playing with his olfactory senses and it was conjuring up visions inappropriate for the office. 'Yes, Mr Porcine?' Beryl persisted.

'Erm, Miss Smythe. Perhaps you could come into my office in, er, say, half an hour and we'll start on the budgets?' Beryl noted his flushing cheeks and the slight glaze of perspiration on his brow. Her tried and well tested 'All Woman' never failed.

'Of course, Mr Porcine.'

'Call me Ernest,' said Ernest, as he grasped at his neck to loosen his tie and headed into his office.

Beryl now had just enough time to contemplate the message as well as sorting out the budget papers. She wiped behind her ears with a moist wipe – she had Ernest's measure sure enough and didn't need to overdo it. When she went through the papers with him, it was plain old Cheryl Ernest talked to, and he was relieved, but also a tiny bit disappointed, that the stirring in his loins was not resuscitated. Nonetheless, it was a productive meeting and at the end of it they had a workable budget for the year ahead; something that poor old Mavis had never managed, Ernest noted.

'Thank you, Miss Smythe, that was very helpful. Please type it all up and I'll get it sent out to all budget holders.'

'Of course, Mr... er, I mean Ernest,' Beryl carefully replied. 'I will do it straight away.'

While Beryl went into autopilot on the budgets; she'd done a million of them before, her brain went into overdrive on how the message got into her drawer. *It had to be Caroline*, she said to

herself. *She must have master keys.* But how would she know about him? This led her to think about the actual warning. Nothing she hadn't been expecting, really; she could deal with it well enough; it was just a nuisance. Her brain was still ticking over as the budgets were put onto spreadsheets, checked, double-checked and printed off for Ernest's scrutiny. It was all complete by lunchtime and she took some rare time out. She opened the window and lit up a cigarette as she thought it through. She only ever smoked in times of real difficulty, and this was one of those times. When lunchtime came, she made a beeline for Caroline. 'I wondered if I might join you for lunch,' she said. Caroline smiled sweetly.

'I thought you'd never ask,' she huskily replied. *Oh shit!* Thought Beryl. Luckily for her, Bert the security guard had been passing at that exact moment. He was very familiar with Caroline's ways. He had never actually sussed her out; he clearly wasn't her type, so he'd had a grandstand view of her approach to others over the years.

'Cheryl!' he exclaimed loudly. 'Sorry to butt in but do you not remember we had an arrangement to look over the Sausage Museum this lunchtime?' In a briefly paused flash, Beryl replied.

'Silly me. Caroline, I am so sorry. Bert is trying to persuade me of the need for a new exhibition case as the Hungary Whopper display has suffered from a little too much wear and tear. Another time perhaps?' and before Caroline had time to pout, Bert had put his arm through Beryl's and whisked her out of the door.

As it happens, another person had also witnessed that exchange; someone even more invisible than a smelly tramp. The cleaner carried on polishing the brass door handles around reception, keeping her thoughts to herself.

While Beryl and Bert sat on the bench eating their sandwiches, Beryl sensed that he too had designs on her. He sat a little too close and talked a little too longingly about friendship. It

was time for her to confess to him. 'You see, I'm still hoping we'll get back together,' she began, dabbing her eyes. 'If only things were different...'

'I quite understand,' said Bert rather sadly, before stuffing the rest of his sandwich into his mouth. 'Better be off,' he said, and he walked away.

Beryl went back to her desk purposefully. Timing was everything and she had to start putting wheels in motion. Phase one was complete, phase two well underway, but preparations for the terminal phase were not quite finished. She took a few minutes out to stand by the window again, this time smoking a special cigarette recommended to her by an old teacher of hers. Clare had confided in Beryl at a school reunion that it was the only way she had ever got through her days at school, and Beryl very occasionally partook. Before you could say spliff, Beryl's action plan was formulated in her mind and all it needed was a little more investigation and a bit more enticement. The time had come to get closer to Ernest and find out what he was really worth. She positively rattled off her work for the rest of the day and spent the last hour finding her way through the office intranet and into Ernest's personal files which, like the man himself, were badly put together and very poorly concealed. She found personal details, and there was a great deal of very revealing correspondence about poor Mavis. There were contact numbers for his wife and family and, most important of all, the exact amount of personal cash he kept in the safe. Beryl's eyes widened with anticipation; there was more than enough to satisfy her. As for the agency, well, they would be none the wiser.

Tuesday morning, Beryl turned up at the office in a shorter skirt, skimpier top, lighter glasses and kitten heels. This would not have been enough for the typical man to notice, but to a randy deprived

old cad like Ernest, it was almost a come-on. He wondered how he hadn't noticed that she was quite attractive, and put it down to his escapades the week before wearing him out just a little. Now was not the time to look back; it was time to start his charm offensive. 'Miss Smythe,' he said.

'Call me Cheryl,' Beryl replied.

'You are looking nice today.'

'Thank you, Ernest,' Beryl smiled at him as if he had paid her the greatest compliment in the world.

'We need to do a little more work on the budgets tomorrow. Can you put something in our diaries?'

'Of course, Ernest,' she nodded, as he unlocked his office and went inside.

On Wednesday, Beryl was wearing a tight skirt which showed off her big round bottom to perfection, and the top three buttons of her blouse were left undone just enough to reveal some virginal white lace at the top of her bra. She wore higher heeled shoes and her sexiest glasses, ready to play the scene where the woman takes off her glasses, swishes her hair and the man says... well, you know the one. When the time came, she gently knocked on his door and went in. His eyes nearly popped out of his head and while he sat, flustered and stumbling, she double-checked every single inch of his office with her eyes.

'Miss Smythe, er, Cheryl,' Ernest stuttered. 'I wonder if you might like to have dinner with me tonight. Nothing improper, but I've found sometimes it helps to discuss things in a less formal setting. And we do have the annual plan to draw up. Beryl smiled at him and sat back, thrusting her bosom out just a little.

'What a good idea,' she said. But just as suddenly her face changed and she frowned. 'I'm so sorry Ernest. I've just remembered, I have to take mother to the community centre

tonight. Can we make it another day?' Ernest was not used to being turned down, but clearly this was not an occasion to pull out his wallet, so what could he say?

'Thursday then,' he said firmly but with a smile on his face. 'No excuses.'

'My goodness,' Beryl exhaled. 'You certainly know what you want,' she teased. Ernest choked a little and loosened the tie round his neck.

By Thursday, Beryl was nearly a sex goddess. She hid her charms on the way into the office under a thin cardigan, but by the afternoon the cardi was gone and Ernest could hardly keep his eyes off her. When the time came for dinner, Beryl walked her wobbliest into his office. Just as he opened his mouth to remind her of their date Beryl's mobile phone conveniently rang. She answered it and her face changed from gleeful anticipation to despair.

'It's mother,' she said. 'She's had a fall. The neighbour's with her at the moment, but I'm so sorry Ernest, I'll have to go as soon as I've tidied up.' Ernest was fit to burst.

'If you must,' he said, trying and failing to disguise his anger and disappointment. 'But you will be able to come out tomorrow, won't you?' he said. 'We have to do it on Friday.' This left Beryl in absolutely no doubt as to what 'it' was.

'Of course,' she purred.

'See you in the morning.' Ernest stormed off in a frustrated rage leaving Beryl in his office, which was quite handy as it meant she didn't have to sneak back again later on.

There was nothing wrong with Beryl's mother at all as far as she knew. The old bag had disowned Beryl many years before when she'd sussed her mother's benefits swindle at the local post office and had appropriated some of the payouts. Beryl had moved

onwards and upwards to much bigger swindles and had never looked back.

Now in position, she opened her handbag and took out the tiny camera which she placed inside the big cupboard in the corner, taking care to loosen one of the large cupboard handles. When she was sure everything was in place, she went home happy and excited. She loved the finale of her dramas; it gave her such an adrenaline rush. That night, just to get herself totally in the zone, she did a little more research to dot the i's and cross the t's.

Ever since her early days of petty larceny, life had taught Beryl a great deal, and what it hadn't, she'd studied. She could edit a film with perfection; was a reasonable hacker of office computer systems; could operate almost any sort of plant and machinery, and now she was becoming a master butcher. She'd studied the similarities of the anatomy of pigs and humans and what didn't quite match, she could put directly into the mince and bone grinder. And she had a complete set of factory keys courtesy of Bert. She could hardly sleep for the excitement.

On Friday, Ernest was pacing his office like a rampant lion awaiting dinner. Beryl was looking ravishing. All day they avoided each other – both knowing that their fun would begin precisely at five o'clock that afternoon. Friday was busy as always; it was the day when most suppliers rang to demand payment, and it was payday for the workers, so the day flashed by. Ernest had been surprised to see an appointment in his diary for four o'clock; an appointment with Farmer Styes no less, so he felt obliged to go. And while Farmer Styes was waxing lyrical about the luscious Beryl, the minx herself was finalising preparations. She opened the window for a last cigarette but before she lit up, she looked at the reflection in the glass and adjusted her hairpin just enough to let a sexy loose strand fall over her eyes.

Suddenly there was a strange noise behind her. She turned around and there was Billy 'Big Nose' Brannigan; now shaved and a little bit cleaner – thank goodness – halfway in through the open window.

'I've got you now, you bitch!' he shouted as he climbed in. 'Did you think I would let you get away with that, Meryl? You *BITCH*. You destroyed everything. My business, my family, my wife... Now it's my turn to destroy you!' Billy came towards Beryl brandishing a very large kitchen knife. Completely taken aback, Beryl shuddered and began to cry; girly, simpering little sobs. Billy stopped in his tracks; somehow, despite all that had happened, this unnerved him. Beryl sank to her knees with her head in her hands, running her fingers through her hair. Billy was almost touched.

'I'm so sorry Billy. So very sorry. It wasn't my fault. I was forced to do it. Do you really think that I...?' Billy put the knife down and walked towards her. *Could it be true?* He wondered; she had always been so sincere. His anger melted away and he walked towards Beryl, smiling at her. She really was irresistible. Beryl looked up, also smiling, then got up with lightning speed, turned round and plunged her hair pin straight into his heart. Billy froze. Literally. Beryl had coated her hairpin in some well-researched and practised noxious animal substance which caused instant paralysis.

'Yes, I'm so sorry, Billy,' she said, her sarcasm almost as cutting as her hairpin. 'Did you really think I wouldn't spot that conk under your filthy dirt and rags? And another thing I'm sorry about, Billy – I'm going to have to make you relive that awful experience all over again.' Billy could do nothing but stare straight ahead. 'You see,' Beryl continued, 'if I put you in here,' and she manhandled him through the door to Ernest's office, 'and into this cupboard...' She pushed him firmly inside. 'Just about here... you will not only be able to hear everything, you'll see it too – right through this

peephole, and you won't be able to look away.'

Billy said nothing. He did nothing. Obviously. But yes, he could hear and he sensed his blood going cold. Beryl had timed it to perfection as always. Less than a minute later, Ernest came in, earnestly.

'I can wait no longer, Beryl,' he said. 'You are driving me insane with your smouldering stockings and your luscious lips. Take me now!' Ernest began pulling at his clothes and bit by bit his pink flabby body was exposed until at last, he stood there wearing nothing but his socks. Beryl, however, was doing something strange. He looked her in the eyes and wondered why she was not responding. Then she breathed in and let out a loud scream, closely followed by another in the direction of the cupboard.

'You beast!' Beryl spat at him. 'I've told the agency about you already. You've got form, Ernest Porcine. Remember Mavis? You're a sex pest and I'm going to show the world what you've done!' Ernest stood still in complete shock.

'Beryl, my love? How could I have got things so wrong?'

'You brute!' she wailed. 'It's all on film. It'll be on YouTube tonight. I'll make sure you never ever do this to another woman.' A look of realisation slowly spread across Ernest's face.

'No, please don't, I didn't mean it... I'll do anything...'

'Anything?' said Beryl. Ernst nodded. 'Then that'll be two hundred thousand pounds in used notes, thank you very much,' she said. 'And a decent reference for Mavis,' she added, showing sisterly solidarity. Ernest knew he was well and truly caught and from his place inside the cupboard so did Billy – she'd pulled exactly the same trick on him. But he hadn't parted with the money, not him, he'd taken a gamble. So the woman he knew as Meryl had edited the video and made him out to be doing, well, all sorts of nasty things that naked men do with objects, animals, hoovers...

Pay up! He willed Ernest in his head. *Pay up!*

Ernest was a coward but a sensible one, and he did just that. He opened the safe behind his desk and wondered, as he counted out the wads, how it came to be that it was the exact amount of cash she had asked for.

'Now go home to your wife,' Beryl commanded. 'And if there is the slightest hint that you have been in touch with the police, I'll...' It had all happened so quickly, but Ernest knew he was beaten. He left the office, head held low, and wondered how his wife would react to him actually coming home on a Friday for the first time in years. He even contemplated buying flowers.

Inside the cupboard, Billy heaved a big sigh of relief. Everything had gone quiet. He'd heard the door close and expected he would just be left there until someone found him the next morning. After all, nobody would be looking out for him; a poor, friendless tramp with nobody in the whole wide world to care for him. Suddenly, the cupboard door opened and Beryl tied a blindfold round his eyes. She struggled a little moving him out of the office and towards the entrance to the factory door, but she was much stronger than she looked.

Then it was Beryl's turn to be shocked. One of the cleaners appeared out of nowhere. Beryl was momentarily frozen; she'd checked the rotas, no one was meant to be there. She wondered how the hell she was going to explain this and as the germ of an idea came to her and she opened her mouth to speak, the cleaner came straight up to them with the slightest hint of a smile on her face.

'I thought you might need a hand right about now,' she said, and she took one side of Billy while Beryl, still open-mouthed, managed the other.

'Why?' she asked.' Who are you?'

'I'm from the agency,' the woman replied.

'The Post-it note?' Beryl queried, to a nodding reply.

'And we've done our own research on this man. Ms Scarlett recognised him from her personal rogue's photo gallery.'

'Is that important?' Beryl queried.

'Oh yes,' the woman replied. 'Better take this,' she added, removing the hairpin from Billy's chest and putting it safely in her very special pocket.

'Well, if this is how the agency operates,' Beryl declared, 'You can count me in.'

As for maybe not-so-poor Billy, as soon as they got him into the processing room, he heard the unmistakable sound of heavy machinery starting up, and somebody making that sort of swishing sound when they sharpen a butcher's knife.

So who was the mysterious cleaner? What manner of outrage was this agency which encompassed office cleaning, bookkeeping, blackmail and murder? And who was the enigmatic Elle Scarlett? We have to go quite a way back in time to when it all began...

CHAPTER THREE

From Little Angels Mighty Elles Grow

Our young sweethearts Angel and David had kept in touch almost weekly by post. Angel spent all her spare time studying the local flora and fauna, which to be fair was almost non-existent in London, so that she could write to him about what she had seen and identified. She also became a vegetarian which irritated her mother considerably. Much as they longed for the occasional brief meetings when their respective parents met, destiny dictated they be separated. While Angel went on to a normal secondary, the gifted David had already been sent to a school in Sheffield which specialised in natural sciences. The gulf was soon revealed in their letter exchanges. 'I saw a fox by the dustbin today', was absolutely no match for 'Went on a field trip to Kenya', but still David remained constant and always wrote of the time when they would be married and live happily ever after. They met only once during those school years and it was a day Angel treasured in her memory. David, who was looking more and more handsome every day, remained sweet and attentive, keeping Angel in rapt attention as he told of his latest exploits. When he had finished talking, he looked her in the eyes and gave her an opal ring; not an engagement ring, but something to wear until he could afford one.

'I'm going away again,' he told her, 'but keep this to remember me by, my one true Angel.' Angel cried then but knew his career

was important to him. University took him further afield, his MA further still, but when he began studying his PhD, he was taken somewhere which began a series of incidents that would change his life forever. 'I'm going to The Andes,' he wrote to her. 'To study the rare Andean cat.' Whilst that encouraged Angel to start reading up about rare species, it was the last she heard of David for quite a while. It was also the making of him.

It was when David was high up in the mountains searching for the cat that he bumped into a presenter making a documentary with an accompanying film crew. This was no ordinary, 'Excuse me' – this was a catastrophic encounter. The presenter was completely at fault because he was dangerously perched on a rocky ledge without wearing his safety harness, mainly because he was an arrogant and vain sort of chap. David had also been standing on that ledge looking through his binoculars. In the distance some foliage moved and, thinking he'd seen a tail, David leaned forward carelessly – sending the presenter spiralling down several thousand feet. David was mortified.

'I'm so sorry,' he apologised charmingly to the film crew and the director who had now come up to the ledge see what had happened.

'It wasn't your fault,' the director replied, peering over, and as close to the edge as he dared. He looked back at David with a strange look almost of recognition. 'I say. Would you just look over there?' He pointed, and David obliged. 'Now this way?' David turned. 'Now can you just say these words, please? To camera?' He held up a board with the presenter's lines written on them and David read them out. The director nodded, smiled and turned to the crew. 'What do you think lads?'

There were appreciative, 'Yes, definitely' and, 'Born for it' responses.

'Well then,' said the director to David, 'how would you like a job as a presenter?' David was stunned.

'But I'm doing a PhD.'

'On what?'

'Endangered species.'

'Well then, that's just perfect. Even better to have an intellectual on board. We'll pay you well, and you can do even more research.'

While David pondered the offer, one of the more thoughtful members of the film crew raised the alarm and as the director and David were discussing terms, a helicopter arrived to search for the missing presenter. Amazingly he was found alive but in a very sorry state. He had hit several trees on the way down which had not only broken his fall, but also his back in several places. As he was hauled back up the mountain, both David and the director turned to look. The director walked over to him, leaned over his stretcher and said kindly, 'Don't worry, Mark, we've found a replacement for you now.'

Thus, David's television career began as the new presenter of *Animal Emergencies*. He was a natural; the camera loved him, the director loved him and most importantly of all, he had such a rapport with the animals that the films he presented took animal programmes to new heights – not just The Andes. He was sensational and the talk of the television industry.

By then, Angel – with three non-committally acquired A-levels – had just turned nineteen and was stunningly pretty but far too trusting. David had been the most sincere and loving person she had ever met so she believed in him absolutely. Her, *I'm taken* could be read by all young men and women at thirty paces and if anyone got closer, the opal ring on the third finger of her left hand was firmly waved in their face. Sadly, nobody told her that opals were often said to be unlucky.

It was her mother who pushed her into a job with a rude

demand for rent and expenses, so Elle signed up with the first employment agency she saw. 'I want a job working with animals,' she had specified. She was thoroughly assessed; her typing skills were adequate, her punctuation and grammar much better than average and she was clearly very bright, but it was her appearance which secured the job at the agency itself.

'Come and work here,' Mr Tadwell, the owner had said. There was nothing like a beautiful intelligent woman to bring in new clients. 'I can't promise you any work with animals around here. There aren't any. But it's interesting work, always varied, and if you're any good at recruitment, you can earn very good money.' Angel took this as a sign, which indeed it turned out to be, and readily accepted. It had saved her a great deal of time pursuing other options. She went happily home to tell her mother the good news.

'Good,' she said. 'That'll be twenty pounds a week bed and board.'

Angel settled in well but apart from looking out for opportunities to work with animals, of which there were precisely none, her determinedness not to progress became the source of much discussion in the office. It was a competitive environment and all of them, especially Mr Tadwell, saw her potential, but she resolutely kept to the junior duties – filing and admin around the office and the bun run on a Friday.

'There's no point me having a career,' she would say to the despair of the other women in the office and, it has to be said, the delight of a few of the men. 'I just want to get married to my wonderful man and have lots of animals and babies.' She would gaze at the photo on her desk showing a smiling David. As David's fame grew, so did the suspicions of her work colleagues that her boyfriend was probably a figment of her imagination, so nobody was prepared for what was about to happen.

One day, one of the lads brought in a copy of the latest *Tit-*

Bits and Tits. He could not help sniggering and the magazine was passed around to more sniggers from the men and squawks from the women. Angel couldn't help but notice the commotion it was causing.

'What is it?' she said innocently. One of the girls, looking extremely embarrassed, passed her the magazine open at the offending page. Poor Angel looked at it first in disbelief, then horror. 'But he never said...'

'Probably a letter in the post,' came a cynical voice from somewhere.

'I have to go.' Angel stood up so violently that her chair fell backwards with a loud clatter and she ran outside with the magazine tightly clenched in her hand, slamming the door behind her. The rest of the staff, who had never heard her say so much as 'That wasn't very nice' before, stood in shocked silence for a moment, looking after her.

'Bloody hell, I wasn't expecting that,' said the man whose magazine it was. 'I'm going to have to buy another copy now.'

Angel ran around outside looking for somewhere to sob. First, she sat on a bench in the high street, but the local weirdo came and sat next to her, so she hid in a telephone box until somebody started banging on the door. Finally, and tentatively, she went into the White Horse pub.

'What can I get you?' the barmaid began then, seeing Angel's distress, she asked, 'Are you OK?' Angel could hardly speak.

She showed the barmaid the article and whispered, 'That's my fiancé.' Without another word, the barmaid poured Angel a brandy.

'Here. On the house.' She came around the bar and led Angel to a small snug in the corner. 'You can tell me about it if you like,' she added, which was all Angel needed. It all came gushing out along with her tears, a great deal of snot, and spit. 'Have you got anyone else to talk to?' the barmaid asked, now being a little fed

up with being sprayed.

'My mother, but she's no use at all. I have an aunt somewhere, but she's not on the phone. And a cousin in Australia but we don't talk much.'

'Ah, but that's perfect,' said the barmaid, now desperate to get rid of the snivelling mess. 'She'll be able to give you a whole new perspective on it all. Go home now and ring her. You need family around you at a time like this.' Subtly, the barmaid manoeuvred Angel out of the pub, trying not to listen to her cries of, 'But he's a man!'

Angel had nowhere else to go so off she went home, pleased to find that her mother was not in – ringing Australia was strictly forbidden because of the cost. Angel looked through her mother's phone book and dialled her cousin. She got through almost immediately.

'Howdy, cuz. You ringing me about that pommy bastard? I saw the pics. Nice tits though.' At Angel's shrieks of grief, even he realised he was being a little insensitive. 'Aww Angel, don't cry. I always thought he was a shit and those programmes...' Angel's sobs made him stop. 'Look, why don't you go see the old gal. She's real good at all this relationship crap.' Angel stopped crying for a minute and thought of her aunt. She hardly knew her; this was the woman that her mother and father never talked about because they thought she was completely insane. What was more, she lived near a tiger reserve in an almost unreachable part of India. But as Angel continued to think about it, she realised that there was no place she would rather be.

'That is a good idea,' she said calmly. 'What's her address?'

Knowing that she had some holiday owing and had saved up quite a bit of money, Angel went to the post office and sent a telegram to her aunt asking if she could go out there.

Two days later, she got a reply. *Would be lovely to see you, dear. Bring cigarettes and Gordon's Gin.*

Angel finally set out on an adventure of her own. The actual location was pretty much kept secret since it was a tiger reserve, but her aunt's directions were clear. After a short flight from Delhi, she got out of the little Fokker 50 and walked down the steps into the searing heat of India. She had been terrified throughout the entire flight and was even more terrified now. *What on earth have I done?* she thought. It was about to get a lot worse. She was in the middle of nowhere! But then she heard a voice, almost obliterated by the noise of the jet.

'Elle? Is that you, Elle?' No one had called Angel that in years. She turned round and there, walking towards her at a brisk pace, was a strange woman in huge brightly coloured sunglasses, a pith helmet, khaki jacket and shorts, below which were a pair of securely tied, heavy walking shoes.

'Auntie Pat?' Angel asked in horror. Now she nearly was at the point where either one end or the other goes. Clenching and swallowing as her aunt approached, she looked behind her as if she might just run back onto the plane, but the steps had been removed and she therefore had no choice.

'Come here, child,' said Pat, managing a friendly, decent sort of hug. 'The wheels are in the car park over there. Hurry, we can't be late.' *Late for what?* Angel wondered. This thought soon changed to, *Are we even going to make it?* when she saw her aunt's old jalopy parked, as far as she could tell, in an open field. Actually it was an old Jeep to be precise, and despite its appearance, it was well maintained. 'Chop chop,' Pat said. 'Get your case.' Angel picked up her case and lugged it all the way to the Jeep. She was even more horrified when she got close to it; there was a chicken roosting in the back and all sorts of junk in the front: old bottles, cans, newspapers, bits of hose. Pat bundled some of it up and threw it in the back, setting the chicken off into a mad clucking. 'Can't disturb the poor old thing,' said Auntie Pat. 'Hetty's very choosy where she lays these days.'

The journey to Auntie Pat's villa wasn't much better. She only ever used the accelerator when they were going uphill. Downhill, to save on petrol, was done entirely by gravity and if it was a particularly steep hill, it was accompanied by a loud 'Whee!' with both her hands in the air. Had Angel dared take her eyes off the road ahead, she would have seen that she was in the most gloriously beautiful countryside. As it was, she was trying very hard not to puke. When Auntie Pat pulled up outside the villa, the outside looked about as promising as the back of the Jeep; there was junk everywhere. An old sink here, a rusting bike there, and chickens and geese running all over the place. 'Quick!' Auntie Pat hustled Angel indoors. She ran straight to the fridge, lobbing her helmet onto the hat rack as she went, took out a saucer with a half a lemon resting in some water and cut two slices. Then she poured out two large gins and topped them with a smidgeon of tonic. Finally, throwing some ice and the lemon in, she looked at the clock. It was thirty seconds to five. She handed a glass to Angel and said, 'Just in time. Bottoms up.' Angel looked at the glass in distaste. She had never drunk gin before, but there was nowhere else for her to go. She steeled herself, took a sip, and luckily she liked it. 'Now dear. Sit down and tell me your problem.'

Angel was very tired from her journey and had kept her tears in for quite long enough. The gin relaxed her eyes and she began to weep. Auntie Pat was horrified.

'Good grief girl. There are far more important things to cry over than men who cheat.' Auntie Pat took a large album, a gallery of grinning trophy hunters posing with dead tigers, lions, elephants, and other poor creatures. '*This* is important,' she lectured, 'Stopping these devils.' Angel sobbed a little less. 'We shan't fall out over this,' said Auntie Pat. I can see you're tired. Go to bed and we'll talk over some fresh eggs. Scrambled, probably, after our journey today.'

Angel looked around the villa. Unlike the outside, it was

spotless and very tastefully decorated with a large veranda at the back looking out onto a beautiful garden. Angel's room was clean and brightly decorated with a large, comfortable four poster bed draped with mosquito nets. There was a small shower room attached so she quickly got washed and then fell into the most comfortable mattress she had ever slept on. She was out like a light and didn't even wake when Auntie Pat came in searching her bags for the gin and cigarettes.

The next morning Angel awoke to a much nicer place. She breathed in the hot air and began to unpack. After a while, there was a smart rapping on the door. 'Breakfast in ten,' said Auntie Pat, and exactly ten minutes later she sat opposite her at the breakfast table feeling very refreshed and not at all tearful.

'Good morning, Auntie Pat,' Angel smiled.

'Good grief child, you're far too big to be calling me *Auntie*. Pat will be fine. And good morning to you, Elle.'

Angel pondered this for a second and then, very bravely, ventured, 'Everybody calls me Angel now.'

'Well that is the silliest name I ever heard, Elle,' Pat snorted back. 'Was that your insipid mother or your wet father's fault?'

'It was David,' Angel whispered, the faintest moistening of tears around her eyes.

'Even more reason,' Pat declared. 'From now on you will be known by your proper name. Now then Elle, we have a great deal of work to do.' Elle sat up, surprised and a little bit curious. 'We've got to find your backbone, Elle. You have the same blood as me so it's got to be in there somewhere. I will teach you what is important in life. You must have standards. The world is a wonderful and terrible place and we need more decency and honesty in it.'

'But...' Elle began.

'No buts,' said Pat firmly. 'We will go and see Dr Gupta as soon as he can fit us in. He will write you a certificate for beriberi or some such and will demand that you take at least six months

off work. You will send it back to your office and you will not go home until we've made a proper woman of you.' Elle sat open-mouthed. 'And please put your tonsils away.' Elle snapped her mouth shut. 'Eat,' came the command, so Elle – by now starving – happily obliged.

Something in Elle, perhaps the wayward vertebrae, told her that this would be a very good experience for her, and she was proved to be right. Pat was a good teacher and Elle was toughened up well. Her first lesson took place at the tiger reserve itself where Pat was a regular volunteer. This was an eye-opener for Elle. She hadn't actually thought about where tigers get their food from and seeing them close up, tearing into large chunks of what used to be pretty little gazelles, made her gag a little. But far worse was seeing for herself the remnants of a tigress carcass skinned and boned alongside the dehydrated remains of her three little cubs. 'All this so that men can get it up and cure toothache,' Pat declared, and Elle felt her resolve and her backbone harden.

Elle soon became acclimatised to the smells and the searing heat of India. It was hard physical work but very rewarding, especially when it came to hand-rearing mewling little tiger cubs. Pat taught her nearly everything she needed to know except how to shuffle a deck of cards. She became leaner, stronger, harder and determined to do whatever she could to help the cause. Her biggest test, however, came when news arrived – even to that remote location – of the sad demise of a certain television presenter.

'Isn't that your horrible man?' Pat had asked at the breakfast table, reading a very out-of-date copy of *The Times*.

'He's history,' Elle declared, chin up and steeled by new courage, but she still shed a quiet tear that night when she was sure Pat was asleep.

At the end of the most informative and useful six months that Elle had ever experienced her backbone was truly in place. The

driving lessons would prove to be redundant in England, but the self-defence classes were going to be invaluable. When the time finally came for Elle to say goodbye, Pat presented her with a copy of her rogue's album, 'So you never forget these bastards.' Then Pat lectured her all the way to the airport. 'Rome wasn't built in a day. Build your career. Take your time. Take opportunities when you can.

'Get a good team of people around you and take it from there. You're a clever girl, you'll find ways of doing things and you can always write to me if you want any help or advice. And never forget...'

'What?' said Elle expectantly.

'Your cousin Robbie is an explosives expert.'

With Pat's advice ringing in her ears, Elle gave her aunt a big hug goodbye and patted Hetty the chicken gently on the head before embarking on the little Fokker to New Delhi.

It was a very different person arriving back at the international airport from the tangled mess of a girl who'd flown in from London. Elle's blonde locks were now cropped into a short, smart bob. She was efficiently dressed and her curves had become lean toned muscle. Her surprised parents welcomed her back and her mother immediately put the rent up, leading Elle to the conclusion that whether she wanted to or not, she was headed straight back to Tadwell's Temps to see if she could get her job back. It was her twentieth birthday and they hadn't even given her a card. Angel might have wept with disappointment, but Elle congratulated herself on knowing what was really important, and birthdays were nobody's business but hers.

Mr Tadwell peered at her when she walked back into the office. 'Angel? Is that you?'

'Yes Mr Tadwell,' she replied. 'Can we talk please?' Mr Tadwell

was already impressed with this super smart-looking young woman and he led her to his office. 'It's Elle,' she began. 'That is my real name. Elle Scarlett. And if you will have me back, I am looking for a career now.'

Mr Tadwell smiled. 'Angel... I mean Elle; it will be a pleasure to have you back. When can you start?'

'Now?'

'Excellent!' Mr Tadwell beamed. 'Patmore's Printing needs a new secretary. Reckon you can handle it?'

'Yes, Mr Tadwell,' Elle replied smartly. 'I think I know what to do.'

After a few *Blimey, you've changed* and *I hope you dropped that skunk before he...* remarks from her colleagues, Elle went to her old desk and sat down, taking in the environment. One of the girls came up to her.

'I see you're still wearing your ring,' she began. 'I was sorry to hear about your ex. Did you forgive him before...?' Elle wrenched the ring off her finger and flung it into a bin. She was appalled at herself that she had kept it on.

'Before what?' she enquired sharply. The girl went a little quiet.

'He died, didn't he?'

Elle harrumphed. 'So I read. It means nothing to me,' she said, pulling out the Patmore's Printing file. It was almost true.

Elle arrived at Patmore's Printing a full ten minutes early. A gnarled old lady called Martha sat in reception smiling with anticipation. *Won't last five seconds*, Martha said to herself. 'You from the agency?' Elle nodded. 'Sit there then.'

Elle clutched her clipboard and pen tightly. The door opened and a man appeared. Mr Patmore was about average height but well above average weight. His shirt barely contained his hairy pot belly which poked out, making a pattern of eights down his front. His dyed black hair was as greasy as a slick from the *Amoco Cadiz*

and his smile was even slimier.

'Miss Scarlett?' he asked and, waiting for Elle's nod, 'This way,' he gestured towards the door, then stood in the doorway forcing Elle to almost touch him as she squeezed by, aghast at the wobbling lump of belly which seemed to have a life of its own. She could smell his BO and his foul breath, and shuddered a little as she walked into the small office. He shut the door firmly behind him but instead of sitting behind his desk, he sat on the edge of it and came very close to her.

'I like your agency,' he greased. 'So long as you are nice to me, I'll give you lots of business. I'm sure they told you what was expected of you.'

'I thought you had a vacancy you wanted filling?' Elle queried.

'Oh, I think you'll find it's you that has the vacancy that needs filling.' Patmore smiled, showing his black teeth, then leant towards her with his hands clearly aiming for her breasts. Elle smacked her clipboard right under Patmore's chin and while he recovered from that, she stood up and kneed him hard in the groin. He doubled up with a loud yell.

'I think, Mr Patmore,' she said menacingly, 'you'll find that we have just written new terms for you. And if you don't accept them, I think you will discover that your business may struggle to find any staff from anywhere in the future.' Patmore grimaced. 'In fact,' Elle began to rant a little, 'I think it might turn out that a serious complaint has been made against you and it might help you in the future to know that I always wear a hidden camera.'

At that, Patmore nearly fainted. Elle was a little surprised with herself too and mentally thanked her aunt's combat training.

'I'm sure that will be acceptable,' he gasped, beaten and bruised, and still bent double. 'Will you see yourself out?' he whispered and, clutching himself, he sidled round the desk to sit down. Elle turned round and left the office to applause from a grinning Martha.

'Well done!' she praised. 'I didn't think you had it in you. He's been asking for that for a long time.' Elle flashed a dazzling smile in return.

'All part of the service.'

That night Elle celebrated her birthday alone in her bedroom with bottles of gin and tonic, a fresh lemon and the local paper. There she began to formulate her plans. She was not going to rush at it, she decided. *I have to establish myself first*, she thought, *and just like Pat said, build up a team. I can't take on the fight against animal exploitation on my own, but I can jolly well work hard and start earning lots of money. And I'm dammed if I'm going to give any of it to my parents.* She began to thumb through the *Flats for Sale* section of the paper, biro in hand.

Elle went from strength to strength and Mr Tadwell was delighted with her; every day she brought in more business.

'That slimeball Patmore has placed another vacancy with us, Elle,' he said to her one evening, 'and that was after you put our rates up. I must say I am very impressed. Carry on like that and you'll be sitting in my chair soon.'

After six months, Elle earned a hefty bonus, enough for a sizeable deposit for her own apartment. She served formal notice on her parents, which certainly served her mother right but left her father somewhat bemused, and now there was no looking back. She took Pat's gallery of rogues and stuck them on her wall to remind her of her mission, and toasted her aunt in her absence. 'To Pat,' she slurred. 'My hero.'

Elle did carry on exactly how Mr Tadwell had hoped; she had expanded the range of staff the employment agency dealt with and business doubled each year for the next few years. Now she was earning serious money, but it wasn't enough – she had amassed nowhere near an amount needed to make a difference

to her beloved tigers and she hadn't found a single one of Pat's horrible hunters.

Just as she was beginning to despair, Mr Tadwell called her in one evening. It was her twenty-fifth birthday and she had nobody at all to share the day with, so Mr Tadwell was as good company as anyone. He greeted her with a big smile.

'Happy Birthday, Elle. I know you don't like to celebrate but since I know the date from your file, I've decided to give you a present that you really deserve. It's time for me to retire and I can't think of anyone better to take over the reins than you.'

Elle was floored. She'd speculated about this meeting but had begun to think it would never happen. It was always going to be the trigger for her real activities. Now her Five-Year Plan needed serious revising and her mind spun off in all sorts of directions; particularly Pat, but it wasn't until she was finally sitting in his office listening to the praise he heaped upon her that her aunt's wise words filled her head...

Always remember that the really big money is in criminal activities.

CHAPTER FOUR

Tacky Takeovers and Murky Mergers

In those early days flying solo, Elle kept things ticking over much as Mr Tadwell would have done. The staff, if not actually liking her that much, did appreciate her skills and were happy enough to be well paid and kept busy. Busy, however, wasn't quite cutting it for Elle; she needed bigger, more, she needed expansion. Just as she reached that conclusion, an attractive olive-skinned woman with glossy black hair wandered into the office. It was late and the last member of staff was leaving so Elle took charge. She was also intrigued; this woman was not the typical office worker.

'Don't worry, I'll deal with this young lady.' When they were alone, Elle flicked the door lock on and ushered the woman into her office.

'What can I do for you?' she asked.

'My name is Mel Morathi and...' Mel had begun confidently then she hesitated like you do when having made it so far, you realise that you might just be making a really stupid mistake. 'I guess I'm not in your normal line of business...' she continued slowly trying to gauge Elle's reaction.

'We're always looking at new avenues,' Elle countered encouragingly.

Might as well spit it out, Mel thought.

'I'm an escort,' she said bluntly, and waited for the response

but there was none; Elle's face was inscrutable. 'But do you know what?' she added, 'I'm sick of being abused by these blokes...' Elle became animated.

'Well then, stop doing it. There's no need to put yourself in danger. You're a pretty girl, I'm sure I could find you a nice job as a secretary somewhere.' Mel looked at her in astonishment then she broke into the deep sexy laugh normally reserved for her clients.

'It's not the Johns I mind. They're OK; besides, I can handle them. It's the creeps that take most of my money I object to.'

Elle's business head was now engaged; this certainly wasn't a line of employment Mr Tadwell had ever considered and it could be lucrative.

'How much do you make in an evening?' Elle asked. And the answer she got surprised her. 'Well, that is extremely good. And you say they are taking sixty per cent?' Mel nodded. 'And what would you expect from us?'

Mel thought for a second. 'That you vet clients, make sure I'm going to safe places, have protection if necessary.'

'How about I take fifty?' Elle ventured. Mel glared at her.

'Well if you're going to be stupid...'

'OK,' said Elle. 'Yes. Maybe I was, but there are overheads you know. Let's talk. I'll buy you dinner and if we get on and we think we can do business together, I'm sure we can agree terms.'

Mel smiled a dazzling smile, so dazzling Elle began to see why she earned so much money.

In the restaurant, Elle and Mel got on well enough. Mel did most of the talking. She deftly avoided Elle's probing about how she got into escorting, although she did mention something about going home to change things one day, but her passion for female equality shone through. Elle's own statements about animal rights

were met with disinterest but Elle was not naive; there were means to ends and what they had in common was far greater; they both really wanted to earn a lot of money.

'As it happens...' Elle began. 'I was thinking of diversifying. More specialists. I haven't got very far with it yet but you might be just the person to kick-start the whole thing off.'

'Then there's nothing to lose,' Mel smiled. 'I'll bring my regulars with me and if the gruesome twosome don't kick up too much, we'll see how we get on.' Elle's face fell a little.

'Are we talking Mafia or Papa's Protection here?'

Mel looked thoughtful. 'On a scale of one to ten, I'd say about a five. But they have a weak spot.'

Elle raised her eyebrows. 'Which is?'

Mel smiled. 'Gambling. They're in hock to Smoky Joe, and he just happens to be one of my best clients.'

Elle thought long and hard about this, and more of Pat's words came back to smack her on the head. Never trust men with silly names. 'What are their names?' she asked. 'I like to know who I might be dealing with.'

'The twosome? There's Ray 'Sunlight' Rodgers and Sammy 'Smiler' Smith.'

Elle, as ever was stunned by the accuracy of Pat's advice. 'OK, Mel. I trust you.

Let's do this.' Elle reached out her hand to shake it; Mel grasped it firmly.

'Deal, sister.'

'Deal!' smiled Elle. 'Now let's put our heads together and see if we can't sort out your pumps.'

Mel threw back her head and laughed so loudly everyone in the place turned to look at her. *'PIMPS!'* she shouted out. 'You mean *PIMPS!'* Elle blushed, but not for long. Mel topped up Elle's

glass and chinked it.

'Baby you have a lot to learn,' she said.

'You'd be surprised,' Elle retorted.

Elle was quick to get to work on her new business endeavour but she was no fool. First, she went to visit Smoky Joe, partly to check him out but mainly to discuss the matter face to face. Elle now carried a piece of paper carefully folded up in her wallet and on it were the images of Pat's gallery of trophy hunters. There were ten in total, nine men and one woman and although it wasn't her highest priority, it made her feel that she was making some progress with her mission by looking out for them. It also made sense to her that if she was dealing with dodgy people, and Smoky Joe was definitely in that category, she should check them against the photos. Anyone who shot animals was automatically untrustworthy, and could not be an ally. But were all her enemies animal killers? It would certainly help form her opinion on their elimination if they were.

Smoky Joe was a thick set tall man with a face like an anthology of short stories but none of them were about hunting animals. Strangely, there was no evidence of any smoking either. He was gruff at first, but as soon as Elle mentioned Mel, he became very accommodating.

'Listen, babe. You don't mind if I call you that, do you?' Elle, lying, shook her head. 'I adore that girl and I know the sort of dicks she works for. You just leave it up to me. So long as Mel is safe and keeps my regular slots, you'll have no worries about those shits.'

'That sounds far too easy,' Elle smiled. 'You don't even want a cut?'

Smoky Joe laughed. 'That girl brings me more custom than I know what to do with. Even if she never brought another John in,

I wouldn't mind. She's a sweetheart and I just want to see her safe. And I never lay a finger on her; not in that way. She's like a daughter to me.'

Elle was surprised at that; how such a mean looking man could have a gentler side. Feeling an intimacy which clearly wasn't reciprocated she ventured a question.

'Why do they call you Smoky Joe?'

Joe's demeanour changed in an instant. 'I suggest you mind your own goddamned business,' he said coldly.

Elle left Smoky Joe's feeling some disquiet but it wasn't until she read the papers a couple of days later, that she really wondered what the hell she'd let herself in for. Two men had been found dead in a back street somewhere in the cheap side of town. They'd been drowned by being dumped head first in plastic dustbins full of water. Elle scanned the article for the names; Raymond Rodgers and Samuel Smith. Bloody hell, she thought. That bastard Smoky Joe did that. And she smiled to herself. 'What a guy,' she said out loud.

Elle's brush with the other side of the law was giving her food for thought; if she was going to turn to criminal activities, she needed some sort of security. Having that on her mind probably distracted her when she arrived at the annual Save the Tiger convention that evening. Almost as soon as she walked inside, a big blundering woman tripped and knocked her over so forcefully she rolled right over a table selling Bengal badges and Malayan magnets, then landed on several rolls of cute tiger cub wallpaper. Before Elle even had a chance to threaten to have the woman taken out, she'd been picked up, thrown over her shoulder, placed very gently on a trestle table and checked over for any injuries. Elle was genuinely impressed.

'Who are you and where did you learn to do that?' she asked

as the woman picked out badges and magnets from Elle's clothing, hair and cleavage.

'Penelope,' the woman responded.

'Coffee?' Elle suggested, and the serious looking woman nodded. Before long, they were friends and like dogs on a lead, were carefully exploring each other's boundaries.

Penelope – who was not very good under pressure and even though Elle was applying almost none – cracked first. She confessed to being a policewoman but insisted that she valued animals above almost anything else. Drawn in, Elle explained most of her business to Penelope, keeping the more unsavoury aspects back until she felt Penelope could be trusted.

A bond was established and they met on several occasions each one bringing them closer together, until at last they came up with an agreement which suited both of them. In return for turning the odd blind eye to Elle's escort services, Elle would help fund, or even actually help with some of Penelope's animal activities. This eased Elle's conscience a little more. It made her feel closer to her goals.

Over the next few years, Elle found out Penelope had a treasure trove of other skills arising partly from her inability to decide on a proper career before joining the police, but also from having a criminal father. She was a damn fine forger and, as Elle was about to discover, a particularly lousy electrician.

Penelope had, in her usual stumbling ways, uncovered something dreadful whilst investigating a strange noise coming from a rundown old barn in the middle of nowhere. She had broken in to discover the most shameful of battery chicken production lines where the poor creatures were kept in the most miserable featherless conditions all to provide stringy meat for the Lickin' Chicken chain of fast food restaurants.

Penelope, who had always loved physics, was so shocked by the electrified cages keeping the poor birds from drinking their

water freely, she tried to redirect the current. Not quite remembering her school experiments, she inadvertently connected the wiring to the light switch. That night, after one brother switched on the light it seemed that the other brother, not realising his sibling was being fried like a, well, chicken, grabbed him, with shocking results.

After the blackened remains were discovered the next morning the discovery became the local news of the decade. However, the fate of the brothers became news chicken feed in comparison with the issues raised by the appalling treatment of the hens.

It was a sobbing Penelope who brought Elle a copy of the paper and confessed what she had done. Elle looked at the article and the pictures of the deceased brothers – before they were blackened, naturally.

'But that's wonderful!' Elle exclaimed to a sobbing Penelope.

'I didn't mean to kill them,' she sniffed. 'Even though they were bad. I must've got the wiring mixed up.'

'Penelope, stop snivelling,' Elle commanded. 'Look.' She banged her finger on the picture on the wall. 'This is my hit list. These bastards shot tigers too. You've done everyone a massive service.'

'They did?' Penelope looked up. 'That's all right then.' She beamed. 'Thanks, Elle.'

Elle's business was expanding in a way she had never anticipated, but the money coming in was good and it all seemed to be very trouble-free. The name Tadwell's Temps no longer really fitted so with very little imagination she came up with Elle's Belles which seemed to be a little more encompassing. She organised a small renaming ceremony and even got the local paper to do a piece on her and the agency. She invited everyone who she thought might

be of use.

For a while, things went very well indeed but that simple little article in the paper was about to get her noticed in a way she did not envisage. It was a few weeks before her thirtieth birthday when the tide began to turn.

It was an especially miserable day for Elle's staff when she stormed into the offices with enough steam coming out of her ears to press several pairs of trousers. The employment agency was still her bread and butter business but she had spent so much time looking for new ventures she'd taken her eye off the ball; something that she knew Mr Tadwell would never have done. She chastised herself for her oversight; failing to notice she had competition was a serious error. She sat in her chair staring at the early edition of the evening paper opened at the page showing the incriminating advert placed by Luigi's Loyal List on behalf of, and she could hardly bear to read it, Patmore's Printing.

Now there was a strong whiff of murderous intent in the air. Previously Elle had only speculated about actually arranging a murder but the years had hardened her. With Smoky Joe, Elle had seen murder almost up close and personal. Penelope's accidental electrocution had filled her with admiration. She was seriously angry; was it time for the next step? Elle broke tradition and in a move which would have seriously offended her beloved Auntie Pat, poured herself a large gin at four forty-five and knocked it back neat. She then sat stewing, waiting for Mel to make her appearance and speculating what Luigi had to offer that she didn't.

What the unsuspecting Luigi de Lupus had to offer was very simple. He had a big wallet, a penchant for the ladies and a willingness to provide them as bait for prospective clients. He'd already established a successful employment agency in Italy so he knew the sector and, courtesy of a certain Arab gentleman he'd met along the way, he'd already got his greasy fingers into some even greasier pies in London. All it took was a chance remark from

this same gentleman about overpriced employment agencies in London and the absence of competition, coupled with a spread about a new agency in the local paper to make Luigi take the next step.

Ripe for the picking my friend, Luigi had been told, and he didn't need telling twice. Elle's business seemed to have just what Luigi was looking for. A new agency with a soppy title and run by a slip of a girl. Perfect for his first backdoor takeover. He spied on Elle's Belles, enticed some of her best temps away and then began to coax her most valued customers using every dirty, and we are talking really dirty, trick in the book.

Elle sat stewing and chewing and while the gin slowly reached her bloodstream, she began to put two and two together. A quick look through her files made her realise that quite a few of her regulars had not given her their business recently and that wasn't all. Rather too many of her ladies had moved on in the last few weeks. Patmore was the biggest surprise; she had no love for him, but he had been a nice little earner for the company since her very first interaction with him, and she wanted to find out more. She rang him.

'I was wined and dined,' said Patmore.

'But I took you out more than once,' Elle snapped.

'Yes, but not to The Secks Cellar,' Patmore shot back. 'Plus he cut your lousy rates,' and with an audible sneer he hung up.

Elle wasn't immediately furious; it would have been hypocritical of her to blame Luigi for those tactics since the sex industry was proving to be a nice little earner for her.

However, the more she thought about it the more righteous she became. There's a time and a place, she thought to herself, and there's no place for that sort of thing in an employment agency. While she was pondering this dilemma, Mel, who was turning in an ever more handsome profit each week, swayed into the office and perched on Elle's desk; an action Elle would not

have accepted from anyone else.

Mel could see something was wrong. 'What's up Elle?'

'It's Luigi de Lupus,' Elle began.

Mel raised her eyebrows. 'The Wolfman?' she asked.

Elle looked perplexed.

'Is he very hairy?' Mel continued.

'I have absolutely no idea,' said Elle, 'but he is trying to ruin my business,' and she banged her finger on the advert in the paper.

'Well if it's who I think it is, he's a walking bathmat,' said Mel. 'Leave it with me. I think Smoky Joe knows him. He has Sicilian connections.'

A couple of days later, Mel came into Elle's office trying to ignore Elle's efforts to throw darts at a grainy picture of Luigi she had torn from the local paper and stuck on the wall. 'Any luck?' Elle enquired trying hard to disguise her impatience.

'Oh yes,' said Mel. 'Smoky Joe knows him well, or rather he knows of him. Apparently, he's like the ice cream barons for employment agencies; he either runs them out of town or takes them over. He's got quite a chain in Italy.' Elle shook her head in amazement.

'Don't ask me how he does it,' Mel continued. 'But he is a nasty piece of work and Smoky Joe has no problems in taking him out.' Elle let the words sink in.

'Do you mean...' she said.

'Hell, yes,' said Mel. 'He says it would be a pleasure.'

Elle was shocked to the core. Could it really be this easy? It would have been bigger than anything she had ever done before. Auntie Pat's words came back to her.

And if you have to take steps, she had said, *make sure that they are bloody great big ones*. Elle looked up at Mel and smiled.

'Let's do this,' she said. 'Amelia Amore, I presume?' Mel nodded.

Amelia Amore, aka Mel Morathi, was as fabulous as her name suggested. In heels, she was six-foot-tall with long flowing natural Chinese red hair, and a figure which would have made Jessica Rabbit's artist go back to the drawing board. No man would be a match for her and Luigi was certainly not up to it, and so the trap was set for a couple of evenings later. Luigi had retired, as usual, to his favourite bar after a particularly stressful but productive day at the office. He almost felt a little guilty; but if he was going to feel really guilty, it might as well be with another woman. That was the sort of guilt he could bear with fortitude having cheated on his long-suffering wife many times before.

Almost as soon as Luigi sat in his chair, such a woman appeared. Dressed in figure-hugging black shiny patent leather from her neck to her feet, broken only with large flesh revealing slashes, Luigi nearly slipped off his stool when he first saw Amelia. She walked in, not noticing him at all and swayed in front of him to take a seat a little further down the bar. Luigi watched mesmerised as she slithered up onto the high stool and crossed her exquisite legs.

'Excuse me, Miss,' Luigi said, in his sexiest Italian accent. 'May I buy you a drink?'

Amelia looked almost virginal as she shyly looked away, but she had already seen the copious chest hair peeping out from his chest and recognised his features from Elle's dartboard. She hesitated for a moment. There was something else she couldn't quite put her finger on. She regrouped.

'Sorry, but no. I was just going to have a little drink to calm my nerves, and then I was going,' she said in her deep sexy voice, hooking Luigi in that very instant.

'But you cannot go,' he commanded. 'I cannot let you out of my sight.'

'But I am meeting my man later,' Amelia said firmly. 'Although I don't suppose he cares if I don't even turn up. I'm sure he's found someone else.' And she blinked away pretend tears.

'Then he is a fool,' said Luigi. 'What man could possibly ignore such a beautiful creature as yourself?' Amelia pouted, which sent Luigi into, well not quite outer space, that came later, but certainly somewhere outside his normal orbit.

'You are so kind,' Amelia said, dabbing her eyes.

'Come with me,' Luigi said. 'Let us go to the theatre or the opera. Stuff this ignorant man. Stuff him I say.' Amelia, drawing out a pregnant pause big enough for an elephant, turned and looked at him.

'If I come with you, he will kill you.'

'What? A monster as well as an ignorant bastard? Let him try! I am Luigi. Nobody kills Luigi.' And with that questionable statement, the evening was more or less settled. Amelia just wanted to check one detail, to be absolutely certain.

'And what do you do for a living, my handsome stranger?' she asked.

'I, my dear lady, am the proprietor of one of the most important up and coming staff agencies in the country. We will soon be the biggest in the country. I have three houses, a yacht and my own personal jet... is on order,' he mumbled incoherently, but it didn't matter, he had her with yacht, or at least he thought he did.

'Have you ever been hunting in Africa?' Amelia ventured. 'I *so* love a man with a big gun.'

Luigi smiled so broadly his mouth nearly reached his ears.

'I will show you my lion's head rug one day. If you are a good girl.'

Now Amelia had ascertained his identity, all she had to do was to entertain the hairy little shit for an hour or two. The evening progressed with opera, during which Amelia had to cover her

boredom with dramatic tears, followed by dinner in a restaurant so exclusive even she'd never been there before.

'How about a nightcap in my favourite hotel,' he asked her suggestively over the Amaretto. 'But I've only just met you,' Amelia protested, 'And what about my man?'

'Forget the imbecile,' Luigi leered. 'For tonight at least.'

'I will tell him I have gone to see my sister then,' Amelia said, smiling at him, and she picked up her mobile.

'As you wish,' Luigi replied, already fantasising about a sister. 'Waiter? Bill please.' And before you could say stupid idiot, they were heading to The Bestissimo Hotel and booking into a room.

Needless to say, it wasn't Amelia's sister who joined them but Smoky Joe's Hitman. So efficient had he been that he was already in the corridor and waiting round the corner for them to arrive. He listened at the door for a moment and when he heard Amelia say 'You naughty man!' he rapped on the door.

'Room service!' he shouted.

'I didn't order room service,' said Luigi slightly puzzled.

'You didn't?' Amelia pouted, 'But why not? I am so thirsty...' Luigi melted. A few bucks more wouldn't hurt.

'Let's see what he has for us then,' he said. And obviously, what the Hitman had, was a gun with a silencer.

It all got very messy. Luigi clumsily wrestled with the Hitman and managed to discharge the gun in the man's shoulder, not causing any serious damage; just enough to be a nuisance. Both of them ended up on the floor and it took one of Amelia's favourite thigh clenches to break Luigi's neck, so at least he died in a relatively happy state of mind. But despite the Hitman's best efforts to clear up, there was blood everywhere.

It just so happened that, at that precise moment, a young lady called Chloe was walking past the room. Alerted by the sounds of the scuffle and a strange popping noise, she listened for a moment outside the room, but when she heard a horrible snapping noise

she became worried. She hated it when guests broke furniture so she immediately opened the door with her skeleton key and pushed it open to reveal a shocked Amelia and the Hitman staring opened mouthed at her.

'It's not how it looks,' Amelia explained. Now it was Chloe's turn to stare open-mouthed as she took in the scene.

When Chloe opened the door, she wasn't at all shocked by the dead Luigi, the gorgeous redhead or the masked man in black lycra. Chloe had almost superhuman powers of perception. She was able to tell a good person from a bad person and even though it was pretty clear what had happened, she instantly knew that the corpse was the bad guy. What really shocked her was the blood splattered on the cream carpet. Without a word, she went straight into cleaning mode while Mel and the Hitman stood there holding on to each other in total disbelief.

'Now. For this I'll need some...' and Chloe rattled off a whole host of ingredients, all of which she seemed to carry about her person in the well-concealed pockets of her utility apron. 'I'd better move this,' said Amelia tentatively, moving towards the corpse.

'Stay right there,' Chloe said in such a commanding way even she was surprised. Chloe had spent much of her solitary life watching detective programmes and anything to do with forensic science and had gained a huge amount of knowledge as a result.

'You'll leave your DNA on the scene,' she stated with authority. 'Your outfit, being patent leather, will have protected your thighs from exposure, but your hands will leave traces.'

'OK then, thanks.' Amelia exchanged bemused glances with the Hitman, who gave a baffled sort of shrug of his shoulders.

'Go sit over there,' Chloe ordered, rather enjoying her power, and the two of them sat on the bed nervously like children on the naughty step. They watched fascinated as Chloe got down to her

work.

As if by magic, all the blood stains were gradually removed from the carpet leaving it spotless. Then Chloe turned her attention to the Hitman.

'Come here,' she ordered, and in the swish of a medical wipe, his blood was removed, even from his shirt, and his wound cleaned and dressed. As he sat down again, Chloe picked up his gun and polished it until it gleamed, returning it to him with a smile.

'Thank you,' the Hitman said, completely nonplussed.

'My pleasure,' Chloe replied, beaming with appreciation.

'But what about the…' Amelia began looking at the corpse.

'Yes, that's more complicated,' Chloe explained. 'Luckily I have my portable acid tank in the cupboard on this floor. I'll sort him out in a jiffy. Might have to cut him up and dangle him a bit at a time…' she added, making Amelia gag just a little. Once she had walked round the body giving it the odd poke and squeeze, she seemed satisfied. 'You two run along now. I can manage from here.' Chloe looked at both of them.

'But can we…?' Amelia began.

'No. All part of the service,' replied Chloe.

'You are an amazing woman!' Amelia exclaimed. 'I may just be able to expand your career.'

Chloe was almost bursting with excitement from all the attention she was getting.

'I am quite well suited here,' she replied.

'I think we can be certain you're worth a lot more than you're being paid here,' Amelia encouraged.

'Fantastic!' the Hitman was shaking and nodding his head simultaneously.

'I'll be in touch,' Amelia smiled, and with that, the pair left the hotel arm in arm, just for appearances' sake.

Mel was blown away, and not in a Luigi way, by Chloe's skills. That evening she rang Elle to tell her what had happened.

'It's done,' Mel began. 'But it went a bit shit.'

'What happened?' asked Elle anxiously. 'Are you OK?' She listened intently to what Mel had to say.

'...and I think this woman could be a tremendous resource,' she said. 'What do you think?'

Elle thought Chloe sounded perfect, but still a little tingly from her very first hit, she wanted to tread carefully.

'Leave it for a week. Make sure it's all sorted. Died down. If she's involved, she's implicated; and I don't want anything to come back on you.'

'Agreed,' said Mel. 'Oh, and I didn't tell you the best bit.'

'Which is?'

'Your gallery; second row, third or fourth from the left. I'm sure it's him.'

Elle ran straight to her wall to look at the photos pinned there. The two brothers already bore big red crosses.

'Well I never. How come I never noticed that?' she said, as she got a big red pen and drew a cross on the photo of Luigi posing with a lion's head. 'That's three now. I must ring Pat. When she gets a telephone installed.'

Mel, as instructed, watched the news and read the papers very carefully for any mention of Luigi. Finally, on the *News at Ten*, there was a small piece on a missing businessman, with absolutely no hints at all as to where he might be. He'd booked a room in The Bestissimo hotel but had never been seen again and was now officially missing. This was all she needed to know; she was in the clear. The next morning she went straight to the hotel and headed for the concierge.

'I'm looking for...' she began.

'Yes?' said the concierge. Mel stopped in her tracks realising that not only did she not know the cleaner's name; she didn't have a clue what she looked like.

At that precise moment, Chloe walked past her without a second glance; she would never have recognised Mel without her wig, heels and makeup. So like ships passing in the night, Mel missed out on an exciting new recruit for Elle, and Chloe headed for strange and exotic shores.

Elle didn't have time to worry about the mysterious cleaner, she was about to meet another one who was nothing at all like the wonderful sounding Chloe. Shortly after Luigi's disposal, a young Filipino woman in floods of tears crept into the reception area of Elle's Belles. Sensing something unusual, Elle took her into her office and gave her a glass of water. As she sipped it, the woman glanced up to the dartboard acquired specially to hold up Luigi's photo. She recognised it and squealed, breaking into more tears and pointing at the photo.

'Did you know this man?' Elle asked, and the woman nodded vigorously.

'He dead now?'

Elle nodded. 'What's your name?' she asked.

'Nettie,' replied the woman.

'And you knew this man?' Elle repeated. 'Tell me how.'

Through gulps, sobs and the odd belch, Elle gathered from Nettie's garbled broken English that she had worked for Luigi, but clearly not as an office worker. Elle poured her a gin and tonic which was happily knocked back in one despite the mild protestation, 'Nettie don't drink alcohol. No way.'

The drink made Elle's questioning much easier in one sense, as Nettie's tongue was considerably loosened; however, perhaps because of the gin, or more likely the sense of safety, the shy tearful

creature began to turn into something of a wildcat, all spits and swear words, some of them even in English.

From what she heard, Elle deduced that Luigi had been running a very shady office cleaning service comprised entirely of illegal immigrants. There were ten that Nettie knew of, all living in a squat in a derelict part of town and forced to stay indoors all day long. Luigi or his sidekick personally provided food for them but when neither man appeared, the food ran out quickly. Nettie, being the most proactive and gobby of the women, had searched the squat and found some old newspapers with Elle's Belles adverts ringed in red so Nettie had come straight to Elle's door.

Elle was shocked at first. She certainly hadn't ever envisaged using slave labour or illegal immigrants but the idea of office cleaning had a huge appeal. It tied in with her other night-time business and she knew it could be a money spinner.

'You go back to the house, Nettie,' she said. 'I'll come by with some food for you all later.'

Nettie smiled; she trusted this nice woman and she left, bowing as she went.

When she had gone, Elle made a quick phone call to Penelope then went to the local supermarket and bought several bags worth of food. When she arrived at the squat, she was first let in by one of the women who was smiling broadly, then she was mobbed.

'You bring pork shit?' one of the women shouted, throwing Elle's purchases of ham, sausages and bacon rudely at her.

'But I thought you were Christians!' Elle wailed as she ducked the missiles. Luckily it was all vacuum packed, so nothing was wasted. Even more luckily, Elle had seen fit to buy bread and cheese just in case some were vegetarians, so when the women ran out of pig products, the bombardment stopped. For a short while, the barrage of abuse gave way to the chomping of bread and cheese as the women tucked into whatever they could. While they ate, Nettie showed Elle to the dilapidated kitchen where they sat down and discussed matters.

'What we do now?' asked Nettie. 'We need work. We need money and papers.'

'You carry on as you are,' Elle told her. 'You should all go to work as usual and I'll sort something out, I promise. One more thing, I'll need passport sized photos of all of you.'

It only took a couple of days for Penelope to put her forging skills to good use and Elle was well and truly buoyed up by the resulting stack of passports and National Insurance papers which would pass muster almost anywhere.

It was time now for Elle to set off on the first of several missions to visit the companies who were using her newly acquired staff. It gave her even more pleasure to see that a couple of them were also defectors from her office services branch, and even more especially, one of them was Patmore's Printing. As she flounced into his offices, Martha looked so pleased to see her she actually applauded.

'So good to see you back, Miss. Things haven't been the same since that other lot took over. Shall I tell him you're here?'

'No need,' said Elle smiling, and she barged straight into Patmore's office just in time to see a movement of hand from trousers and a colourful magazine being stuffed under his desk.

'What the hell do you want?' he shouted at her, all red-faced and flustered. 'I dropped you, remember?'

'Ah, yes, well that was before poor Mr Lupus met his tragic death.'

'Plenty more agencies out there,' Patmore retorted, determined to face her down.

'Yes,' said Elle coolly. 'But not many who also employ women trafficked from the Philippines.'

'I don't know nothing about that,' stammered Patmore.

'Oh, I think you do.'

63

Elle thrust some papers headed Cleaning Services Contract, under his nose. He sat back in his chair in despair. Patmore wasn't so stupid that he didn't realise he'd been shafted again, and not in a way he enjoyed, so he signed the contract without even looking at it. Much later on that evening and over a large Scotch, he read the terms and conditions and wept into his glass.

Elle's thirtieth birthday arrived and she was, once again, contemplating her Five-Year Plan. Yes, she had made some progress; she'd even knocked three of the rogues off. It wasn't enough but yet again, the business wasn't making enough. Even though she had quadrupled the size of the agency and now had an official cleaning services section with twelve legitimate staff members, it wasn't big enough. More than that, Nettie was becoming quite a handful. First things first, she decided. She needed someone to head up her cleaning team and once again her thoughts turned to the woman that Mel had so lauded. Yes, Elle needed a Chloe, and she was determined to track her down.

CHAPTER FIVE

The Bestissimo Bombings

Chloe-May Chopra was almost born into invisibility. As a newborn baby, her unremarkable birth and exceptional quietness immediately afterwards meant that she was almost completely forgotten seconds after her arrival. In fact, if it hadn't been for a half-drunken new father turning up at the hospital, she might have been left in the Moses basket forever. The 'May' got completely forgotten after a few days too.

It didn't get any better; as a small tot in her pram, she was regularly abandoned by her somewhat disinterested mother until her father on impulse bought a shockingly patriotic bright green and orange buggy with white stripes and blue wheels that nobody could miss. Even if her mother got distracted, the locals spotted it and Chloe was regularly pushed back home by kind souls.

This set Chloe up nicely for when aged five and on her first school trip, she was left behind by the teacher. By then she knew almost every route home and managed to arrive at her house before anyone even noticed she had been missing.

In addition to highly developed homing skills acquired because of her useless mother, Chloe was forced to spend a great deal of time second-guessing her and that, coupled with some help from a slip in the inherited gene pool, gave her the most extraordinary perception.

It was almost as if she could read people's innermost thoughts. Thus if she stood staring at a fish tank in a zoo, a thousand people would pass by and not even notice her, but Chloe would have memorised all the fish and even known what most of them were thinking about.

Unfortunately, neither of these skills counted for much at school, at least in an educatory way. There was a certain amount of kudos gained from her teachers by anticipating their responses to her dismal homework efforts and sometimes even writing them on their behalf to save them time. But in terms of her own progress, even if her teachers had something of use to say, each parents' evening was railroaded by her mother. She would embark on a long and winding rant about her own lost education. This always ended in her confident assertion that she would have been a prizewinning chemist if it hadn't been for that blasted auntie in India who talked her into marriage with Mr Chopra's eldest. She would then inevitably receive a tap on the shoulder from a parent queuing impatiently behind her, and would quickly sum up by thanking the teacher and dabbing her eyes before sashaying out to her car. There she would be surprised – mainly because she had completely forgotten the purpose of the visit – to find Chloe already waiting for her.

It wasn't totally her mother's fault that Chloe left school bereft of decent qualifications; Chloe simply hadn't found her own path. She had rather tied herself to her friend Harry and had coasted for years without ever thinking about what she wanted to do or make of herself. The day Harry told Chloe she was emigrating to America, Chloe's world, such as it was, fell apart. As oddballs often do, they had found themselves shunned at school by all the cool kids. Then they bonded. Harry's abundance of ideas compensated for Chloe's limited vision and her good nature and perception brought peace and happiness to Harry. But with Harry gone, Chloe had no idea how she would cope on her own. To be precise, she

had no ideas at all.

That summer, it was a very bored and somewhat languid Chloe who was stuck constantly at home much to the annoyance of her mother who could no longer avoid or ignore her. Eventually, following much nagging of Mr Chopra, he was persuaded to take his daughter into work one day. This was prompted by him foolishly telling his wife that they were looking for a junior cleaner.

'Anything to get the silly girl moving,' Mrs Chopra had said. In those days when jobs were often given based on personal contacts or families, Chloe was instantly taken on for a trial period.

Chloe shone from the very first time she picked up a cleaning cloth. She was instantly absolutely obsessed with dust, grime and stains and even more importantly, their removal. She became a top-notch cleaner and excelled in finding the correct solution required to remove any number of stains from a plethora of surfaces. She was, in truth, an undiscovered master chemist. Suddenly Chloe had a purpose in life and she took to it like stains to underwear. It was a year or two before Chloe built up enough self-esteem to hold her head up at least as high as anybody else and having broken this monumental barrier, it was time for her to decide what to do with the rest of her life.

Unlike most of us with aspirations way above our abilities, Chloe was content with who she was and what she could do. She loved the challenges cleaning set and relished the thanks and praise of those she served. So that was her ambition in life; to clean for the benefit of other people. With newly found confidence she cut loose from her parents and found herself a cheap grotty bedsit which became her first project. Within a week it was transformed into her own little palace. Chloe's new route home from work took her past a big swanky hotel, The Bestissimo, which was all glass and shimmer. She often gazed at the building full of wonder and curiosity. How I would like to see inside, she said to herself every day, and one day such an opportunity presented itself.

It was late in the evening when, as she walked past, she spotted something somewhat incongruous in the bottom corner of the window. It was a little note bearing the legend:

> CLEANER WANTED
>
> APPLY WITHIN

Chloe didn't need telling twice. She snuck inside the hotel and discreetly removed the notice. Then looking around, saw an important looking man standing to the side of the marble reception. He smiled at her and beckoned her over.

'Can I help you, Miss?' he asked kindly.

'Yes, I've come about the job,' Chloe replied, waving the card in her hand.

The concierge had a little difficulty reading the moving notice but put two and two together and directed Chloe to the Head Cleaner's cubby hole. There she was given an assessment on the spot; well more of a large stain really, and naturally, she passed with flying colours.

'Very impressive, Miss, er...

'Chopra.'

'When can you start?'

'Tomorrow!' Chloe squealed. 'I have holiday owing from my old job.'

'Tomorrow it is then.'

Chloe had never been so excited in her life; it was about to get a great deal more exciting.

'Welcome to The Bestissimo Hotel,' the Head of Housekeeping beamed at Chloe as she sat in her impressively small office.

'This is our founder, Bessie Wainwright,' she turned round pointing to the framed picture hanging on the wall behind her

desk. It was a photo of a very important looking woman with dark skin and a wonderful welcoming smile full of gleaming white teeth.

'And one day, if you are very lucky, you will meet her yourself. That was taken when she won the *Best Business Magazine* award for Newcomer of the Year,' she added.

'Oh, I do hope I will meet her,' said Chloe, well impressed. 'Thank you so much.'

Chloe's first week was pretty normal and mainly involved learning the geography of the hotel and having some basic induction training. Then the real test came; like all newcomers, she was given the very worst job to do. And how the cleaning team sniggered when Chloe's arrival coincided with the departure of the latest big thing boy band who were on tour. The suite they had occupied was so disgusting, there was even vomit on the encrusted vomit.

'In you go,' said the head cleaner, pushing Chloe through the door with one hand whilst covering her mouth with the other.

After opening all the windows and breathing in some fresh air, Chloe leapt to the challenge like a frog leaping for flies, and there were quite a few of those around too. Within an hour, the rooms were tidied, cleaned, disinfected and restored to a pristine condition. Even the obscene graffiti carved on one of the bedsteads had been infilled, sanded and revarnished. The Head of Cleaning was both astonished and delighted but mainly gobsmacked.

After that, news of Chloe's performance spread like salmonella through the hotel, and before you could say, *Acid burn on bedside table* she was the talk of the housekeeping department and quite the little star. Stars typically are rather lonely sorts, so Chloe's social life remained the same; zilch, but at least people knew who she was and what she could do. Then suddenly, thanks to Mel and the Hitman she had been given an even greater new challenge than the dirtiest band in the world could have given her;

a whole corpse.

The next morning Chloe set her alarm for an hour earlier than usual. She'd had an extremely late but very interesting night and now she knew precisely the durations and concentration ratios of acid required to dissolve human flesh. It had taken a long time to finish off and she'd had to fumigate the room thoroughly before taking herself off home. Luckily Luigi had paid for the room for the whole night and wasn't due to settle up before ten the next morning by which time she hoped the fumes would have dissipated. But before she could double-check the room she bumped into the Head of Housekeeping.

'Just the person,' she began. 'Erm, what's your name,' she beckoned, 'come to my office now. I've got something important to tell you.' Chloe followed her, more than a little worried. She sat down and listened carefully.

'We are about to open a hotel in Azerbaijan,' the Head of Housekeeping began, 'and I have been asked personally by our beloved founder and chief executive Bessie Wainwright herself,' she paused to look at the photograph, '...to nominate an employee to go there to improve hygiene standards.' She finished with a smile nothing like as splendid as Bessie's, but sincere enough, looking straight at Chloe. Chloe still didn't quite get it and shook her head.

'I'm choosing you,' the Head of Housekeeping explained. 'It will be a fantastic experience,' she said. 'Cleaning up in the dirtiest city in the world. What do you say?'

Well, there were only two choices, and Chloe couldn't resist the challenge. 'Yes,' she said.

The second Chloe's plane landed she was hit by the terrible smell. The Head of Housekeeping had certainly been right about that bit. She made her way to passport control by following the other

passengers; she'd never travelled alone before. It took the woman at the desk quite a while to verify her passport, but eventually she gave up and waved Chloe through. On the other side, Chloe found herself in a very unfortunate situation. She had brought tiny samples of her chemical portfolio with her in her ample handbag; just enough to replicate her wonderful techniques. But the officials in Azerbaijan were highly suspicious so she was detained until they had analysed what her samples actually were.

Chloe was naturally passive and went along with it without arguing. They gave her a nice room, almost like a hotel room, above the security centre at the airport and said they would be in touch when they had cleared her portfolio. There, she had full use of the internet and there was a television in the lounge downstairs which she was welcome to watch. She wasn't allowed to touch the remote control but luckily the guards' choice was usually American detective and action serials especially those which dealt with weapons and chemicals; precisely what Chloe would have chosen herself. So in what could have otherwise have been a very boring week, she became quite an expert in all sorts of dangerous things.

Chloe was almost disappointed when her week was up; by then the guards had completely forgotten who she was and nobody had actually remembered to check out the contents of her handbag, so it was simply given back to her. After lots of hugs and kisses goodbye, she was sent back into the arrivals building where she felt a little lost and unsure of what to do. She did know she urgently needed her suitcase; a week of washing one's smalls in a sink was more than enough for anyone to take. Luckily, her suitcase was still going round the carousel. She grabbed it immediately and walked outside to where she thought the taxi rank was. There she waited for what seemed like hours before a single taxi spotted her and stopped for her. As she found out later, she was in completely the wrong place, but at the time, she was

just relieved that she had been spotted.

'Where to, Miss?' said the rather polite young man as he put her suitcase in the boot.

'Bestissimo Hotel?' Chloe responded hopefully. The taxi driver smiled broadly at her.

'Oh yes,' he said. 'The big new one.'

Unfortunately, or maybe not, at the exact same moment Chloe got into one side of the cab, three young men with high aspirations and a gun climbed into the other side. The one with the gun sat next to the driver and held it to his head. He muttered something sounding very unpleasant which caused the driver to turn the taxi round and head off at a cracking pace.

Meanwhile, in the back, Chloe looked at the two other young men and smiled weakly. They looked at her in complete astonishment. They muttered to each other and there was a great deal of shoulder shrugging.

'I'm Chloe,' she said offering her hand. 'Pleased to meet you.' The terrorist in the front turned round to look at Chloe, and he spat over the back of the seat losing his chewing gum. Chloe dipped into her handbag and retrieved one of her own recipe wipes, collecting up the spittle and gum in one easy move. She smiled winningly at the gunman who then also shrugged his shoulders and turned back to make sure the taxi driver was on course.

When they arrived at their destination, which was clearly not the hotel, Chloe saw that the gunman, who she deduced was the leader, was about to shoot the taxi man. Displaying a remarkable and previously hidden talent for mime, she explained that the blood from his head would splatter all over them and the car which would make it very easy for them to be identified. Far better, she demonstrated, to knock him out with a light blow to the back of the head, and drop him at least two hundred yards away from their hangout. If they did it just here, she pointed to a specific spot on the man's head, he wouldn't remember a thing about it.

Chloe's logic was unarguable. The gunman nearly smiled at her then followed her instructions to the letter dispatching the driver as instructed, and dumping him in a different part of town. The cab was swiftly stripped of its identifying features and driven to the gang's hideout. One of the gang took Chloe's bag from the boot and she was invited in. Chloe smiled her acceptance. Well, they did seem like such nice young men.

When she got inside Chloe let out a yell of despair which startled the lads. The hideout was naturally a complete hovel and without a second thought, Chloe grabbed her suitcase and pulled out some bits and pieces. Now it was time for the lads to howl; who and what on earth was this woman? The leader held the others back as if to say, I will deal with this, but before you could say Dyson, Chloe had whipped her hand-held out of her case. While the three desperadoes stared in amazement, she whizzed round managing as best she could with her little vacuum cleaner. The gang watched in astonishment as bit by bit, their hideout became if not quite sparkling, a damn sight cleaner.

When he was sure that Chloe had finished, one of them asked her to sit down while another brought her a nice cup of tea. When she was comfortable, they introduced themselves as best they could in broken English. Baghir, who Chloe thought was the most handsome, was the leader. His friends Hasan and Tagi were brothers. Chloe deduced that they had all been friends from school and their ambitions were simple. They wanted to change their world for the better. Baghir had picked up something on the internet about an attempted attack on a Western hotel newly opened up in town and they wanted to stop it.

'Chloe?' Baghir asked. She nodded and smiled and since that seemed to be the limit of their English, the conversation rather trailed off after that and nobody was really sure what to do.

'May I go now?' Chloe asked. 'I have a job waiting for me at The Bestissimo Hotel.'

At the sound of that name, the three shook their heads violently.

'No,' Baghir spoke. 'You stay here. Be safe.' Chloe could almost see something flash through his brain. 'The taxi man know this?' he asked. Chloe nodded.

'I asked him to take me there. He seemed to know it.'

The three lads rushed outside and headed straight for the taxi, Chloe following behind. Very gingerly Baghir opened the bonnet then jumped back in shock as a very rudimentary bomb was revealed. Chloe's eyes widened. She recognised this device. It would explode on impact and therefore wasn't wired. She knew exactly what to do and squeaked with excitement. She'd been dying to have a go at a bomb. In another spectacular mime, she explained that she would deal with it. She went back inside to take a couple of things from her suitcase, then putting on some magnifying glasses, she set to work on the bomb while the lads stood well back watching her every move.

Without even having to admit this was her first time, Chloe managed to first neutralise the bomb and then she began to separate out its components to make sure it couldn't accidentally explode. Once they realised all was safe, the lads cheered her and went back inside. Chloe, strangely enough, felt safe with these young men. They were polite and respectful. She had not been tied up or even locked in; they seemed to be accepting her as one of their own.

'You sleep here tonight?' offered Baghir, taking her into a tiny but adequate room. 'I will sleep with them,' he added looking back at Hasan and Tagi.

'It's very kind of you,' Chloe nodded. 'But just for tonight as it's so late. Tomorrow I must go to the hotel.'

Since they were all hungry, Chloe offered to rustle up some supper, and despite the rather limited selection of ingredients, they ate well. The three of them sat cross-legged on the floor so that

Chloe could sit on her own and they all gazed at an old black and white television. She couldn't understand much of what was being said, but suddenly the screen went blank and what happened next shook her to the core. There was a news flash and some live footage being shown. Somebody had just blown The Bestissimo hotel sky high.

Chloe was now very concerned. She had almost laughed off the bomb in the taxi, being so pleased with her new-found skills, but it was apparent that this was part of a much more sinister plot. There had to be more than one bomber, and by the look of the footage, several bombs had been used. She didn't dwell on her own fate, but she did worry for others. The hotel had been good to her and she felt that she owed it to them to try to help find out who did it; but how? She was in a strange and foreign country where the only place she felt a connection with had been destroyed and she didn't even speak the language, much less understand why it had happened. Even so, she felt ever more drawn towards these three young men who she instinctively knew were on the side of good.

'Chloe,' they said to her as one. 'Stay with us. Fight with us.'

'Let me sleep,' she answered. 'We will talk tomorrow.'

Chloe slept remarkably well considering what had happened, the sheer exhaustion overwhelming her whirling brain. The next morning Baghir woke her early with another cup of tea.

'Good morning, Chloe,' he said. 'When you want we will see mother. She is teacher. She teaches English. That is good, yes?'

'Yes,' Chloe smiled. 'That will be good.'

When Chloe had drunk her tea and had sat in quiet contemplation for a while, she went to join Baghir in the main room. His mother's house was not too far away, and so they walked to it through derelict building sites and bustling markets. He was very protective of her and she was quite taken with his good looks and shy manner. Gunman? No, freedom fighter, she

decided.

Baghir's mother greeted them at the door. It was clear that Baghir had explained some of what had happened.

'I am Ulka,' she held out her hand in greeting. 'Please come in and sit with me.' Chloe took her hand and went inside. The house was simple, but beautifully laid out, and she saw it was spotlessly clean.

'You have a lovely house,' she gushed.

'Thank you. Now please sit,' and Ulka patted a big cushioned sofa in the main living area.

'My stupid son,' Ulka began, 'tells me you are a clever lady. Now that is not stupid at all, for I can see with my own eyes and hear what you have done to know that. But he tells me that you will help him fight the gang responsible for this terrible outrage. And I want to know if this is true.'

Chloe took a very long time to answer, but while Baghir paced, Ulka sat expressionless; a picture of calm. This was an important decision and it needed time and space. Chloe's mind was racing with so much stuff she could hardly cope. Then she took a broom to her head and swept out all the superfluous stuff which was mainly her un-doting parents and her non-existent friends. What she was left with was quite simply that, had it not been for these boys, she would almost certainly have been killed. The people who did this would presumably do it again somewhere else and needed to be stopped. Therefore, her life did have a purpose and it was indeed to help find the bombers. It was blindingly simple.

'I will do whatever I can to help,' she said. Baghir whooped, but Ulka looked solemn.

'Then you will stay here with me,' she frowned a little. 'I have a nice house. The boys are good but so dirty.' Then Ulka laughed the dirtiest laugh Chloe had ever heard and it was impossible not to join in. When the laughter subsided, Ulka showed Chloe to a

very nice room, complete with a very comfy bed and, most importantly, a computer.

'Make yourself comfortable,' said Ulka. 'I have preparations to make; we will commence our lessons after lunch.

Chloe looked around the room; there was no cleaning needed so she wondered what she could do. Then having made her decision, her mind soon turned to her job and whether anybody was worried about her. She turned on the computer and searched all she could but came up with almost nothing about The Bestissimo explosion in Baku, and wondered whether it had been hushed up. There was nothing on The Bestissimo website either; all references to a new hotel had been removed. It looked as though she was officially a non-person.

Chloe decided to check her emails in case the hotel had tried to contact her and was completely taken aback to find that she had one email waiting but it wasn't from the hotel; it was from Harry. Harry always wrote to her on her birthday. She looked at the computer screen in bemusement. Today was her birthday and she'd completely forgotten. Well, everybody else always did, she wallowed, why should she be different? Everyone except for dear Harry. She opened the email and read it with a little smile. *Happy birthday Chloe!* But there was more. *And what the fuck are you doing in Azerbaijan?* Chloe sat up. Of course! Harry was the one person in the whole wide world who was interested in what she was doing, how had she found out?

The answer was obvious really. Harry was spectacularly good at all things computing, Chloe remembered. Just then another email from Harry popped up.

Remember the exam thing back home? Well it happened here too, so I've been slung out of the college course, but they were so impressed with me they given me some work as a researcher so it's fine. I'm doing OK.

Chloe smiled to herself remembering the time Harry had

hacked into the school computer.

Lovely to hear from you, she typed back. *How did you know where I was?*

Easy peasy. That was nothing. I saw about the hotel. Are you in danger?'

Yes, possibly I am, Chloe replied. *I was just wondering...* she began. Instantly the reply came back.

Yes, you dufus. What do you want me to find out?

Chloe grinned so broadly, that even when Ulka came into her room, she was still smiling.

'You look happy,' Ulka remarked.

'It's my birthday,' Chloe replied. 'And my best friend in the whole world has just wished me a happy one.'

'Then we must bake you a cake,' said Ulka. 'And who is your friend who so kindly writes to you?'

'Harry,' Chloe replied. 'Harriet Hackett.'

That evening, Ulka threw Chloe's first ever birthday party and Chloe was surprised to find how much she enjoyed it. She was feeling more at home with Ulka and the boys than ever she had with her own family and she discovered another skill. With a little help from Ulka, she was picking up the language very easily. The only slight friction that evening came when Chloe insisted on cleaning up afterwards and Ulka refused to let her. By the time they had finished the argument, the lads had done it all, admittedly very badly, but it would have been churlish for either to complain.

'Thank you for giving me the best birthday ever,' Chloe said.

'Thank you,' they replied in unison.

CHAPTER SIX

Chloe's Calling and Penelope's Progress

Chloe spent the whole of the next day studying with Ulka. She learned more of the language and Ulka gave her a tour of the city together with a potted history and culture lesson. Chloe absorbed it all like one of her super sponges.

The following day Ulka gave her the ultimate test. Chloe was taken to a local market. As they walked past a huge stall of brightly coloured carpets and rugs, Ulka hesitated beside a particularly fine red patterned rug and Chloe saw that it would be perfect for Ulka's living room. It was also good hard-wearing natural wool and tufted, not Berber, so easier to keep clean. In perfect Azeri local slang, Chloe first asked the price of the rug. The seller was insulted and almost spat back at her. Unabashed, Chloe answered him. 'You imbecile son of a female gnat. My arse could produce a finer carpet than that. I'll give you thirty manat.'

Well, it wasn't quite a typical phrase, but it shocked the carpet seller and he settled at thirty-five manat. Ulka was delighted and laughed all the way home clutching her new purchase at a price even she couldn't have beaten.

'Baghir? Come. Meet your new sister Chichek,' she said, 'She has passed the test with airborne rainbows.' Baghir and Chloe exchanged shy smiles, but they weren't the sort Ulka had envisaged.

Chloe had told the boys about Harriet, well not quite all, because, quite frankly she wasn't at all judgemental and besides it wasn't any of her business. They were hugely impressed with anybody who could hack computers and waited with eager anticipation for her to call. At the appointed hour, Chloe and the boys were huddled round the computer on webcam waiting for Harry to show.

Harry had been busy. She'd started searching with *Suicide bombers* and now she was on *World War Two* and *Kamikaze pilots*. This, by one of those wondrous twists of fate, led her to Hara Kari, often misspelt as Hari Kari and then somehow she ended up with a strange video on the screen. It was made by a sorrowful young man called Hari and Harry was mesmerised. Never before had she heard such awful poetry. She cringed at first when she wasn't laughing but then she felt a little ashamed of herself. Here was a fellow human being who was in some sort of torture and clearly needed help. Plus he was quite cute looking too.

He was different, she was different; the difference between them being that she didn't care.

He clearly had not yet arrived at that wonderful state of self-acceptance. With the eyes of an outsider, she thought she understood his torment and decided she could help him.

Taking an unusually personal step into the unknown, Harry left a comment on his video.

'I feel your pain. Would you like to talk to me?' She had no idea how recent the video was, so she left it there not really expecting to hear from him, besides she had a lot more searching to do to find Chloe's bomber and more importantly the organisation behind it all. And find out more she certainly did, but before she called Chloe to report back, she comforted herself that she had at least attempted to contact Hari so he would know that somewhere out there, someone cared about him.

At Ulka's house the screen wobbled and flickered a little, but

suddenly Harry was revealed, somewhat to the disquiet of the three young men.

'Is that man or woman?' Hasan said a little too loudly. Baghir elbowed him, but it was too late.

'I gotta bigger dick than you, little boy,' came Harry's barbed reply. Surprisingly, they not only understood what Harry had said, not one of them doubted it.

'What have you got for us?' asked Chloe, anxious to get some more information.

'Well, shitloads,' said Harry, who was clearly beginning to pick up some unedifying American ways.

Chloe, Ulka and the boys moved closer to the screen to listen to what Harry had to say, with Ulka translating the more complex bits.

'There's a very small unit assembled just to take out The Bestissimo hotels. It seems that there's an Arab man pulling the strings but no clue yet if there's a bigger fish out there.' This caused great amusement to the boys who didn't quite understand what she meant.

'Secret Service don't care, they're watching bigger fish in Ukraine.'

'Fishes?' Hasan giggled. 'Are we catching fish with string?'

'She means criminal gangs,' Ulka translated. 'Shush!' she added which worked perfectly well in both languages. Harry carried on regardless.

'I've got intel they're about to do the Rostov branch, day after tomorrow; same ploy, suicide taxi drivers probably including your little pal from last week, Chloe.'

'Damn!' said Chloe. Baghir rolled his eyes in irritation but held his tongue. If only she'd let him finish the man off.

'I'll get you car ID tomorrow,' Harry hissed. Over the line they could all hear her mother calling her in the background.

'Harriet? Tea's ready. Hurry darling or...' With that, the line

went dead. At Harry's end, however, a message from Hari popped up on her screen.

You are very kind, it read. *Yes, I would like to talk to someone. But first, there is something important I must do.* So Harry, being absolutely starving, left him to it.

'What do we do now then?' Chloe asked. 'Where's Rostov?'

'Russia, not too far over the border,' Ulka replied. 'I have relatives in Rostov and I know people,' she said knowingly. 'Getting in is no problem. Getting out alive may be.'

Ulka peered into Chloe's eyes. 'Chichek, are you sure you want to do this thing? It is dangerous. The boys here, they do what is right for our country. But you, this need not concern you.'

Chloe stood firm. 'They killed my colleagues,' she said 'And it was my fault the bomber got away. I have to do this.'

Ulka took in a deep breath of resolution. 'Then I must teach you Russian. It is essential. We start tonight.'

Ulka and Chloe were up half the night until Chloe was able to manage some basic phrases, certainly enough for a native of Azerbaijan to get by. Both women went to bed tired and anxious; Ulka for their safety and Chloe for the sheer adventure of it all. The next morning came too quickly for both of them. Ulka knocked on Chloe's door and went in as Chloe was just finishing getting dressed. Under her outer clothes, she wore her utility apron, crammed with small vials of various substances.

Ulka smiled. 'You travel light, my daughter,' she noted.

'Yes,' Chloe confirmed, realising that Ulka was indeed far more of a mother than her own had been. 'If I don't make it back, will you please accept my suitcase as a parting gift from me? You'll find my micro cleaner with adjustable nozzle and convertible lint remover and my special stain remover which does everything from chewing gum to primate faeces...' Ulka smiled as Chloe continued to list her utensils and their properties.

'It will be an honour to accept,' Ulka said. 'But I swear if you

do not come back, I will bring your case back to you wherever you are.'

All they needed now was the car registration numbers from Harry, and the second her email arrived, their goodbyes were said. Ulka made the boys promise that Chloe would not get involved in any fighting; she was only there to defuse bombs and make things safe.

'And you have college next week,' she scolded. 'And exams soon. Come back quickly.'

As the four of them set off in the old converted taxi, Ulka dabbed her eyes a little, then went inside to inspect Chloe's suitcase. It did indeed look very impressive.

The journey took them almost the whole day, and crossing the border was a little slow, but eventually they arrived safely at their destination a few miles from Rostov. Ulka's auntie, who was very old, slightly deaf and nearly blind, lived there in her tiny house. She was clearly expecting them and welcomed them into the aroma of some wholesome smelling soup.

The house was comfortable enough but unacceptably dirty and Chloe, being far too hyper to sleep, gave the little house a thorough going over as best she could with an ancient besom and a knitted dishcloth.

The lads crammed into a tiny bedroom while Chloe had the relative privacy of a large comfortable old sofa downstairs which was fine once she had taken off the covers and given them a good shaking outside.

There was freshly baked bread for breakfast washed down with strong coffee which was all gratefully received. It was clear from their conversation that Auntie had absolutely no idea what their plans were. When they were on their way, it was also clear she had no idea who they were either, but she still waved them off as they continued their drive into Rostov.

'I hope you catch your fish. Come and see me again one day.'

'If we get separated,' Baghir declared, 'We meet back at Auntie's.'

Chloe had later realised her mistake in taking the grungy black saloon car when she first arrived in Baku; tourists were normally greeted with old London Black Cabs. Taxis in Rostov, however, were gleaming shiny black saloons due to cleaner air and better maintenance so even without the IDs from Harry, they were quite easy to spot. Even so, they were all somewhat surprised and excited when they found the first taxi *en route* to the town centre on the very same isolated road they were following. Hasan read out the registration plate to confirm and with a 'Hurrah!' Baghir put his foot down and gave chase.

The driver realised something was up and sped up, going off road and through a wooded area. As the others clung on to the sides of the car and each other, Baghir, who was demonstrating all the skills of a joyrider in London, followed it move for move. He saw the big tree ahead before the bomber did and slammed on the brakes just in time. He reversed back as fast as he could to escape a massive BOOM after which the whole area was subsumed in thick black smoke and splattered with bits of old car and failed bomber.

When they recovered from what they had just seen, the four of them realised two things. Firstly, that there was no time to waste, secondly that they all needed the toilet. Chloe handed out her special sanitary wipes as they took turns behind an old garage just off the road.

Once they were back in the car, Baghir put his foot down and sped into town. Chloe had wanted to ask whether it had been the same taxi driver as before but knew that without trying to piece him together again, she would never find out and none of them had the time or the inclination to do that.

When they arrived in the centre of town, they located the hotel and then cruised the roads around it looking for suspect

vehicles.

'There!' Tagi shouted, and they spotted another dingy taxi sitting in traffic. The number plate checked out.

'My turn!' Tagi announced, as he chewed gum and patted his chest where his gun was clearly protruding from his badly fitting holster. He snuck out of their car and ran across the road, catching up with the taxi and jumping in alongside the driver. He knew instantly from the man's expression that he had the right one, although on reflection he realised anybody would probably have reacted badly to somebody jumping into his car. He pulled out his pistol and without a second thought, shot the man cleanly in the head.

Chloe had jumped out behind him and was heading for the front of the car. She looked at the man's face, trying to ignore the mess Tagi had made but it wasn't *her* driver. She did, however, note that she had been almost spot on, no pun intended, about the amount of blood and the splatter pattern over the back of the car. But this was no time for *I told you so*. Instead, she opened the bonnet of the car. The bomb was there, but this time it was wired. 'Shit,' she said. 'Wasn't expecting this.'

All Chloe's research had led her to believe that you always cut the green wire, but these were yellow and blue. She had to think fast. What to do, WHAT TO DO?

By now there were some very worried and unsettled people still sitting in their cars. A couple had witnessed the shooting, but most had just heard a noise and were getting worried. Chloe came to her decision.

'BOMB!' she shouted in Russian as loud as she possibly could, and she didn't stop to watch the pandemonium that ensued as fellow drivers cottoned on to what was happening and began to flee their cars.

Baghir had anticipated traffic problems and was waiting in a side road. Chloe and Tagi ran after him, just managing to jump in the car in time for him to make a clean getaway. As they moved off, they heard the unmistakable sound of an explosion behind them. No time to stop, Baghir drove further on. Then Hasan shouted out.

'It's there! Approaching the hotel.'

They all turned to look, then Baghir looked ahead and just beginning to approach the entrance was the third taxi. Chloe went a little cold as she recognised the driver's face.

'No shooting,' she warned. 'Too many people around.'

Baghir put his foot down again and swerved right in front of the taxi, causing it to brake suddenly. Chloe jumped out and opened the bonnet; no wiring this time, she got to work as quickly as she could while Hasan and Tagi dragged the driver out and began to punch him senseless. Suddenly there was gunfire over their heads. Close. Too close. The local police were just catching up on recent events and had sent a team to The Bestissimo in case of attack. There was no time for the lads to try to explain what was going on, they had to escape. A Russian jail was no place for them.

Baghir drove alongside them. 'In the car,' he yelled, Hasan jumped while Tagi spat on the driver as a last gesture, before following Hasan into the car.

'Chloe!' screamed Baghir, but Chloe was too busy defusing the bomb. Now they saw the police cars; they were being chased, they had no choice, Baghir began to pull away.

'I'll be fine!' Chloe shouted at them. 'See you at Auntie's,' But as Baghir drove off, he saw in his rear-view mirror what Tagi and Hasan had just turned round to watch. As Chloe raised her hand to give them a thumbs up that she had defused the bomb, they all heard shots and she fell to the ground. Tears filled their eyes as Baghir put his foot down and they sped away.

'She is a true heroine,' he said and Hasan and Tagi sniffed their agreement through their tears.

Harry, momentarily out of contact with her friend but receiving reports of the attempted bombing was scared sick for her friend and was frantically searching the internet.

Suddenly she received a message from the strange young Russian.

'I was stopped again,' he wrote.

'Tell me about yourself,' she asked. 'I know you have lost someone dear to you from your video, but tell me what happened. It might help.'

Hari did not reply directly; instead, he shared with Harry more of his atrocious essays and poems. The more Harry read, the more fascinated she became and she gleaned his story from his terrible writings. Then he wrote something which confused Harry.

If I ever find the woman who did this to me, I shall surely kill her.

But I thought you loved Anna?

With all the many pieces of my broken heart.

Tell me about her then, typed Harry, and she read patiently while Hari had poured out his soul to her in the form of more of his terrible poetry.

Oh, woman who refused my love, one began. *How must I bear a rejected heart in my bosom?*

Harry tried very slowly and carefully to pull him away from his lost love and maybe, although she hadn't quite realised it herself, towards her.

Hari, I'd love to see you in person. Can we talk face to face? I haven't got a camera yet, but I will have soon.

Hari was both surprised and pleased that this Western woman who seemed to understand him wanted to look him in the

eyes. Maybe she would join him; maybe even on his next mission whatever that was going to be?

The next day Harry found a message that he was waiting to speak to her. She had been really excited when she turned on the screen, but her excitement turned to shock when she saw his appearance. Although now fading, his face was still swollen and covered with bruises.

What the hell happened? she asked him.

My mission. He'd replied, adding sincerely. *One day I will tell you all.*

Harry, despite being terribly clever, never made the vital connection that this was the man who had tried to bomb the hotel. She did, however, assume it was some sort of suicide attempt and this made him her top priority; her mission was to save him from himself and that meant burying his dreadful video and poetry so deep in the Internet it would never be found again. He'll thank me one day, she thought, when he realises how embarrassed he would be if people heard his shit writing.

So what had happened to poor Chloe? Well, firstly, she hadn't been shot at all. She'd spotted Tagi's gum on the ground, and worried that he might be traced through his DNA, she'd ducked down to pick it up at the exact moment the policeman had shot. In any case, he wasn't aiming for her; to be honest, he hadn't seen anything behind the bonnet of the car, he was just trying to look like he was doing something, and boy did he love shooting.

Chloe realised that the boys had driven off and she did what she was very good at – she melted away through the *mêlée*. Her first thought was to get to the hotel and as soon as she decided it was safe, she wandered over there to find out what was

happening.

The second she walked in, she was shocked to the core. The floor hadn't been swept, the windows were dirty and there were cobwebs hanging from the chandeliers. She marched straight up to the concierge and gave him a good ear battering. Within minutes, the Head of Housekeeping had been summoned, and Chloe began a detailed critique of precisely what was wrong.

'And who are you?' squealed the admonished Head of Housekeeping.

'I am Chloe Chopra. Specialist Cleaner for The Bestissimo Hotel in London.'

This was almost like royalty for the poor Head of Housekeeping. She was both ashamed and honoured. Within minutes, Chloe had been allocated a fine room and was made more than comfortable. She even managed to contact the Head of Housekeeping in London, who was astonished to hear from her.

'Er, I remember you,' she said without much conviction. 'Weren't you meant to go to Azerbaijan? We assumed...'

'I'm fine,' Chloe assured her. 'I missed all that. But now I'm here, I think they can do with some help. I don't mind staying for a week or so if you want, but I do need to come home soon, and I need money.'

While Chloe waited for everything to be confirmed, she thought about contacting Ulka and the boys; especially Baghir, but in her heart of hearts she knew her destiny lay back in England. It wouldn't be fair to tie him down, she decided. He's so young and only just starting out. For a moment she wondered if she should say nothing; let them assume she had died. After all, she had no easy way of contacting them, but as soon as Harry rang her at the hotel, she changed her mind. She didn't even question Harry this time as to how she had found her.

I'm fine Harry. I'm staying here for a while but there's something I need you to do.

Anything Chloe.

Can you contact Ulka for me? Tell her I'm safe and make sure that the boys are OK?

What even that dick? Harry had replied.

Yes. Even him. They were the good guys. And you need to make sure that the Russians know it too. Please, Harry. Ulka was always worried that they'd be thrown in prison for what they'd done and they have to go back to college.

Just for you, Chloe. But you must promise to come and see me soon. I have bacterial issues with my bedroom.

A few days later, Chloe came back to England and when her suitcase appeared on the carousel, she grabbed it quickly. She took off her jacket to change it for a coat and it happened by a fundamental tool in storytelling otherwise known as coincidence, that Mel was also at the airport that day. Mel couldn't have picked out Chloe from a line-up of one, but there was something she did recognise.

'I'd know that utility apron anywhere,' she said. And she marched over to where Chloe was standing and held out her hand.

'Mel,' she announced. 'Long red hair, killer heels, corpse in The Bestissimo bedroom.'

Chloe peered at the woman for a couple of seconds.

'Ah yes. Acid bath, career progression.' She paused and offered her hand. 'Chloe Chopra. Nice to meet you again.'

'You must come with me,' Mel urged. 'There is someone I know who is dying to meet you.'

Elle was instantly impressed with Chloe and without hesitation offered her a job. She invited Nettie in to meet her new boss and gave them some space. After a brief discussion about microfibre cleaning cloths, Nettie gave her approval.

'You nice girl. Not like shit Luigi,' she said, which Chloe took

as a great compliment from the needle-sharp woman. The whole arrangement was cemented with a G&T toast to Chloe which even Nettie was invited to, although Elle took care to give her a much greater tonic to gin ratio.

'And before I forget, thanks so much for what you did with that horrible Luigi character,' Elle smiled.

Chloe blushed. 'My pleasure. I could see he was a nasty individual and what he did to those poor girls...' Nettie hiccupped in agreement.

'I wonder what else he was up to?' Elle ventured.

'Perhaps you could get Penelope to have a dig around?' Mel suggested.

'I know someone,' Chloe said a little too quietly but even if the others heard her, they were too distracted by the growing rumbling outside. Elle knew this noise well, so it seemed did Mel and Nettie who made for the door standing carefully on the left-hand side. Chloe, sensing something or someone who was very distressed but not having X-ray vision joined them.

The noise grew to a clamour and the door burst open to reveal a tumbling Penelope who stopped just before Elle's desk but not in enough time to avoid the coat stand. As she picked it up and tried to stick the arms back into place the others discreetly slipped out.

The first thing Elle noticed was that Penelope was wearing only the dregs of her uniform.

'CID at last?' Elle ventured hopefully.

'DID more like,' Penelope replied dolefully.

Finally detecting Penelope's even more miserable than usual state, Elle smiled. 'I have gin.'

Penelope slumped ungraciously on the chair while Elle went to her cupboard to get another glass into which gin, ice and a slice of lemon from the little fridge were promptly added. Before she could open her mouth, Penelope spoke.

'Dismissed in Disgrace,' she explained. 'I'll never get another job now,' she moaned.

'What on earth happened?' asked Elle, handing her the glass, and between large gulps necessitating a couple of refills, Penelope told her tale.

'We were picketing a fishing game at the local funfair because it was giving out goldfish as prizes,' she began, and this was indeed true. But what Penelope glossed over was that her animal army had been snatching goldfish from little kids making them cry and making their mothers very angry. The owner of the despicable source of animal cruelty had telephoned the police and before you could say goldfish bowls, Penelope had found herself toe to toe with one of her fellow officers.

'Then that nasty little cow spotted me,' Penelope continued. The nasty little cow in question was a very smart and universally despised fast track officer; very ambitious and exceptionally full of herself. Gradually, the story emerged.

In one of those moments of monumental stupidity we all sometimes have, Penelope had taken the statistically impossible option that she might not have been recognised and had legged it to her car. She'd ploughed down the motorway as fast as her poor old but considerably souped-up banger could take her. Might as well go down for a shit as a fart, she had thought as she put her foot down; one of her father's sayings that had wedged itself firmly in her brain. It was no good; her little Fiesta was never going to outpace a brand spanking new patrol car.

'It's an unfair cop!' she had pouted at WPC Smart when she was pulled over and arrested.

Penelope had actually been a damn fine copper right up until that day. Corruption and speeding they'd called it, although when they realised the corruption, the speeding was thankfully forgotten. Then they dropped the corruption charges, because, well putting it bluntly, she knew too much about what everybody else had been

getting up to. What was more, WPC Smart was getting up everybody's noses so much that no one above her could bear the idea of her lording it all over them and having to curtail all their illicit activities if Penelope blabbed. So instead of a long and protracted process, Penelope was summarily dismissed with a compromise agreement and a reasonable payoff. She still fumed at the injustice of it all. It wasn't corruption, it wasn't even a backhander, it was simply a contribution to her animal crusaders group, but she was not confident she could challenge the force. Besides the money at the time seemed very tempting. It was enough to fund a door drop and poster run about bad practises at We R Pets.

Now, money gone, Penelope had been glumly sitting on a park bench, her blue serge trousers had long since had a row with her bright white socks and the button on her trouser waistband was now pulled to its last fibre of thread. She wasn't exceptionally big, but she did have the perfect build, and the strength come to that, for a lightweight Sumo wrestler. All sorts of thoughts of new careers were running through her head but it wasn't until she looked up and spotted the welcoming legend ELLE'S BELLES that she sat up and finally made the connection. Elle dealt in careers of a sort, but not one that Penelope herself could contemplate, but who better to ask for advice?

'So I came here, Elle.'

Elle, needing more than a second to think it all through, poured the pouting woman another gin.

'What? With all your knowledge? Anybody would be glad to have your skills. How are you on computers?'

Penelope moaned out loud. 'Rubbish. I'm just rubbish,' and she began to sob into her gin.

Elle began postulating; she certainly knew that Penelope wasn't rubbish. Ungainly, clumsy, yes, but does she have her uses? She knows how the police work. She's had gun training. She's hot on security. She can handle a car like a Formula One driver...

'Come and work for me,' she said.

Penelope gulped. For all her strengths, Elle had underestimated how dim she could be.

'Er, I'm not sure that I would fit into that line of work,' she stuttered. Elle laughed a little too loudly and Penelope's bottom lip quivered just a little.

'No dear Penelope. I meant for me, as my right-hand man/woman. My security advisor. My protection.'

'Oh?' Penelope perked up. 'That sounds interesting.'

'Don't get too excited,' Elle said. 'It won't be very interesting at first, but I'm sure as time goes on, it will become downright thrilling.'

'That's good enough for me,' said Penelope, now beginning to beam. 'Did you know I can strip a car down in ten minutes flat, retune an engine, break into any car on God's earth and deactivate any CCTV camera in the Western hemisphere?'

Elle's mind, like Penelope's car, went into overdrive. 'Yes,' she said noncommittally. 'I'm sure that might be of use.'

'And you already know I am as good a counterfeiter as my dad. At least he says so.'

'Yes,' said Elle again trying to sound disinterested, but inside she was slapping her thighs and high fiving her reflection. She'd struck gold. Well, maybe not quite gold, she reconsidered as Penelope loped out of the office, promptly tripping over her own shoelaces.

CHAPTER SEVEN

What the Devil Did Happen to David?

Delilah was not really a bad person, she just had an obsession with animal skins. Born and brought up in the Rockies, hunting animals was in her blood and although she hadn't been hunting since her daddy died some years before, she did it vicariously through the stories and films of the men she knew around the town, which was most of them. She always wore something derived from animals, but when she was performing her exotic dances, it had to be bear fur and it never failed to drive the customers wild.

There had been much excitement in her little outpost of a town recently; a film crew had come to town and they were filming her favourite TV animal show. Delilah could gawp for hours at the gorgeous skins of the creatures captured on film, but none were more gorgeous to her than the hunky presenter, David Swallow. Delilah was bursting with excitement at the prospect of seeing him in the actual flesh. As it turned out, it was the other way around.

David's career had blossomed from those early days in the Andes and the programme's ratings were rocketing. Now a seasoned professional, he was far too busy filming and writing his dissertation to come home to see his one true love, Angel, but still, he wrote letters whenever he could from whichever hotel or lodge he was staying at. His letters always ended, *We will be together soon my love*, and to be fair, he meant it. None of the tons of fan

mail had yet reached him; he rarely read newspapers and never went on the internet except to undertake research, so he was completely oblivious to his astronomical fame.

When the filming of *The Real Yogi Bear* was finally finished, the film crew organised a special surprise for David. They had realised fairly on from their conversations with him that despite his detailed understanding of nearly every conceivable form of animal copulation, he had never actually dabbled in the human kind. In short, he was still a virgin. The crew chose their moment carefully in the hotel bar when David was in his room writing. A quick show of hands confirmed the nature of the surprise they were going to give him; he was going to lose his cherry.

When he emerged downstairs to join the crew at the bar he was immediately whisked off for a night of steamy entertainment. He struggled a little as they pushed him through the doors of the infamous Bare Bear Bar; the pictures outside were already way beyond anything he had ever seen before, but when he went inside, his eyes nearly popped out of his head. A whip-round of the money kind was swiftly organised and David was soon shuffled into a small room furnished in red velvet to enjoy a private lap dance with a local girl known for giving extras when required.

The crew were right about David; never in his entire existence had he encountered a single human female in the actual flesh, and certainly not anything so spectacular as Delilah. Clad entirely in bearskin, she blew him away with her routine. As each piece of second skin came off and was wrapped round his neck, face and hands, he felt for himself the exquisite touch of animal fur on human skin. He had handled animals many times before, but this was different. He had never felt anything so sensitive, vibrant and downright sexy before. He was completely smitten with Delilah and as the pile of clothing grew beside him, he couldn't take his eyes off her, or his hands off her clothes.

Delilah too was star struck. David was the most famous

person she'd ever met. The only man who'd even come close before was an aging singer about whom her mom had nursed not so secret desires for years. She'd recognised him from her mom's pictures but she never told her mother that she danced for him, but then again her mother didn't know she danced quite the way she did.

The chemistry between David and Delilah was palpable and their bodily conversation was heading for a room even before they'd spoken to each other. The bar did have provision for such use, but Delilah decided that it was too seedy for someone as special as David.

'Meet me outside at ten,' she whispered to him. 'You can come back to mine for coffee.'

A red and very flustered David emerged from his private dance to cheers from the film crew, followed by whoops when he told them about his assignation.

'You've got til midday tomorrow,' Kenny, the head guy told him. 'The flight's at two.'

Steeled by a couple more drinks, when the appointed hour came, David went nervously to meet his date. Delilah was waiting as agreed and without a word, led David to her old Mustang. He went to speak but she shushed him with a finger to her lips, and started the stuttering engine, then pulled out and drove him to her boudoir.

Delilah's log cabin was simple enough, but to David, it became a paradise. Delilah sat him down on her genuine bearskin sofa while she slowly stripped off. When she was naked, she started to take David's clothes off so slowly he thought he was going to burst. Well, actually he did burst. Delilah had no idea it was his first time and just took it as a compliment. Before long they were congressing like rabbits at a speed dating convention; first on the bearskin rug, then on the wolf coffee table and finally on the lynx skin bedspread. They had both eyed up the moose head on

display, but sensibly realised that they were too tired to make use of that too. When they were both completely exhausted, Delilah made some hot chocolate and they fell asleep in each other's arms.

The next morning, David had all but forgotten about Angel. He was as deeply in love as a humpback whale is in the sea hiding from a Japanese whaler ship. He looked at his watch, it was getting late. Then he looked back at Delilah. There was no way he was going back home, not yet, but he had to tell the crew members.

'I must go back to the hotel, my love,' he said.

'Aw honey, do you have to? I wanna stay like this with you forever.'

And looking at her wrapped in furs all sexy and pouty, that was exactly what David wanted to do too.

'I'll be back my sweetheart,' he said. 'With my suitcase and clothes. Now that I have met you, I can't leave you.'

'Shucks baby, I'm coming too. Just to make sure you come with me. Besides, you'll need a ride there.'

They dressed absurdly shyly with their backs to each other. Delilah, who had learned from the experience of wearing out her male friends, cooked them a good full breakfast of eggs, bacon and potato fries which they savoured and washed down with strong coffee. When they had finished, they made their way to the hotel where they were surprised to be greeted by a small crowd gathered outside. The locals and even some of the national press were there and wanted to grab a few shots of the crew before they left.

Everybody was shocked to see David Swallow, the star of the show, emerge from a car with a brass blonde hooker. But at least she was a local girl, so they cheered anyway.

David, like a rabbit caught in the headlights, gave a nervous smile then turned to talk to Kenny.

'I've decided to continue my research here for a little while

longer. I'll be back on the show as soon as you can say bear ass.'

Well, nobody quite knew how to take that. It certainly didn't sound like the English gentleman presenter, but assuming he was just trying to be friendly they all cheered again. There was much snapping and flashing of cameras which David endured with absolutely no idea of the consequences. A couple of days later, it was a photo from this very scene which ended up in *Tit-Bits and Tits* under the heading Nature Boy Falls for Naturist Girl.

Delilah and David were beginning to get to know each other a bit better, or at least David was getting to know most of Delilah's body parts, but there was nothing wrong with her brain either. She knew who she was, what she knew and most importantly what she did not know, which made her a good deal cleverer than those judgemental people who think they know everything. For the first time in her life, she had a man of her own and they spent a happy and blissful six months together.

David couldn't bear her dancing at the Bare Bear Bar anymore; she was his, so he'd put his increasingly manly foot down and she relished his possessiveness. One day, however, a recorded delivery letter arrived. David blanched as soon as he saw the logo of the TV Company splattered over the envelope. The letter was brief and to the point.

'If you're not back next week, you're off the show.'

'I have to go back, my sweet,' David told Delilah that evening. 'You know I do.' And Delilah did know it and being good natured and understanding accepted his decision gracefully. After all, she decided, he'd be back as soon as the next series was finished. But the days were getting colder and there was something she had a hankering for. There was nothing so nice on a cold night as a new bearskin rug. Now, however, because of David's demands, there was no chance to ask any of her former man friends to get her one. She started a conversation that evening.

'David honey, have you ever thought about going hunting?'

David shook his head. 'I have devoted my life to preserving animal life; not extinguishing it.'

'Aww but lover, you're not in silly ol' Engerland now. Out here everybody hunts. It's our way of life and you're not a man here if you don't hunt.'

Delilah's words hurt him. Not the bit about not being a man, it was more about not understanding their way of life that got him. How could he, who knew animals inside out, not realise that humans had their needs too? Especially, as he now understood, the bedroom ones.

'Tell me about hunting then. Surely it's not a fair fight; a man with a gun is always going to win.'

'Oh my,' Delilah exclaimed. 'It's about as fair as it can be. Let me tell you what's not fair.'

'Tell me then,' David teased, and Delilah began her story.

'Well a good ol' time ago my daddy went to Africa. One of his pals from the city thought it might be fun to shoot some really dangerous animals, so off they went on safari.' David shuddered but Delilah poked him.

'Shush and don't judge till you've heard the whole story.'

Chastised, David nodded and listened.

'Well, daddy was taken out on a truck an' all. And there were rangers too and all they did was chase some poor critters round. It weren't no fair fight at all. Not one bit. But daddy's friend had paid a whole heap of dollars money so they had to go through with it. They killed a lion which had no way to escape and they didn't even get out of the truck.'

'That's shameful,' David said.

'That's just what my daddy said. So when he came home, he took his friend out to hunt bears.'

David was surprised. 'How did that help?'

'Well, when you hunt bears it's just you and them. No trucks, no rangers; the bear has as much chance to get you as you have

it. And our bears sure are smart.'

'So what happened?' David was curious.

'Well, that time the bear won,' Delilah declared with a slight moistening of her eyes.

'You mean...'

'I do. My poor darlin' daddy died that day. And the bear ran off with some of him that we never found again. But that was a fair fight. That's how it is and we never took up against that bear or nothing.'

David hugged Delilah tight and his mind began ticking over.

That night when they were in bed together, with perfect timing Delilah asked, 'Honey, have you thought any more about going hunting?'

'Yes, I have Delilah. Do we have to talk now?'

'Well, I wanted to know if you're going to take me.'

'Anything, anything,' he replied. 'Just don't stop.'

'It's getting colder again and I'd really like a new bear skin rug.'

'Delilah, you know I'd do anything for you.'

'I know my darlin'. So you'll get me a bear?'

'Yes, yes YES!' he had replied on the cusp of ecstasy.

Delilah's loud squeal of delight in reply was not as a result of her own ecstasy, more at his response. She couldn't wait to be back out hunting and so looked forward to having a new skin to cure. When they were lying next to each other and he was falling asleep, she told him that she would book them a hunting lodge in the morning but being too excited to wait, she went online straight away to have a look at what was on offer. There was one place she had never been to before; it was a little off the beaten track and could be tricky, she'd heard, but the bears there had the most perfect colour skin. David awoke the next morning to her *fait accompli*.

It had never occurred to David, in his ignorant arrogance, that

bears could be dangerous to him. He was used to animals and they usually responded well to him. He did, however, correctly guess that he would need a pretty big gun to fell one. When he went to the gun shop the owner recognised him from the television and without a word, handed David a gun big enough to take out a herd of elephants, but only if you knew how to use it.

'On the house, sir,' he said. 'Pleasure to see you partake. I had you down for one of those god damned Bambi lovers.'

The very next day David and Delilah set off in a hired off-roader into the mountains.

Delilah's excitement was infectious. She was in heaven; just breathing in the clear mountain air made her realise how much she missed hunting. And seeing her ample bosom heave made David realise how he wanted to put his head between her breasts.

When they arrived, Delilah fixed lunch and then they went out on their first expedition together. Delilah led the way; she knew what she was doing, or at least she thought she did. David followed, happy to admire the scenery which mainly consisted of Delilah's expressive round bottom.

'Shush,' Delilah waved her hand behind her, and David stopped dead still. He looked up to see a bear but something strange had happened to him. Instead of seeing one of God's creatures, a fine young specimen of a brown bear, he saw a new rug for his love.

Now came the tricky part; he had never actually fired a gun before and this was a real biggie. Delilah spotted his hesitation and came to his rescue.

'Now you hear, y'all, you take this and hold it right here and put your arm here then your hand here and when you're ready you just squeeze. Gently, like you would my titties.'

David got into position and took aim at the creature without

a second thought. His aim wasn't bad, but the kickback from the gun sent him sprawling backwards and the force of the bullet meant he'd blown half the poor creature's head off. He was horrified. The skin was still OK, but the missing head bit was definitely going to spoil the overall look of any rug.

'I'm sorry my sweet. I'll try again tomorrow. But that's our last chance you understand. I have to go back the day after that.'

'Aww. Thanks, honey. You're the best,' said Delilah giving him a big kiss. 'I'm gonna miss you so much.'

The next day did not go so well at all. Momma bear was very angry that her oldest had been taken and she was in a very bad mood. She was also crafty and much smarter than the average bear. She left her youngest playing just outside the lodge to tempt David out and it worked. David gazed at the beautiful creature with just a glimmer of his old animal lover's eyes.

'Oh my gosh!' said Delilah when she saw it. 'That'll have a soft lil ol' hide like silk.'

'Yes it will,' said David, as if the scales had dropped from his eyes. 'I'll get it for you.'

He didn't see the momma bear standing behind the lodge but Delilah did. She screamed at David to get away but he didn't stand a chance. Momma bear slashed him across his face, tearing half the flesh from his bones. He fell back, dropping the gun, and she slashed at his trunk then grabbed his left arm, wrenching it off just below the elbow. Delilah bravely grabbed the gun that David had dropped and fired it straight at the bear. She missed but the bear went running off with her cub close behind. Delilah nearly went after the cub but David's moans distracted her so she ran over to him instead.

'Oh my,' she said. 'Where did your face go?' which wasn't a particularly inspiring thing to say to someone in David's position.

David was a complete mess of blood and gore but unlike his prey the day before, he was very definitely still alive. Delilah knew what do; she'd seen something like this before when her daddy died. There was nothing that could have been done to save *him*, he was missing his head. But his friend had been almost in one piece. Delilah often wondered what had happened to her daddy's head. For now, let's savour the notion that one day in the future, a bear hunter will discover a grinning human skull stuck on a ledge in a bear cave, just like a trophy.

Delilah kept calm and first, she called the local medics. Then she ran inside to grab one of her best silk stockings to tie round his arm to stop the bleeding. Looking around, she found the rest of his arm a few feet away dropped by the momma bear when she ran off. It looked beyond saving, but she picked it up anyway, just in case and shoved it in the freezer.

She thought about stroking David's face while they waited for the medics, but she was worried she might dislodge an eye, so she stroked his groin instead leaving David in both agony and ecstasy.

When David was admitted to the hospital, one of the admin staff recognised his name if not his face and immediately metaphorically wrote him off. Very soon afterwards rumours circulated all around the media that he had been killed while filming. The TV company heard the rumours too and since he never reappeared on the appointed day, assumed it was true.

The gossip columns were full of him for a day but as no more information came out, and Brad Pitt was making a new movie, by the following day nobody gave much of a shit. David, for all the world knew or cared, was dead. Actually, he just dodged death by the skin of his teeth. Luckily for him, and unluckily for momma bear, she had just missed the jugular and so his fate rested with the little hospital in the Rockies.

The hospital was very used to patching up bear victims and did a decent enough job, even managing to reattach his arm, although they doubted he would ever be able to get much use out of it in future, but David remained in a coma. The lovely and kind

Delilah didn't just listen to Tammy Wynette songs, she lived them, and so was determined to stand by her man – especially after he added her name to his bank account. One of Delilah's ex-clients ran a private clinic way up in the mountains so Delilah, with extraordinary generosity, paid for David to be moved there so he could recuperate in peace.

David's coma endured for several years and when at last he regained consciousness it took him a long time to regain any mental faculties. Naturally, nothing had been done to help mend his body although some bits had reattached inside, sometimes even in the right places but he was somewhat bent and distorted physically.

David, even in his waking hours, never once thought to tell his parents about his accident. They, however, when the grief had subsided became extremely interested in his wealth, and a little concerned about the whereabouts of his body. They wrote to the TV company who really didn't know what had happened and didn't particularly care. But there was one admin assistant who had also been a fan and she took it upon herself to trace David's last movements. After writing to everyone who had been involved on the show, she eventually reached one of the crew who mentioned the Bare Bear Bar. So it was that a letter addressed to *The blonde stripper in bear fur* finally made its way to Delilah's door.

When Delilah received the letter, she had no idea what to do. David was just about conscious by now, and he was adamant that he was going to use all his money to provide for her, after paying the hideously high medical bills he'd just found out he was incurring. Not to mention the astronomical plastic surgery bills he suspected he might need in the future. The one thing he was sure of was that he no longer wanted to be David Swallow so being dead seemed to be the best option. Together they worked out a convincing enough story about his entire wealth being left to an animal foundation and what was recovered of his body being left

to medical science. Not being as adventurous as their offspring and disincentivised by the lack of funds, his parents accepted this. He lived on in their memory and in a photo, which was given pride of place on the mantelpiece.

David's physical recovery was slow. He was still bandaged from head to toe although both his eyes were saved and he could now see. He was free to decide what he wanted to do with the life that had been given back to him. He was a non-person; he had no identity, no past, just a future; and this began to play on his mind. At first it was terrifying, then he realised that no, it was probably the most liberating thing that could happen to anybody.

In ignorance of his appearance, he began to harbour thoughts of returning to some sort of work. Delilah was encouraging. She had been at his bedside almost day and night since the accident and was getting very bored, not to mention frustrated, and looked forward to getting her man back. When the day came for some of the bandages to be removed, both David and Delilah were very apprehensive about what would be revealed. It started well; half his scalp was almost untouched so his blond hair had grown long on one side, but his face was horribly scarred. Delilah, swallowing her disgust, ran her fingers through the good side of his hair and flopped it over his face.

'You look kinda cute like that,' she remarked. 'Like you used to but sexier.' She was joking; he really looked like Andy Warhol on a really bad day and with terrible scars down his face, but she *was* trying to cheer him up. It worked to the extent that David actually gave her a very weak smile again. Delilah was thrilled to see this but hoped she wouldn't see it too often, at least, not close up.

Delilah tried to encourage David back to normality by bringing in old videos of his TV shows; she had recorded loads of them. At first, he watched them with good humour but something had gone horribly wrong inside his head and he found that he was physically repulsed at the sight of all those animals. He stopped

watching, assuming it was his medication making him ill, but inside he was in turmoil.

When all the bandages were removed and he was confronted with the whole of his broken battered body with bent and sticky out bits, the turmoil only increased. The final blow came when he caught his old show on TV. He grimaced when he saw the new presenter was, in fact, the previous guy again, who looked fine if a little nervous and walking with a bit of a limp. That made David realise that with all the surgery in the world, he would never look good again and it made him very severely angry.

David's anger, coupled with his very damaged brain, began to eat away at him. In his old life, he'd known that a mother bear would do anything to protect her cubs, but the David who lay in his bed stewing was furious. How dare that creature do this to me? What right has a god damned bear to take away a man's career? How stupid was I to waste my time studying and protecting animals? They don't deserve to live.

The other final blow came when Delilah's doctor friend gave David the very bad news that David's money had run out and in another month he would be politely asked to vacate his bed. Some wiring in David's head connected his newfound revulsion for animals to his hatred for them to a lack of money. So like a horrible slimy old lamp in the dingiest street in the grubbiest place, an idea came to him. He grabbed at Delilah's old videos and ran them one by one, fast forwarding all the animal sequences, looking only for the really interesting bits; how much money came from illegal poaching. Bingo! His new career plan was beginning to form.

After the accident, Delilah had become everything for David; eyes, ears, carer and treasurer but now he was about to be discharged, or to be more accurate, thrown out, the pressure was on. She'd offered to go back to work but David was having none of it.

'Not while I've got a breath in my body,' he ordered her.

Banned from stripping, Delilah had to find new ways to make money. She'd already made some headway, but more out of boredom than need. The day after the accident she'd gone back to the lodge to clear up. She'd skinned the first bear and cut off a piece of flank to make some bear burgers. The rest was left as carrion, but the pelt itself she'd taken home and given it to one of her man friends to cure. She'd almost forgotten about it until she saw an advert in the paper campaigning against the use of fur in fashion.

'Oh my,' she said. 'What a gorgeous jacket. I wonder if Billy Bob has kept that ol' bearskin?'

Luckily he had, and he gifted the fur back to her without even thinking of asking for one of her favours; well not a very big one anyway.

'How's your man doing now, darlin'?' He enquired.

'He's mending mostly,' came her reply.

'Always here to help,' he'd added as he handed her the fur.

Delilah had then discovered that she had an undiscovered gift for sewing. At her very first attempt she'd recreated that little sleeveless jacket and she was thrilled with it. On the very first day she wore it out she was amazed at the reaction to it. Everybody wanted to know where she bought it.

'You made it? Aw sweetie. Can you make me one too? I'm a size twelve. I'll pay you whatever you want.' Stunned by the reaction, Delilah made her pitch.

'Is one hundred dollars OK?' asked Delilah curiously.

'That cheap? Honey, I'll have two for that.'

Delilah was starting to make a little money on the side. She'd had no idea at the time that David's savings had been so depleted. Now she knew, she began to crank up production but she worried that it wouldn't be enough to keep them both, especially with David needing plastic surgery as he very definitely did. A week or so before David was due to come home, the fur gilets were selling

very well and at two hundred dollars a time, Delilah was beginning to earn serious money but her fortunes were about to change.

One day one of Delilah's old friends, a hostess at the Bare Bear Bar came knocking at her door.

'Hello, it's me,' she said shyly.

'Why hi, sugar, what can I do for you?'

'It's kind of private,' the woman said, and she whispered in Delilah's ear; Delilah nearly blushed.

I wonder, Delilah thought.

Well to cut a pelt short, the hostess was thrilled with what Delilah made her and promptly ordered more for her friends. Delilah was delighted, so were the customers at the Bare Bear Bar. The especially good thing about a fur thong was it took up so little material that Delilah could make hundreds of them for the same amount of pelt she used for a gilet but she had no idea if the demand was out there. She thought long and hard and penned an ad for her local shop window which she knew only women would understand.

'Do you wanna have a fun fur over your fun fur?' she wrote. 'Discreet Service. Call Delilah on 8334 988333.'

The very next day she received a call from a shy caller with a very high-pitched voice.

'Well I need your measurements honey,' she said. 'It's got to fit right, you can't have a baggy fur.'

'What measurements?' said the caller, perturbed.

'All of them, sugar. Around your hips, your hoo-ha, and your thighs...'

The caller said something which really did make her blush. 'Ah OK, I guess I can do them for guys too...'

The following day there were three calls, the day after that ten, and as word spread, it seemed like the whole darn town wanted one of Delilah's thongs. She couldn't wait to tell David about it and was bursting with excitement when she went to the

hospital to see him.

'I just don't understand it,' she said. 'They'd be so itchy...'

'I don't think they're for day wear,' said David, amazed that Delilah could be so dim.

'Oh my!' Delilah exclaimed. 'You mean that I'm making sex clothes? What would mamma say!'

David thought for a moment and something in his brain began to tick. 'She'd say that we need to go bigger,' he said, becoming rather dominating. 'There's clearly a market for them. You keep on turning them out. I'll do some research and we'll get some advertising out there.'

'You will? When are you coming home?'

'Tomorrow,' said David. 'I'm coming home, my sweet.'

'Awesome!' said Delilah.

So the day came and Delilah took David home and showed him some thongs. She'd showed him some other things first but he couldn't seem to raise any enthusiasm, so she took him to her sewing corner instead.

'What should we call them then?'

'Genuine bear pelt thongs?' David suggested.

'That ain't very exciting sounding honey. How about Muff Muffs?' David cringed under his blond mop. 'And Dong Thongs!' added Delilah laughing.

'If you say so, my sweet,' said David. 'They do have a sort of ring about them.'

'Who'd have thought all these fine people would want my do dahs?' said Delilah and in a much clearer light bulb moment, a new company was born. Delilah's Do Dahs.

Delilah was ecstatic at the thought of her very own business. She'd always wanted to make her own way in the world and now she was on the verge of doing exactly that but better; she had her

man back home. She'd thought a lot about David over the last few months, and although he looked pretty hideous, she'd been with worse, and deep down she really did love him. She'd seen him in hospital many times but now when he was standing in front of her looking so pale and thin, she worried about him. There was something different about him now. He was a changed man.

David was indeed a changed and angry man but he hid it well and even though he could have blamed Delilah, he was still a little in love with her although he was now somewhat deficient in the trouser department. He'd had some time to think about their future and he knew it was his responsibility to look after her. Her growing business sparked off some ideas of his own. From the moment he came home, David seemed to spend all his time glued to his computer.

'I'm researching markets,' he told Delilah, and in a way he was. He was also beginning to build up his strength.

Delilah wasted no time getting her side of things moving. She went out hunting for bears and even started a side business in burgers which she sold back to the town. At first, she sent all the pelts out for curing, but as business got better, she realised she could do the whole thing herself much cheaper. Well, if not quite cheaper, without performing little favours for her hunter friends because even she knew that David would not approve of that especially now he was home. She turned her little lodge into a factory office and rented a cabin nearby big enough for a processing room and a sewing room. She hired a couple of girls to sew and off they went. The more they made, the more they sold. It was amazing! The whole world seemed to want their furs.

Delilah was now well and truly into her own routine just as David began to take a real interest in the business and he began to start interfering, or as he would put it, offering constructive advice.

Delilah tried not to argue with him because he wasn't really well yet, but he was beginning to needle her. She almost wished he'd go away and tried dropping hints about him doing some actual research, somewhere else, but David wasn't yet up to travelling.

'Soon Delilah. When the time is right,' he'd say. 'Now what about changing this stitching here...'

It was with great delight that one day Delilah received a letter which would change both of their lives forever.

'Oh my,' said Delilah as she read its contents. David snatched it from her.

'Delilah's Do Dahs have been nominated for the Newcomer award, by the *Best Business Magazine*,' he read. 'You are invited to join us in London for the awards and presentation ceremony.'

This was Delilah's chance. She never much liked travelling and hated the idea of all that publicity which is perhaps surprising for a stripper, but maybe it was more because she saw a way to get David out of her hair at last.

'I just can't go there, honey,' she said. 'You're the presenter an' all, you know how to talk and stuff, I'd be just plain useless at all that. Can you go? Please darlin'?'

David couldn't fault her logic but he had to think it through. The last thing he wanted was to be recognised as *That guy off the telly; shit, what happened to him?* Besides, he was dead, wasn't he?

'I'll think about it,' he said, just as the telephone rang.

Delilah took the call but as usual, David listened to the conversation. It sounded like a difficult call and Delilah was getting flustered.

'Let me speak to your boss, little girl,' the caller had said in such a rude way, Delilah automatically handed the phone to David.

'This is the manager here,' David said. 'How can I help you?' David listened carefully to the request. It wasn't long before an evil smile began to creep across his face.

This was David's dawning; he was on the verge of a breakthrough and he could turn it into a nice round trip.

'No problem at all sir,' he said. 'We are just about to open an office in India.'

CHAPTER EIGHT

Awards, Alliances, and Adversaries

David, with a new identity and passport, was stepping out with not a little trepidation.

It was his first trip since the accident and even longer since he had been back to England. *The Best Business Magazine Awards Ceremony* was being held in a very nearly swanky hotel in London called the Swilton. The best newcomer award was regarded as more of a talent spotting gong, and its endowment on new businesses induced high expectations for all sorts of companies over the years. Almost all of them had failed.

This year, one of the talent scouts was a young lady, a reporter who had purchased her own muff muff and was delighted with it. All the fashion magazines seemed to be full of them and that, to her, was more than a good enough reason for Delilah's Doo Dahs to make the shortlist. Her rather more seasoned colleague had nominated a much more formidable player; Bessie Wainwright for her Bestissimo hotel chain. Delilah's Do Dahs never really stood much of a chance, and Sovan Wildwald, aka David, knew this but he also knew that in order to attract the right sort of attention he had to put himself in the spotlight. He hoped that the publicity generated from contending the award would bring forth precisely the sorts of enquires and demands he was looking forward to supplying.

By the time David checked in to the hotel he was well used to strange looks. The passport staff on both sides of the pond had been unable to hide their grimaces. So he ignored the stares of the reception staff and wandered along to the bar. He was feeling a little out of sorts with the journey and the time difference and needed something to calm him a little. He ordered his drink and sat in a corner as far away from everybody as he possibly could, sending out vibes that would have penetrated a concrete bunker; he clearly did not want company.

'Hello,' said a big black bustling woman as she strode up to sit opposite him. 'Are you here for the awards? My God, what happened to you?' And the phenomenon that was Bessie Wainwright was about to impose herself on him.

Elizabeth Eugene Wainwright had come a very long way from her humble beginnings as the only daughter of West Indian parents. Neither did she know how prophetic her initials would become. Demanding and snobbish from the day she was born, she shunned her own mother's milk because of the unmistakable flavour of pepper sauce. From that day on, she would only drink British formula baby feed and as she grew would only eat traditional English fare. So fussy did she become about the meals she was served and their appearance, it drove her poor mother half mad. Knowing little about bangers and mash, she spent hours studying cookery books, shaping meat, moulding potatoes and counting peas.

Elizabeth's bus driver father couldn't bear her at all. She constantly lectured him on his pronunciation and ticked him off for his generous intake of rum. An early attempt to lose her on his longest bus route failed when she found her way to the local police station and gave them his ID number.

With no hope of changing their daughter, the only thing that

brought the poor parents comfort was Mr Wainwright's vasectomy. Normally reserved for slightly older people with several children, Mrs Wainwright had never been so grateful for her nursing profession when one of the doctors, who had met the awful child, agreed to do a favour for all of them. There would be no more offspring and they would endeavour to make sure she was out of their hands as soon as she was eighteen.

The young Elizabeth resisted all attempts at a shortened name and was very rude to anyone who called her Betty, especially if they sang *that* song but was somewhat taken when her primary class school did a project on Elizabeth the first deciding that Good Queen Bess sounded rather splendid. Elizabeth became Bess, which inevitably, and purely for PR purposes, later on, became Bessie.

Bess had been banned from the primary school kitchens after her interrogation of the dinner ladies led to their first ever strike, so it was a long time before she could infiltrate another institutional kitchen. Her chance came on her first day at secondary school. It was also the day she finally met her match. At break time she marched straight into the kitchen and began to inspect the equipment and the contents of the fridge, freezer and cupboards. Mrs Huggins was not one to allow anybody in her kitchen. The second she spotted Bess, she stood arms akimbo in front of her.

'And where do you think you are going, Miss?' Mrs Huggins asked.

'If I am to eat at this establishment, I insist on checking the kitchens,' Bess said haughtily, taking a step towards the oven.

At this point, Mrs Huggins, who had a great deal of experience in handling little madams, grabbed a giant ladle from the worktop and planted a firm smack on the top of Bess's head. Bess was mortified; her head hurt a little but her pride was smashed to smithereens.

'Now, young lady,' Mrs Huggins said. 'If you ask nicely, I will

show you around the kitchen. But if I get any more trouble from you, you'll be tomorrow's dinner.' She glanced menacingly at a large bloodied meat cleaver lying on the chopping board. Bessie took a sharp intake of breath. Nobody, but nobody had ever spoken to her like that. Ever.

'You can't...' she began, but Mrs Huggins held her ladle aloft.

'*Please*, Mrs Huggins,' the formidable lady lectured. 'Always remember your p's and q's'.

Bess stood there for a minute processing the information.

'I am s s s sorry, Mrs Huggins,' and it really was the hardest word. 'I am exceptionally interested in food preparation and I would appreciate it very much if you would show me round your kitchen.'

'That's better, dear. Of course I will.'

Mrs Huggins, being a good and sincere woman did just that. Bess too had been taught a very valuable lesson; she had learnt the art of insincerity. From then on, to the outside world Bess was the most affable person in the world. Inside she remained a cold calculating bitch.

Clearly destined for a career in hospitality, Bess's business brain wasn't bad either. She could spot a USP before most people even knew what it was. She couldn't see the point in wasting time at university and set her sights on a small bed and breakfast establishment in Blackpool. Her parents were only too glad to give up their life savings for Bess's start-up capital.

'Take it,' her father said to her. 'Just don't ever come back home.'

Bess began her research and did it well and thoroughly. She found ways and means to regularly feature in travel magazines. She had an uncanny ability to spot a reviewer at thirty paces and oozed charm like an éclair oozes cream. But Bess was no wallflower. A grafter, she worked exceptionally hard and by the time she was twenty she had seen off the immediate local

competition and bought out the B&Bs either side to construct her first seafront hotel, called Big Bessie's B&B. She grabbed the attention of the local press and more importantly the local bank manager whom she bullied into lending her more money so that she could expand.

Bessie carved out a niche market; small enough to be personal but with the economies of scale of a bigger enterprise, and before long she had established a small chain of hotels. Then she took the biggest gamble of her career; she sold up and invested every bean she had in a new hotel in London which was intended to be the flagship hotel of her new luxury chain, Bestissimo. The gamble paid off and before long Bessie's hotels were west in New York, south in Sydney and east in Azerbaijan and Rostov. She was just contemplating going north to Scandinavia when she was nominated for the best newcomer of the year award. Her moment had come and there she was at the Swilton trying to lord it over the competition which at that precise moment in time was David, who was increasingly trying to avoid her gaze, her conversation, and her appalling perfume of roast beef and Yorkshire pudding. He failed.

Bessie, despite asking the question, had no interest at all in David's accident and he didn't manage to get a word in edgeways. She prattled on endlessly about her hotels and how wonderful it was to be nominated, taking David's nervous twitch for agreement. As the alcohol soaked in, her nastiness seeped out and she began to belittle the other contenders, especially the one that made the thongs. This was too much. David had had enough and he got up and left without a word, leaving Bessie open-mouthed behind him.

Just then an Arab gentleman, who had been sitting, or rather slouching down in a chair behind David, got up, followed him to the lift bank and tapped him on the shoulder. David turned round trying to look as ferocious as it was possible to look with his mop of long blond hair, expecting to see Bessie. Instead, he saw an oily

olive-skinned man in the finest suit David had ever seen.

'My goodness, my friend,' the man said, 'I thought she would never stop,' and he smiled such an enticing smile, David's face changed – at least the bits capable of movement did – from angry to perplexed.

'Let me introduce myself,' the man continued. 'I am Iqbal. Will you please join me in my hotel room? I believe we may have something in common. I have also been insulted by that miserable excuse for a woman.'

David hesitated but glanced over his shoulder which brought an angry and fast approaching Bessie into view.

'Yes,' he said to Iqbal, who had already summoned the lift and he got in with him as the doors closed to the sound of a very loud, 'Well how rude,' from Bessie.

A few minutes later, David found himself sitting in one of the hotel's best suites, high up the building.

'Let me introduce myself properly,' Iqbal oozed. 'I am a specialist. I deal in very, very rare things.' He glided over to the fully stocked leather-clad bar and poured two large whiskies. 'I have contacts all over the world. And you Mr Wildwald, are expanding your business interests in animal skins. Understand this my friend, I can get you anything you want. Anything.'

David leaned forward, impressed. 'Tell me more,' he said, and Iqbal did exactly that.

Iqbal Tahan never intended to be a bad guy, that sort of happened to him partly because he owned what they'd now call a bitch resting face. He found out early in life that a little squint could send the other kids screaming back to their mummies and he wasn't slow to capitalise on it. By contrast, his smile was as enigmatic as the Mona Lisa's but far more engaging. As a young teen, he'd caught an episode of *Minder* which was showing in a coffee house,

and he'd been transfixed. By the time Arthur Daley had weaselled out of an impossible situation involving the intended assassination of a Lebanese businessman, Iqbal had found his vocation. His father had always been a bit of a dodgy trader, but Iqbal was determined to be the dodgiest of them all.

It was when the local kebab shop ran out of halal lamb that Iqbal made his first buck. He rustled some mangy looking sheep, shoved a few dirhams into the hands of a farmhand and Alakazam! Fresh halal meat.

He learnt his most important lesson early on after he'd been roundly beaten up by a dissatisfied customer. The poor man had discovered in the most embarrassing of circumstances that the material Iqbal supplied for the production of burqas was actually, in a certain light, transparent. From that moment on Iqbal decided that what he really needed was a minder. Somebody else to do the actual dirty work and take the rap, the insults, and the bodily harm.

Iqbal did not have a particularly good academic education but his early life in the relatively cosmopolitan state of Dubai gave him a unique perspective and he learned to speak bullshit incredibly well. He also had a wide and genuine interest in all religions, driven entirely by his discovery that people were prepared to pay almost anything for certain artefacts or pilgrimages. He was soon able to converse sensibly with almost anyone on the planet and he met people from every country in the world. Anything he didn't know he researched and as his skills grew, he got so good he could have sold Rastafarianism to an Imam given half the chance. But he still hadn't recruited his minder.

Iqbal's meeting with David was planned after he had set up some lucrative people trafficking for an Italian businessman in London who wanted cleaning staff. Yes, Luigi Lupus. He'd also pocketed a nice backhander for a tip he'd given him about an

employment agency he'd just read about.

He made it his business to read every single paper he could find on the bus or train or wherever and since he was in town, he'd had a nosey around and had found out about the *Best Business Awards* in the paper. Blagging himself an invite and a room for the night was child's play to him and an afternoon researching all the nominees on the hotel's computer was no hardship – especially when it looked like it would pay off.

Delilah's Doo Dahs struck him at once. Iqbal had relatives all over the world, some even as greedy and evil as himself, and best of all, some were already dealing in animal pelts and trading in other animal parts. All he needed to do was collar Mr Wildwald. But first, he had the displeasure of being collared by the very nosey and bossy Bessie.

Iqbal had heard of Bessie before the awards ceremony. A few weeks back he'd read a particularly vicious, or some might say accurate, article which exposed her true disposition.

Bessie gives good interviews and is always sweet and kind to reporters, the article began, *But catch her unaware after a couple of Shags on the Beach, and she turns into Bitter Bessie the nefarious nit-picker, the competitive cow*, it concluded. He'd also read that she'd tried to sue them and he knew that gossip columnists were as slippery a bunch as himself. Besides, no real harm had been done to the business. Personally, he couldn't be bothered about her at all. But she, in her inimitable way, was about to make an enemy of him. While chatting to him and after a long boast about her hotels she'd added with extreme conceit: 'And I'm going to civilise those barbarian Ruskies next.'

Iqbal had friends and family in Russia and as the hackles began to rise, he politely enquired.

'Super. And how will you do that?'

'By bringing my hotels to their people,' Bessie had replied. 'I'll teach them what it feels like to sleep in a proper bed on clean

sheets. Big Bessie Wainwright is coming to tame the Big Bear. And then I'm going to start on the Arabs.'

That was enough for Iqbal, he despised Bessie from that moment on. It would be a pleasure to see her humiliated, he decided. Having given her the slip while she was in the ladies, he'd spotted David coming to the bar. He correctly guessed the chair David would head for and sat behind it waiting for the inevitable to happen. He was correct and now he and David were friends with a common enemy.

And so the two men, Iqbal and David, already had something in common. It was only a little step further forward to a proper business deal.

David had quizzed Iqbal enough to judge he was telling him the truth. And what David needed were contacts on the poacher side which was precisely why he'd come to London. So he listened carefully to Iqbal and the more he listened, the more delighted he became; Iqbal seemed to be everything he was looking for. It was all stacking up nicely; now he could relax a little.

When they had finished talking business, Iqbal smiled a most villainous smile.

'And if that battalion of a belittling Bessie Wainwright of Bestissimo Hotels wins the award tomorrow, we might both have an interest in putting her in her place.'

David laughed and clinked Iqbal's glass.

'You are so right,' he agreed.

Then Iqbal put his head close to David's in a way David found most unsettling. 'And remember, Sovan,' Iqbal began 'or should I call you David? You should know that you are dealing with someone who keeps his word, my friend.'

David visibly blanched at that, well to be fair he was so pale no one would have noticed. It had never occurred to him that he

could be unmasked so easily and he decided there and then he would never be the face of his business again. If, however, Iqbal was as good as his word, which was certainly looking good, David could simply delegate. Anyway, he rationalised, it was too late to back out. Iqbal not only knew who he was, but what he needed to get. After realising that the only way was forwards, he took in a deep and a little creaky breath.

'I understand,' he nodded.

'And do not worry my friend,' Iqbal continued. 'I understand that everybody has their reasons for what they do and rest assured, I am the only person in the world who knows your former identity. Sadly, I also know that nobody will ever recognise you from those days.' David dropped his head a little in sad agreement.

'But my friend,' Iqbal lightened up. 'We have made a splendiferous connection. Let us drink some more to celebrate our new friendship because later you may be drowning your sorrows over that pathetic little award.'

When David went back to his room to get changed for the ceremony, Iqbal rang his cousin Ratib, aka Rat, for good reason. Rat lived near Delhi, and on Iqbal's assurance of much buckshee coming his way, promised to find Iqbal a proper driver to take this businessman friend of Iqbal's to the tiger reserve. Rat, being genetically very similar to Iqbal, was also a bullshitter but did not have Iqbal's integrity or attention to detail. He found the first idiot he could, bunged him a few hundred rupees and demanded he pick up a man from the airport muttering something about a tiger.

'It is arranged,' Rat told Iqbal. 'There will be someone to meet the flight.' And that meant that Iqbal could now fulfil his promise to set up the rest of the meeting between David and his dealer at the tiger reserve.

The next day at the awards ceremony, Bessie did indeed win the

award and afterwards her extremely patronising and self-congratulatory speech became so unbearable that everyone in the banqueting hall was thoroughly sick of her. Protocol demanded that the commemorative photos be taken and so all the nominees were called to the stage. The photographer couldn't avoid having Bessie in the picture but he was none too keen on David's appearance, so David found himself pushed to the back along with Iqbal who just loved having his photo taken. It was a very sulky David who skulked back to his room to reassess; publicity didn't work with a face like his with or without a new identity. Thank goodness he had found Iqbal. But where was he? Just as he was getting concerned someone pushed a note under his door.

'I have found somebody for you. He will meet you at the airport and take you to where you are going,' it read. Newly enthused, David jumped into action and while he threw his toilet bag into his suitcase and left the hotel heading for Heathrow, Iqbal sat in his own suite rubbing his hands with glee. This promised to be his best deal ever; constant demand and an almost never-ending supply, well at least until the animals died out.

A few hours later, David found himself in New Delhi airport searching through the milling crowds looking for his pick-up. Finally, his eyes alighted on a sign held up in the air; 'MR TIGER' it said. David was furious and he marched towards the man.

'Hello, Mr Tiger? I am Sunil. I am your guide and chauffeur.' He gave a deep bow.

'Put that down, you idiot,' said David, tearing the sign from Sunil's hands. 'My name is Mr Wildwald.'

'I am very sorry, sir. I was not told your name, only that you need a ride to the tiger reserve.' David scowled at him.

'I am really being very sorry, sir. Let me take your good self's bag please?' David let Sunil take his suitcase and he followed him

slowly because it was a big case and Sunil was a small man, to Sunil's car. After a bit of a struggle, Sunil heaved the heavy case into the boot.

'I am pleased to welcome you aboard my humble cab, sir,' said Sunil as David got in the back. 'It will be taking us nearly four hours sir. We will be stopping at a cafe for refreshments and some,' he paused, 'some relief.' he glanced behind to make sure that David understood him; David nodded.

The car sped off through the busy noisy streets of New Delhi with Sunil, like everybody else on the road, honking his horn at every car, camel, and cow he saw. During the drive David used the time to concentrate his thoughts on precisely how he was going to maximise his revenge on, and more importantly his investment in, the animal kingdom. If people really wanted tiger skin thongs, what else they would like? Delilah's Do Dahs was nothing compared to the potential for much darker and devious demands.

Sunil chattered complete gibberish almost the entire way but it was only when David realised that the car had stopped, he actually began to listen to him.

'Mr Tiger, sir. I am unbelievably sorry,' Sunil said. 'I do not have the directions to where we are to meet whoever it is you are supposed to be meeting.'

'Call me Mr Wildwald,' snapped David. 'Drive to the next town and I'll make some calls.'

'Very good sir. There is only one problem with that, sir.'

'What?' David was now getting very irritated.

'I am begging your pardon, sir, but we have run out of petrol.'

'WHAT?'

David was now beyond irritated, he was angry. He got out of the car and kicked it; then looked around. They were, as he suspected, in the middle of nowhere.

'Where is the nearest petrol station?' he ranted.

'Excuse me, sir, but I am having absolutely no idea, sir.'

'Then what the hell are we going to do?'

'Ah, well I have an idea, sir if you don't mind, sir.'

'Go on.'

'I will walk along the road until I find a house and I will ask to buy some petrol. It is very remote in these parts. It is quite common for people to be keeping the jerrycans.'

David sighed. 'Go on then. I'll wait here.'

'Excuse me, sir. There is just one other problem I am having.'

'What now? David roared.

'I am not having any money, sir.'

At that, David kicked the cab so hard it made a dent in the door. Sunil cowered, almost squatting on the ground with his head in his hands. David turned round as if to hit him, but stopped himself which was just as well because then they both heard the unmistakable sound of a car. Well to be truthful, had Pat been driving downhill they would just have heard a loud 'Whee,' but she wasn't, so they didn't. She pulled up alongside.

'Spot of bother?' she asked. David could hardly take in this strange vision of a woman, but any port in a storm.

'Indeed there is, madam,' David turned to point very rudely at Sunil. 'This complete idiot, this imbecile, who is meant to be my chauffeur has not only lost his directions but has run out of petrol.'

'Oh dear,' Pat said. 'You poor man.' But she was talking to Sunil. She hated loud bossy men and she could see in an instant that Sunil was very upset. Besides, there was something she instantly disliked about David.

'You,' she said, pointing rudely at David, just to let him know how it felt. 'Where are you going?' There was something about Pat that made David hesitate. He certainly detected her grit, so he decided not to tell her.

'I am so very sorry, madam,' he simpered. 'I'm a salesman and

I've had a very bad day. Do you by any chance store any petrol that we might buy from you?'

Pat considered this. She was extremely careful with her petrol consumption but she did have a half-full jerrycan back at her house somewhere.

'You wait here,' she said to David. 'You,' she beckoned to Sunil, 'You come with me.'

Pat drove Sunil back to her house, which was only ten minutes away. She invited him in and made him a nice cup of tea which was followed by a pretty thorough interrogation.

'All I know about this man is that I mustn't call him Mr Tiger,' he said. 'Although I believe he is going to the tiger reserve.'

'That is very interesting, Sunil.' Pat was beginning to get distracted; the clock was perilously close to five pm and she had no time to talk further. 'Come round here,' she beckoned, and took Sunil out through the back door and began rummaging in her garage for the jerry can. 'Here. It's not full but should get you to the next town.'

'Thanking you so very very much, madam but I am not having any money.'

'That's all right, dear,' Pat smiled a tiny hint of impatience in her voice. 'I trust you. Come back when you're ready with the can filled up and we'll call it quits. But I want to know everything you can tell me about the man you are driving.' Suddenly Sunil stood up straight.

'I remember. His name. It is Mr Wildwald.'

'Good,' said Pat, eyeing her watch. 'I shall write that down. Be off with you and come back soon.'

Sunil did return the next day, with a full can of petrol and a large bottle of gin, 'I am being most dreadfully sorry, madam,' he said.

'Well yes, Indian gin has its uses but...' Pat stopped. 'You weren't talking about the gin, were you?'

'No madam,' Sunil replied, nodding his head vigorously. 'It is about who this man Mr Wildwald met. He telephoned somebody from the town where we got petrol and he got new instructions. I cannot remember the old instructions but I do remember that the new ones were not at all like the old ones which I cannot remember any more. I remembered that much, madam.'

Pat listened intently, understanding almost nothing. 'So what were the new instructions, Sunil? Where did you leave him?'

'Ah, that is easy,' Sunil grinned. 'As I have been there myself now. I had to take him to a far far gate of the tiger reserve and leave him there. I did try to look, but I saw nobody there at all. It was very strange almost as if it was a secret meeting.'

'Thank you, Sunil, yes, very strange indeed.'

When Sunil had gone on his way, Pat took out a map of the tiger reserve. There was only one gate so far away. I wonder. It looks like I shall be doing a little investigating myself.

She glanced at the clock. After my gin.

CHAPTER NINE

The Fall of the Bestissimos and the Rise of the Wallows

Sunil's incompetence had not ruined the whole day; Iqbal's contact was genuine enough. The trader had turned up at the appointed place and was very accommodating. David was extremely satisfied and the mix up with the taxi was soon forgotten in the afterglow of David's dealings. He now had confidence in Iqbal and had started on his new journey with as secure a supply of all things tiger as he could have dreamt of. Skin, bones, whiskers, teeth... in fact any part that didn't have some sort of nonsensical treatment properties, David decided he could invent one. They'll be making wine out of tigers one day, he prophesied.

On his flight home, David had lots of time to think about things. Firstly, he had to decide how he would develop the new lines alongside Delilah's factory and the plain truth was that he couldn't. Much as he loved Delilah, he wasn't entirely sure if he could trust her after hearing her anger about lion hunting. Besides she needed protecting and there was no reason she should be implicated if, God forbid, his new business was ever exposed. No, he decided, the new lines had to be developed carefully, made discreetly and most importantly entirely separately from anything Delilah handled.

The next decision was about where they should be made and how could he cover locations all over the world. That was a toughie and he decided he would talk to Iqbal about that; he was such a well-travelled man. Finally, he had to decide about his own role. His face clearly was not his fortune. He pondered yet again whether he could put himself through plastic surgery; it would cost thousands but then again he could be making millions, but that was all still a long way off. Then there was scientific research; his old love. If he earned enough money he could do whatever he wanted; maybe even become immortal. Then the idea popped into his head. Genius, he said to himself. Pure genius.

When David's flight touched down, Delilah was there to meet him at the airport with a hug worthy of any of her prey.

'Damn David, I've missed you so much,' she said. 'It's darned good to see you home at last.'

'Put me down Delilah,' said David, suddenly aware that she had put on a not inconsiderable amount of weight. 'I'm very tired and we need to talk. Let's get going.'

Delilah pouted all the way home but cheered up a little when David cracked open the bottle of Asti Spumante Delilah had put in the fridge. 'I wanna hear all about it,' she said. 'You mustn't worry we didn't win. It was so good we even got in the running.'

David told her all about his trip to London, skipping quickly over the awards ceremony and inventing a few tales about meeting other businessmen and women along the way. Most importantly he was topping up her glass at frequent intervals. When he sensed she was woozy enough, he dropped his bombshell.

'You've been amazing, Delilah, the company and everything has been so successful...'

'Don't tell me there's a but comin',' Delilah drawled.

'I think it's best I quit the company,' he said firmly. Even slightly drunk, Delilah was shocked.

'But why honey?' she slurred. 'What the devil are you gonna do with yourself?'

'Delilah my love, there is a huge demand out there for thongs made out of all other sorts of other materials.'

'There is, honey?' she asked, frowning a little as she tried to remember the telephone conversation she'd taken a few weeks back. 'You mean in India?'

'Yes, Delilah. And in lots of other countries. Some people do not like the idea of using real animal skin. And fake furs these days are getting very good.'

'Damn, you're right.' Delilah fell back in her chair. 'I know about people protesting and stuff. I always thought they were just dumb. But why shouldn't dumb people buy our thongs too?'

'Exactly. I've decided that we will go international and I am going to bring in custom from all over the world.'

'Gee that sounds exciting. But does that mean you'll be going away more? Can't I come with you sometimes too? You know I'd love to see a bit more of this lil ol' world.'

'In time, my sweet,' David replied. 'But until I start getting in the orders, I'll need you here. Who else could run the company?' Delilah sighed; she knew he was right. 'I'm thinking first that we should open a new factory in China. Labour is cheap there, and so are synthetic materials. This time next year we could be a global company. Imagine that, Delilah? Delilah's Do Dahs all over the world?'

'David darlin' I do love you. You're so darned dynamic. I think you're the best businessman ever and that damned Bessie woman can just darn well go to hell.'

David froze. He hadn't even mentioned Bessie by name and even Delilah had heard of her. It wasn't just Delilah either, the next day and the day after that the papers were full of her and her award. Bessie's face began to taunt him mercilessly from the business pages of every paper, and on the cover of every magazine except *Playboy*.

As he stewed, his brilliant brain began to do what it did best and he began to formulate a plan. He needed new locations to exploit, why stay in hotels when you can own your own? The next day he outlined his idea to Delilah.

'I think that perhaps we should go into the hotel business. It will help us expand our business and it seems like hotels are the new thing.'

'Oh my! That would be the darndest thing ever, but do we have the money yet?'

'We will soon,' said David. 'Don't you worry about that.'

As we all know, it sometimes takes a very long time to achieve our targets in life or to be truly diabolical, and so David was stewing for quite a while before his plans came to fruition. Delilah's Doo Dahs was expanding rapidly and with the addition of a sweatshop in China, production was high and the money began pouring in.

A few trips abroad made him realise that on business trips, it was often best to travel to second-rate hotels. Dodgy deals on Indonesian civets or Asian pangolins were facilitated far more easily there. Such places were so inefficient that they were totally discreet. David's stew was now matured, ready to serve and particularly cold; you might even say cold-blooded. It wasn't too great a leap for him to turn the idea into a vision of building a hotel chain to rival The Bestissimo. It didn't really matter that some of the hotels he had his eye on gave more comfort to cockroaches, mice and rats than human beings; they were cheap to buy and the locals were even cheaper to hire.

China was the obvious place for his first purchase. He bought a rundown ancient boarding house near his factory which was notorious for a terrible fire in which many people died and was on the market at a knockdown price. After all, David thought, who outside of China knew or cared about its history? So the Gansu

Wallows hotel, complete with an English-speaking local manager in charge, was opened to the world, or at least some of the low life inhabitants of it. Even still, despite having his foot on the bottom rung of the hotel chain ladder, the condescending figure of Bessie Wainwright haunted him with her finger wagging and thong wronging. By the time he had acquired another three hotels in Sumatra, Nepal and Kenya, she had become a gigantic chip monster sitting on his shoulder. It was time for another serious talk with Iqbal.

'Hello my friend,' said Iqbal over a very bad line. 'I am just arranging the counterfeiting of a few million Power Ranger dolls for the ignorant masses. What can I do for you?'

'Hello Iqbal. I have a proposition for you. We've worked very well together for a number of years now and we trust each other, don't we?'

'Most certainly, dearest David. It has been of great mutual benefit.'

'Precisely. But what if we formalised our arrangement? Went into something much bigger?'

'That sounds very interesting,' said Iqbal, who had been expecting to hear from David about his hotels. He had researched them and most of them provided him with good bases too.

'How would you like to be a director of a new hotel chain?' David said.

'I think that is a very interesting proposition,' Iqbal replied although, in fact, he was a tad disappointed having been hoping for a partnership. But sometimes, like not being the gofer, it was also better not to be the top man. While he paused David added.

'And if you wanted to use them for some of your other activities that would be no problem.'

'I like your thinking, my friend. And where are these hotels?'

David explained the locations which clearly, Iqbal already knew but it didn't hurt to show interest.

'And what is your marketing going to be, David? How will we make them successful?'

'Do you remember our conversation about those ridiculous Bestissimo hotels?'

'I remember it very well, my friend. We were planning to raise their roofs I remember,' Iqbal's eyes were gleaming.

'And you had the means to do it I think,' David speculated, feeling Iqbal's enthusiasm. 'Just think, after a little bad publicity, we could buy them out for a song.'

'My friend, you are a genius,' Iqbal enthused. 'I am going to Azerbaijan very soon. I believe there is a new hotel there. It can be target practise. I will get on it straight away.'

Iqbal was as good as his word. Recruiting suicide bombers turned out to be much easier than he had imagined. Like all good training camps, some students simply didn't pass muster and were rejected, but their training had fuelled them so much that they were all bursting to, well, burst. And they weren't so choosy when it came to a mission. All it took was a little ad in the back page of *Jihad Weekly* and Iqbal had two recruits both experienced in improvised explosive devices for the Azerbaijan job. Iqbal preferred working in threes, just to cover eventualities but he was running out of time so he took a chance on placing an ad in a local corner shop resulting in the recruitment of the poor young man by the unfortunate name of Hari, who was looking for just such a mission.

Hari's mother Vladlena had been a huge George Harrison fan and had rather ineptly named him after her favourite song. So from an early age, he stood out from all the Borises and Mikhails and not surprisingly became another odd kid, not unlike Harry. He was a sensitive, delicate child who loved literature but had been filled with a passion for tragedy from the moment he read *Anna Karenina*. It didn't help that aged fifteen and just starting college,

Hari met an Anna who despite being absolutely nothing like the woman embedded in his soul, stole his heart merely by sharing her name.

Rampant teenage hormones combined with his tragic leanings turned into an overwhelming love and desire for her and much to the amusement of Anna and all the other kids, he followed her around everywhere like a lovesick puppy. Anna let him do it, just until she attracted the attention of her own intended amour; but for Hari, love was blind and pretty damned stupid too.

Hari and Anna progressed to the same university and it was there that Hari had set his heart on betrothal and marriage before graduation. He planned his surprise for her seventeenth birthday and on the day itself, Anna arrived at her locker to find a huge bouquet of roses – which barely hid a crouching figure – waiting for her. When Hari stood up, revealing his full military uniform, alas, four sizes too big as he was so slight of build and not really cut out for fighting, Anna smiled. In Hari's mind at least, he was Count Vronsky emerging from a railway carriage. But to his beloved Anna, he was a complete tosser.

Anna's smiles turned into giggles then shrieks of laughter which brought hordes of students over to see what was happening. One of them, a young man by the proper Russian name of Vladimir, was Anna's intended, and he was destined to be the one to end Hari's dreams. Vladimir dramatically dropped down on one knee and looking at Anna said.

'Come with me Anna. Leave this wretch to his posies. Marry me, Anna.'

Anna pushed aside the roses, accidentally elbowing Hari in the eye and while students cheered and applauded the happy couple, Hari ran from the university never to return.

It was after Anna's rejection that Hari began to go down a very terrible route indeed. Vladlena, much as she loved her son, soon got very tired of him wailing around their house, still nursing

his black eye and thinking of ways to die. Sending him to his room only elicited reams of terrible poetry, all of which he insisted on reading to her.

His first pathetic attempt at suicide – overdosing on a laxative because he didn't understand what purgative meant – ended with him spending a grim and bitter three days trapped in the confines of the outdoor lavatory. His mother would not let him inside due to the appalling smell. But it was his second attempt which really did attract his mother's attention.

Vladlena heard a strange noise overhead; first the small thud of a chair being kicked over, then a loud thump as Hari came crashing down, having forgotten to secure the rope properly to the overhanging joist. When she had finished laughing at his incompetence, she hugged him to her bosom and spoke sincerely to him.

'Haruska,' she said tenderly. 'We all have hearts that are broken by that special one,' and she turned her eyes skyward as if she were mourning somebody in her past. It wasn't very convincing, but he couldn't argue, she was clutching him too tightly. 'You need to find a job,' she said. 'Something to keep your mind occupied and to earn some money.'

She felt him nod under her grip. 'I will teach you how to drive,' she said. 'Your grandfather was taxi driver. That is a good and honourable profession and, my little turnip; you will earn more money that you will ever get from your poetry.'

Hari, maybe dreaming of a car crash on a level crossing but certainly feeling a bit bruised, let this idea sink in. Walking everywhere was such a drag and buses never ever came, so if nothing else he could get out a bit more. Maybe he could follow Anna around and try to persuade her to come back to him? He agreed with his mother's suggestion and the lessons began.

Hari was also adept with his old clunky computer and searched for driving tips online.

He quickly found a chat room where other teenagers were looking to take their driving tests. One day, however, one of the boys said something very stark about wanting to die and he openly invited the others to join a new type of chat room, a secret one. Hari, keen to share his experiences, joined the group but listened carefully before talking about himself. One of the boys was talking about becoming a hero by sacrificing his own life for something he truly believed in. Hari didn't believe in anything that much, but he couldn't think of a better way to make his case to Anna; that if she didn't come back to him, he would die for her. In an instant, he decided that he must find a fitting cause to give up his life for.

Not surprisingly, there were very many options available to him; the demand for suicidal idiots was strong. But Hari had a single condition and without agreement to it, he would not accept a mission – that his heart must be retrieved, whatever its state, then boxed up and sent to Anna. With remarkable honesty for terrorists, the reply was always the same.

'That would be too dangerous,' they said. 'Yes, we can maybe take the heart from the scene, but a parcel can be traced. We must maintain our anonymity at all cost.'

It was the very day that Hari passed his driving test that he walked past that little shop he'd never even noticed before and he would have walked past it again too had it not been for a broken paving stone. He landed nose up to the side window of the shop staring at that small notice of Iqbal's.

> **Driver wanted**
> **for terminal mission**

'This is fate,' Hari declared, and on the exact same day that Chloe had picked up her card from the window of The Bestissimo Hotel, Hari went straight inside the store and likewise grabbed the card, waving it under the nose of the shopkeeper.

'Are you sure, young man?' The storekeeper said, but on Hari's determined nod, he went to the back and made a telephone

call.

'Wait here,' the man said, calling Hari to the grubby storage area behind the shop. Within minutes an immaculately dressed businessman of Arab appearance appeared. This time Hari's terms were acceptable.

'That would be no problem, Hari,' Iqbal lied; he wasn't stupid or honourable, there would clearly be no comeback. 'We have specialist agents who will do this for you. Rest assured you are doing something extremely worthy. These hotels are destroying the livelihood of our fellow nations and they are intending to spread all over Russia. Why should we meet the standards of this ridiculous Bessie woman from Blackpool? We are Russian and proud and we will have our own hotels as grubby and badly run as we like.'

The deal was struck and Iqbal began the preparations. There were explosives to be obtained, cars to be acquired, security to be checked and most importantly, training to be undertaken. Obviously, personal safety issues could be ignored but the drivers had to understand their targets and how best to detonate their devices.

As the date approached, Hari was fully prepared except for the making of his final video. He looked at many others of those who had gone before him for inspiration but they were full of venom and spite. His was to be a literary masterpiece, homage to his eternal love, Anna. With his poetry in hand, he set the camera up and lamented for a good half hour in his terribly badly rhyming verse concluding with a promise that Anna should keep his heart for all time. Wiping back the tears, not of sorrow, but pride in his outpourings, he switched off the red button and sat back to catch his breath.

While he basked in his achievement, he glanced at his instructions and cursing, realised that he had forgotten something. If there was nothing about The Bestissimo Hotels, his terms would

not be met. He looked back at the camera and spat out a small diatribe about foreign hotels in Azerbaijan spreading to Russia and how he had died for the cause, but being Hari and a little incompetent, he forgot to press the red record button. No one can be sure if, had he recorded the ending correctly anyone would have seen Hari's masterly literary achievement of poetry inspired by unrequited love. It's possible that the mention of the hotel would have been enough to bring it up in a search. It really deserved to be seen by millions; it was spectacularly funny. Instead, it was destined to lie unnoticed, to be seen only by Chloe's friend Harry before being permanently consigned to obscurity.

With no contribution at all to the mission from Hari, it was still successful and the Baku Bestissimo was toast. The hotel in Rostov, however, was still standing. Iqbal's triumph for the former event was followed up by a good dose of bullshit about the latter. He explained it to David over the telephone later that evening.

'I took the decision not to do it in the end, my friend, it is enough that the intention was there,' he said, with his most sincere voice. 'I want to be able to use my man for other more important missions and don't forget, whilst The Bestissimo brand is kaput, there is a hotel that perhaps someone like ourselves can purchase at a good price.'

David, initially sceptical, now followed his logic. Rostov was logistically and strategically a very important location and to have a really good base for his operations in Russia would be no bad thing. 'You are so right, Iqbal. You have carried out your end of the bargain, now it's my turn. Are you ready to formally accept my offer now?'

'I am listening,' said Iqbal, and David went on to outline a package which consisted of an impressively small and therefore taxable salary, but a substantial bonus payable in any currency, including non-monetary ones, of Iqbal's choice. Iqbal was in two minds; whether to accept immediately, or whether to hesitate a little. And while he hesitated, that hesitation secured him an even better deal; David upped the salary by ten per cent, and they figuratively shook hands on the matter.

'I will put together such a team,' Iqbal told David. 'We will be international. We will find hotels wherever they are needed for your devious developments and we will secure your supplies, whatever you so desire.'

David poured himself a whisky telling Iqbal to do the same.

'We start with London Bestissimo. I have the funds; you put in the offer and we will build a chain of hotels as big as any that have ever been seen.'

He and Iqbal figuratively chinked glasses.

'David, I think that you are the cleverest man I have ever met. Here's to you and your wondrous hotel chain!' He raised his glass before taking a large swig.

David thought for a moment. How much could he really trust Iqbal? Surely a hotel bombing was good enough surety in a relationship? Emboldened, he carried on.

'But my real desire Iqbal is something which will make all this look like child's play.'

'Tell me more,' said Iqbal, now extremely curious. David whispered down the phone. Iqbal sat back; even he was shocked.

'No, no my friend. That is not possible,' he said.

'Nothing's impossible for the right money,' David replied smugly. 'Some of our existing clients have intimated that they will pay millions for this. We will earn a fortune.'

Iqbal went quiet for a moment. 'I see now where you are coming from. Tell me, how many of our clients have expressed an interest?'

'At least fifty of them; minimum pledge, one million dollars each – if I get them.'

Iqbal stroked his chin. 'My friend,' he said. 'You will need to give me a few days, weeks even to do this. Maybe years. I will set off tomorrow.'

'No,' said David. 'This is something I must do myself, and yes, it will take many years and I am the only person in the world who can do it. Your job is to hold the fort for me now, Iqbal; that is what I need you to do. I will be around, but I am relying on you to keep the hotels and our animal trade continuing. I myself will be devoting my life to research.'

'As you wish,' said Iqbal, as he wondered how on earth David could pull off such a terrible yet wonderful plan.

David was rejuvenated. He still looked frightful, but at last, he had a new purpose even if it was a little wishy-washy round the edges. Once again Bessie's face adorned the papers and magazines but this time David delighted in reading about her downfall. As Iqbal had said, The Bestissimos' reputation was now ruined. Business was finished; who wanted to stay in a hotel targeted twice by terrorists?

Bessie's fall from grace was speeding up as her bank manager called in her loans, and her repayments faltered. It was a slippery slope. She was going down faster than a skier on speed and as she was the personal owner, there were no shareholders to help share the pain. Her last transaction was to sell her flagship hotel in London for £1 and that pound was invested in a nice hot cup of coffee which she drank outside the building which had been the realisation of her dream.

There was however someone who did not relish Bessie's misfortune; someone with a nose for foul play and someone who was destined to provide the really impossible piece of sky in the big jigsaw which finally finishes the whole puzzle, or at least the sky bit of it.

Veronica Holmes had been plagued all her life by her name. She'd been the butt of so many jokes, that in her retirement from her administrative job in the city, she had given up the resistance and decided to become a sleuth. She adopted a bloodhound, or at least a dog with long ears, from the local dog's home and inevitably named him Sherlock. The closest to an address in Baker Street that she could afford was a maisonette in East Walthamstow. With precious little family – her only nephew Steven seemed to have grown out of their once regular marathon Monopoly sessions – she had all the time in the world to devote to her new hobby.

Every evening she would take the papers from the local library and scan them for interesting mysteries, keeping cuttings of all references to whatever it was that had happened. She also relieved the library of spare copies of all their business magazines and these she kept intact and neatly filed in order in a pile behind her sofa.

Veronica actually came close to solving a case once; it was the Iced Bun Scandal when a whole tray of cakes had disappeared from a locked room at the back of the bakery and had seemingly turned up in the window of a rival. Sherlock had found a side entrance with a dodgy loose panel and had burst through it revealing the route of the thief. But the baker, outraged that a dog had infiltrated his bakery, took all the credit for the discovery himself, giving Veronica, who had been rather hoping for one of the retrieved buns for her troubles, nothing but a rude, 'Piss off.'

Veronica still seethed with the injustice and it increased her determination to solve another case. When her eyes fell upon the Azerbaijan hotel bombing story on the international pages, she matched it with an article about the missing Luigi Lupus, also last seen at a Bestissimo hotel. When she found the later story about the attempted bombing of the Rostov Bestissimo she was on high alert. At last her stash of magazines would be of use. Not surprisingly she found many articles about Bessie Wainwright and

her incredible rise to fame in the business world. She even found a photograph showing Bessie and the other nominees for the Best Business Newcomer Award. And there, in the picture, at the very back, she could just make out a very shady looking man wearing dark glasses who had floppy blond hair covering half of his face.

'Well aren't you a wrong'un,' she said to the photo. 'I'm going to track you down and find out what really happened to poor Bessie.'

There were several names associated with the picture and she wrote them all down meticulously. By a process of elimination, she decided that the shady man was S Wildwald, and so armed with this she decided to find out what she could about him.

In her working life, Veronica had been an administrator beyond compare: a legend in her own filing room. Always overlooked for promotion, mainly because she was too good to lose, and strangely unattractive to either sex, she devoted her life to her files and had a vast knowledge of the City and its workings. So it was with relish she trod in the footsteps of her former life and travelled up to the City.

Poor Sherlock wasn't allowed to come; Veronica firmly closed her ears to his whining and whimpering and proceeded on her mission. Once there she was in her element; reliving the old days and searching the records. Sadly she found very little. Mr S Wildwald was listed as a director of a small limited company called Wallows Ltd, but not for very long. There was an old address for him somewhere in North America and she discovered that his first name, Sovan was Cambodian, but from the picture, he certainly didn't look South East Asian, or at least his hair didn't. That was all that she ever found out, so she left disappointed but unprepared for a nasty shock when she got home.

Sherlock's earlier whimpering were not those of a jealous dog being left, they were those of a very old dog much older in dog years than Veronica was in human years. She found him slumped

in his basket unable to even wag his tail when she came in. All her research was bundled away, labelled and promptly forgotten; Sherlock was far more important.

For the next few weeks, Veronica spent all her time and most of her money looking after him, ignoring the vet's advice that she was wasting her money and it would be kinder to, well you know. But Sherlock was her only friend and she didn't think she could cope without him. He went downhill fast and the day the inevitable happened she was distraught.

She arranged the best doggy funeral she could afford on her meagre pension and satisfied that she had given her devoted friend a good send-off, she started to contemplate a life without her faithful companion, which was no life at all.

With no one else to look after, Veronica stopped looking after herself. She neglected her washing, her personal hygiene deteriorated and she stopped eating properly. A paltry five weeks after Sherlock died, Veronica followed and it was only because her nephew Steven came to visit that her body was discovered. It was a while however before Steven fully understood the scale of his future inheritance.

CHAPTER TEN

Elle's Elite Team Building Meeting

Elle was taking a little time out to reflect on things. Yes it was true she hadn't done as much as she'd liked to help animals, but then again, her resources were growing and she had the makings of an incredible team. And she'd now eliminated three of Pat's terrible ten trophy hunters even if she'd had nothing to do with them personally.

She raised her glass to herself and with a loud, 'Here's to the next five years,' knocked back her gin and patted herself on the back. 'You're on your way, Elle. And you're rich.'

'But what's your next step?' she asked herself, the gin clearly working its way into her system. 'You're going to call a meeting right this minute,' she answered. 'An elite team building meeting. You're going to get Pat's slideshow out and you're going to create the most formidable team on the planet.'

'That's jolly good,' she said to herself. Better start ringing around.'

Elle's first call was to Chloe, who as it happened was already on the phone to Harry.

'It's very specialised stuff. It's not just cleaning. There'll be bombs and chemicals and all sorts. I'll be like a secret agent. How good is that?' Harry was delighted and jealous.

'That is exceptionally cool,' she replied. 'I'd love a job like that

too. Oh, by the way, I've cleaned up the boys' records. They should be back at college now.'

'That's great! I'll tell Ulka. Hey sorry, Harry, the boss is on the other line. I'll see what I can do. Speak soon.'

'Elle?'

'Meeting at mine. Now.'

'On my way.'

Elle welcomed Mel, Chloe and Penelope in with an unusual gin shaped smile on her face.

'My lovelies,' she gushed. 'We have so much to talk about.' As the others took seats in Elle's flat, she set up a projector and screen and began to talk passionately about animals. Penelope was animated, Chloe interested but Mel was bored. All of them knew in varying degrees about Elle's interest in animals but none of them had seen her quite like this before. She was dramatic, angry, caring even, and clearly a little drunk. The last slide held the images of the remaining seven trophy hunters.

'First I want you to memorise all these faces. They may or may not be doing other despicable things to animals but we must look out for them wherever we go.' She paused for a slurp of gin.

'We must also research these terrible criminals and find out who they are and where they are. And we must raise more money; lots more money. I bet that low life Luigi had millions stashed away; why shouldn't we find it and put it to good use? There is this wonderful tool, the internet. We need help. Do any of you know anyone who can help?'

Mel got up, looking at her watch, and left with a slight shrug of her shoulders. Chloe fidgeted in her chair. Penelope dropped her head and shook it sadly. Chloe could hold it in no longer.

'You need a Harry!' she squealed. Penelope sat up in amazement; she'd never heard Chloe so animated.

'I remember now,' Elle nodded. 'Tell me more.'

To most people, Harriet Hacker was a weirdo but she possessed that very rare quality common in weirdos and sadly lacking in most of us. Harry had one hundred per cent integrity. She knew who she was, and at a very tender age, she knew exactly who she wanted to be. Most importantly, she didn't give a shit about what anyone else thought. What a hero.

Or heroine. Both really.

From her first day at school when one of the boys stood squarely in front of her to block her way to the climbing frame, Harriet made her stand. She went as if to shake the boy's hand and by reflex, he stretched his hand out to hers. She grabbed it firmly and like a demented shot putter, she began to spin him round in a circle about her. Round and round he went, faster and faster and faster until finally she let go and he went spinning off, landing on his bottom on a grass verge several yards away.

'Beaten by a girl, Simon?' How the other boys laughed. But when they turned to look at Harriet, in her checked school dress, now rather crumpled, they didn't know quite what to do.

'I'm Harry,' Harriet stood defiantly, and despite the obvious attire, not one of them doubted it for a second.

'After you, Harry,' one of them pointed at the frame. She turned round and, in an instant, had run up it like a monkey up a tree. When she hung from her knees and did a somersault off it, the other boys were seriously impressed. Only Simon sulked and skulked away.

From that moment onwards, Harry was one of the lads and they would have cheerfully punched anyone who said otherwise. That same evening, Harriet took her mother's dressmaking scissors and cut off her long hair, making a terrible mess of it. Her mother, horrified at first as she tried to shape it a bit suddenly and fondly remembered her own tomboy childhood and decided it was just a phase. The next day she agreed to Harry's demand for boy's shorts instead of dresses, and proper lace-up shoes. This was going too far for her father though; he went into a shock he never really came out of. Yes, he admitted to himself as he sat in his potting shed at the bottom of the garden with a can of beer, yes it was true he'd hoped for a son. But if it had to be a girl, he wanted a pretty little thing; not a girl-boy.

Secondary school, that awful time when hormones rage and acne explodes all over heads perched on awkwardly growing bodies and all sorts of new bodily fluids make an appearance, was bound to be a major challenge for Harry. For the first year or so, her trousers were overlooked, mainly because nobody knew she was a girl. The morning register for Harriet Hacker was met every day with an almost inaudible mumble so none of the other kids really noticed. The problem only really manifested itself when the time came for her to select her exam subjects and that was because of a dinosaur of a Computer Sciences teacher.

Harriet always had an inkling that computers would be her thing and was devastated to hear her form teacher announce to her and the class:

'I'm sorry Harriet, but Mr Stickler says only boys can study computer sciences in this school.'

The other pupils were shocked too.

'Who the fuck was Harriet?' they asked each other.

'Why don't you join in with the sewing instead?' the form teacher suggested. 'It's much the same thing and it's a lot more practical.'

'Is it bollocks,' Harry replied rudely. 'Put me down for computer lessons or I'll complain to the Equal Opportunities Commission.'

Well, that sort of settled it and Harry joined in classes with the other boys, who quite frankly, neither noticed nor cared. Surprisingly though, Harry did decide to take up sewing.

Boy's clothes weren't beginning to fit so well and it was a skill she thought would be useful. It was there in the sewing class she first met Chloe and they instantly hit it off. Chloe was struggling with her vision of a specialised apron and Harry, seeing her frustration translated it into a design complete with a pattern for Chloe to use. Chloe was thrilled and by return made Harry something extra special to keep her computer clean. Both of them were delighted but Harry was particularly pleased with herself. This, she decided, wasn't sewing at all; it was design, and it was wicked.

From the very first C prompt, Harry was hooked on programming. The combination of data management and problem-solving was to her like blackmail was to Beryl. It opened up a whole new world of adventure and discovery at a time when to most people it was a chore. She had a natural sixth and even seventh sense for the sorts of things which computers could be made to do and she was soon way ahead of her teacher when it came to new developments; so much so, that the teacher would often leave her to finish the class lesson.

Harry's first breakthrough, or perhaps that should be hack-through, was when she got into the examination board's files at a time when hackers were almost unknown and security was very low. It wasn't to make money, or even cheat on her own behalf, it was a last-ditch attempt to keep her friend Chloe at school. Sadly it hadn't worked. Chloe had been both flattered and bemused.

'But I don't want to go into the sixth form,' she'd said.

'Then who will I talk to if you're not here?' Harry had replied entirely selfishly but Chloe was resolute.

'We'll always be friends,' Chloe had assured her. 'I couldn't manage without you to talk to.'

It was just as Harry had managed to get into some low-level UK

government websites that her mother broke the news to her. She didn't even need to hide the screen; her mother had absolutely no idea what she was doing.

'Darling, daddy's got a new job in Chicago. We're going to have to move to America,' her mother had announced. 'There's no easy way to say this...' she added, before realising she'd already said it.

Stumped by her own ineptitude she left, giving Harry a few seconds to let the news sink in. Harry couldn't have been happier. With Chloe leaving school, America was the place to be. Her only slight concern was that she hadn't seen her father in years.

'Fantastic!' she shouted out.

Harry took to Chicago like Al Capone did to tax evasion. It was the most exciting place she had ever been, which wasn't saying much, but more importantly, it was stuffed full of organisations she could hack into.

Her mother found her a place at a college in town where she settled in well. Nobody even realised she was a girl, Americans being used to everyone having odd names, and so Harry could be precisely who she wanted to be until they discovered her aptitude for hacking. Whilst the establishment ejected her forthwith, one of her lecturers had been so impressed he gave Harry some paid assignments. All of these were very intrusive, often highly personal but extremely useful as hacking practise.

Harry had set up an email address for Chloe and taught her how to use a computer before she left and she wrote to her often. Harry knew all about her cleaning skills and had been pleased to find out about her new job but hadn't heard from her very recently. On Chloe's birthday, she'd begun to wonder what she'd been up to. Simply asking her would be far too easy, Harry decided. Much more interesting to find out the hard way instead.

When Harry found Chloe's name on a flight to Azerbaijan, she was very surprised. Never one to be unprepared, she began to search for things about Azerbaijan which might appeal to a cleaner. The first thing she turned up in a search for spots was a picture of an Anatolian leopard. It did look rather cute, so she read up a bit more on it. It was a piece by someone called David Swallow, who looked even cuter, as part of his dissertation. Curious, she tried to discover more about him but all she could find was that he had graduated with a first-class degree in Zoology, an MA in large mammals, and had then begun a PhD in endangered species. There was a brief reference to a TV programme, but absolutely no evidence of it at all. Having reached a dead end, she parked it and wrote to Chloe.

'...and then out of nowhere was this email from Harry.' Chloe droned on.

Elle had heard enough. The lure of Luigi's loot was too large to ignore and organising international animal initiatives would not come cheap. It was worth a punt.

'Let's call her.' She hooked up her laptop to the screen with Chloe and Penelope sitting beside her.

Elle's trust in Chloe's judgement was not increased by seeing Harry on screen but she was too consumed by impatience and she made her decision.

'Harry, to be honest, I'm really not sure if my organisation needs someone like you, but if you wouldn't mind checking a few things out for me, I can pay you for that and we'll take it from there.'

'Sure,' Harry responded. 'Fire away.'

So Elle fired and two days later she was astonished at what Harry had discovered. Not only was she able to tell Elle the names of every single individual and company Luigi had ever had contracts with, she uncovered his secret bank accounts and asked for Elle's account details so she could transfer the money before the authorities got on to it.

'Thank you, Harry,' Elle smiled politely while stamping her foot on the ground with joy. 'How about we agree a retainer for your

services with bonuses for special jobs?'

'Awesome,' Harry approved. Harry had a new job and Elle had found an incredibly useful member of her team.

After that, Elle and Harry often chatted online late into the evening. Harry was a very good source of potential information for Elle; there were often problems which could be resolved by a bit of hacking, or people to be selected for, well let's not dwell on that too much.

Harry, as promised, had not been idle since Chloe's adventure but was now reanimated by Elle's call for her to start international research. She had never given up on the case of the missing bomber and had managed to dredge up some very old footage. She'd found film of the incident near the hotel and she could just make out a man being kicked on the ground then being picked up by an ambulance but there were no images of his face and so the trail had stopped.

Elle had also given Harry a new interest in animal protection. She'd taken a keen interest in tracing the seven remaining trophy hunters but also, while tracing Luigi's money, she'd discovered that one of his ex-customers was an importer of certain fur items. Curious, she'd tracked down the supplier and ordered a couple. One she kept and one she'd sent to Elle. When it arrived, Harry hadn't quite expected the reaction she got the very next day. Soft kind compassionate Elle had reverted to the steel hard bitch.

'What the fuck is this you've sent me?' Elle held the article aloft in front of the webcam.

'It's a genuine bear skin thong,' replied Harry, taken aback. 'But totally legitimate.'

'How disgusting,' Elle replied looking at the label. 'Delilah's Doo Dahs?' she cringed. Who the hell would wear anything as revolting as this?'

Harry squirmed in her chair. 'And itchy,' she said, swiftly adding, 'I would imagine.'

Elle went quiet for a moment. She couldn't legally challenge the fur trade, however much she despised it, but there was something she could do. Her finances were looking good. Not only that, she had a cracking good team and it was about time she put them to the test. If she was going to stop international criminals abroad from plying their despicable trade, it wasn't going to be done by inviting them to tea and asking them to stop. No, she had to get her team fighting ready to face up to the big boys and what could be a better test than a spot of local sabotage. It would be the perfect team building exercise.

She looked at the clock. Pat would have some good words of advice, and more importantly she actually had a land telephone line now but it was just five o'clock there and Elle did not lightly disturb Pat's routine.

'Thank you, Harry. You may have given me an idea.'

Elle waited a full ten minutes before ringing Pat.

'Smashing,' Pat enthused. 'Nothing like a spot of breaking and entering. Now dear, did I ever tell you about that chap who took someone to a tiger reserve? No? Well now, what was it?'

Pat often spouted half-remembered things in her post-gin phase and most of them were ignored, and rightly so. Still, Pat's enthusiasm for an outing was all the encouragement Elle needed and she called Harry straight back to set her researching fur farms in England.

The more Harry read, the more disgusted she was at the scale of animal cruelty for human vanity. It wasn't difficult for her to locate a particularly nasty mink farm reasonably accessible to Elle, and she rang her with the details. She didn't tell Elle she had a possible match for one of her seven because she didn't want to raise expectations but she had a sneaking suspicion that she'd managed to pinpoint the sole woman on the list. She also guessed it was unlikely the woman in question would be at the factory. But she did tip off Penelope, who still had a few grubby contacts in the

force.

The next morning, Elle called the meeting of her elite team and Mel, Chloe and Penelope duly arrived. Mel, when she heard the agenda, was as usual, dismissive. Fur was crucial to her outfits and she was no hypocrite.

'When fake gets better,' she muttered on her way out. Penelope was naturally on board and raring to go, even Chloe was supportive.

'Those poor animals!' she exclaimed. 'They don't even clean the cages properly.'

'OK,' Elle began. 'Penelope, you concentrate on logistics and access. Chloe, can you investigate the cleaning company they use? We'll meet up again with Harry this afternoon.'

'On it!' both women spoke together. Penelope had not been idle these past few years. There had been quite a few bodies buried but apart from her own animal ventures, Elle's promised action had not materialised. Now something was brewing, she couldn't wait to get started.

Chloe too had rather missed the excitement of her escapades in Azerbaijan. She also really missed Ulka and pined for Baghir but being who she was had done nothing about it. She had hoped for a chance to go out there again, but as Elle had told them many times, 'First things first. If we can't manage something in England there's no hope of us doing anything overseas.' And Chloe was nothing if not patient.

Later that afternoon they all met in Elle's office with Harry on webcam. Penelope had already given Harry the low down on the security and Chloe had discovered all they needed to know about the cleaning company; especially that they operated during the night shift. Elle's strategy was simple. Take out the factory cleaner, or cleaners, and substitute Chloe. Chloe and Penelope would then

open the cages and let the animals out.

Harry had joked, 'You'll be the moles in the mink farm.' More seriously, she went on to explain there was local technology involved, and she would not be able to intervene remotely.

'I could probably take out the local power station for a few hours,' she suggested helpfully, 'but that's as far as I can go from here.'

'Damn,' Elle cursed. She had been too used to Harry's remarkable technical ability to realise that there could be a problem.

'No, we can't take the whole station out. That's too drastic.'

While they all sat thinking, there was a knock at the door and Nettie appeared.

'Why you all look so sad? Your men got the droop? I know good fix.'

Elle laughed. 'I don't have a man Nettie.'

'Ah,' Nettie nodded with meaning. 'Then that's why.'

Nettie surprised Elle nearly every day with her knowledge, so she took a punt.

'It's not men we need Nettie, it's someone good with security systems.'

Nettie laughed heartily. 'Hey, no security man get one past Nettie. I flexible and I fix cameras good so he thinks I clean while I on phone to mum.'

Elle sat up. 'Nettie, are you telling me you can fix security and telephone systems?'

'Sure. How else I phone home?'

'What do you think about fur?' Elle asked tentatively.

'I don't give shit about fur,' Nettie replied. 'But I like you. What you want?'

Carefully Elle explained to Nettie the plan to break into the fur farm

and release the mink.

'Give me one hundred pounds for mum and I sort it.'

'Deal,' Elle shook Nettie's hand, which sent her off into more infectious hearty laughs.

Chloe was delighted; she had great faith in Nettie and was beginning to get enthusiastic again.

'You leave it to us, Elle,' said Chloe, beaming.

'Just get us in with the cleaners and we'll do the rest,' added Penelope, already wriggling with excitement.

Elle beamed with pride; this was exactly what she wanted from her team.

On the appointed evening, Elle sat in the office drinking gin very slowly. She was trying to visualise what was happening and was getting nervous with good reason. It had started well; Penelope had got them there discreetly and a generous bribe to the cleaner on duty had been enough for her to throw a sickie. Chloe's persuasive substitution was promptly approved by the duty security man and Penelope was now safely in place at the back entrance waiting for Chloe to open up. The problem was that Nettie had misjudged a security patrol and had been discovered tampering with the cameras. It had taken all her flexibility and some very unconventional tricks involving ping pong balls to distract the security man sufficiently so that he did not raise the alarm. Nor did he continue on his rounds as he was astonished and extremely excited by Nettie's display.

Chloe now had the opportunity to get down to the cage room, open the back door and let Penelope in. Between them they let all the mink out of the back door where they scurried out into the depths of the countryside and towards the innocent unsuspecting wildlife.

When all the cages were empty, Chloe and Penelope high fived each other, then went back to retrieve Nettie who by now was in the firm embrace of the security man.

A quick flick from Penelope's illegally retained truncheon soon sorted him out and the three women walked triumphantly back to the car, Nettie with a gait somewhat resembling John Wayne after getting off his horse.

When they were safely away from the compound, Penelope stopped the car and spoke to the others.

'The owner of this place lives just up here, near a really deep canal,' she said, hoping that the others would cotton on. They all peered at her a little suspiciously.

She continued throwing the words out there and hoping they would hit. 'It's one of the seven. The only woman.'

'We throw her in canal?' Nettie asked, her grin widening. 'Make big splash?'

Chloe was quiet. In the early days when she had no one important to her in her life other than her very distant friend, she relied entirely on her instincts about people to judge them. Now having experienced something very close to love for Ulka and Baghir she realised there was more to people than just what they did. Some people would have regarded Baghir as a terrorist simply because he had a gun; sometimes you had to dig deeper. When Chloe did speak the others listened.

'I know what this means to Elle, but I can't condone the killing of someone I haven't seen properly. On balance, given the state of those poor animals, I would say go ahead but if there's a chance to speak to this woman, we should. I need to know why she does what she does.'

Nettie was having none of it. She shrieked with excitement.

'Go go go!' she urged Penelope. 'Let's give bad woman a good bath.'

Penelope, however, took in what Chloe had said. 'No, I'll go and knock on her door. Give her a chance to explain.' And with that, she drove them to the woman's house which even by the silhouette of moonlight was extremely impressive. The canal,

banked by deep steep walls, ran sparkling alongside the house.

Penelope parked the car and they looked around. It was so beautiful even Nettie was silenced; that was until the front door burst open and a large woman carrying a huge shotgun materialised. She had just heard about the break-in and being a natural hunter was about to set eyes on her prey. She saw the car and began running towards it. Even worse, she just caught the faces of Nettie and Chloe and began screaming.

'Bloody foreigners! I knew it, coming here to interfere with things. You should've buggered off to your own country, no one will care here if I give you some lead filling and line the canal with you!'

Penelope turned on the ignition to scarper but something wasn't right. The team looked at each other; they sensed something. Even the woman stopped in her tracks. No one could have predicted what happened next.

Everyone began to hear a strange noise, was it rustling, scampering, pounding maybe? Suddenly a moving column of fur came careering round the corner; several hundred coat-loads the woman noted before she realised they were heading in her direction. It probably hadn't helped that she was wearing her own mink coat. She turned and ran but the creatures were extraordinarily specific in the direction they were chasing her and the team could only gaze in wonder as the woman ran ever close to the canal.

'Faster!' Nettie urged.

'Well I never!' said Penelope.

'Clever little creatures,' commented Chloe.

At last, there was nowhere for the woman to go. She turned round and took aim with her shotgun. She couldn't get them all, but maybe they would run away.

Just as she was about to pull the trigger, a very small mink nipped at her ankles. That and the force of the kickback left her

teetering on the brink. All it took was one more mink to push her over.

When they heard the splash, the team rushed to have a look but there was nothing to see. The canal was very deep and the water very dark.

'She gone,' Nettie concluded, and they turned round somewhat stunned by what they had witnessed.

The strange mood didn't last long and by the time they got back in the car, they were cheerful again. Penelope couldn't wait to ring Elle and tell her.

'We can't be absolutely sure,' Penelope cautioned, 'but she definitely got a very deep soaking.'

Elle was delighted with the success of the mission and even more so at maybe knocking another one off the hit list. She sat back in her chair grinning like an escaped mink. Now was the time to start thinking big. If she could pull off something like this, she could aim higher, further, bigger. Why not go after tiger poachers? What about the rhinos and elephants? With each glass of gin she downed, Elle's ambition grew.

'I'm gonna change the world,' she slurred, as she poured the last dregs of the bottle down her throat.

By the time the three arrived back at Elle's, they were in ebullient mood. They had worked brilliantly together and were beginning to realise what a good team they made. When they got to Elle's, they were amused to find their normally impeccable boss drunk, completely incoherent and very, very affectionate.

'You want Lady, Missy? You go somewhere else,' Nettie untangled herself from Elle's clinging arms.

'Brilliant. Bloody brilliant women,' muttered Elle, as she began to fall asleep. 'World wake up, the wonderful women are coming.'

When Elle did wake up the next morning, there was a present

waiting for her in an envelope on her doormat. Chloe had carefully cut a clipping. It read *Fur Farm Founder Fatality*. And the photo perfectly matched the woman on the hit list.

'Four down, six to go.' Elle dragged a red pen across the woman's smiling face before rushing into the bathroom to be horribly sick.

And so the missions began. For the next five years, wherever they found evidence of animal abuse, at least that they were capable of interrupting, Elle's team were on the case, honing their skills, ratcheting up the body count of unscrupulous animal dealers, pimps and business competition and all the while avoiding detection. Harry and Penelope, working together, found another trophy hunter who for entirely honourable reasons gave up their life. Elle was, at last, seeing real progress.

When Elle's thirty-fifth birthday arrived, she didn't notice how grey her hair had become or how thin she was; all she cared about was moving the mission forward. They were ready. She called Harry and gave her the final go ahead.

'We're going international. Start your research now. And look out for those last four trophy hunters. They're out there someone; two American and two Japanese.'

Harry began to search with renewed enthusiasm.

CHAPTER ELEVEN

Iqbal Overwhelmed and Undermanned

Iqbal was naval gazing. It had been several years since the bombings and he'd just been too blasted busy to concentrate on a proper strategy. There were far too many balls in the air. Now he had a big problem.

In the early days of working with David he had made a point of keeping on some of his own activities, a sort of insurance really, and one of those had been a half-share in a big game hunting enterprise. The money had been spectacularly good. It seemed that there was no end of rich foreign tourists desperate to shoot defenceless animals for the glory of posing for pictures with their kill and the prize of a decapitated head stuffed and mounted to take home with them. Unfortunately, something had begun to go wrong.

One day, a particularly experienced American hunter had paid extra to go out hunting on his own; so rich and overconfident was he. Iqbal had personally authorised the expedition but being smart, had produced a considerable amount of additional paperwork designed to make sure that if anything went wrong, there would be no claims against him. Yes, they'd checked the Jeep; the petrol tank was full and the tyres properly blown up with a spare on the back. Yes, they'd checked that the guns were oiled and working and the ammunition was intact. Yes, the man had

personally assured them that he was happy with the arrangements and would see them in a few hours. So naturally, they had waved him off and wished him good hunting.

Iqbal could only speculate what happened after that. When the Jeep was eventually recovered several miles away, they found the tyres ripped to pieces by, he assumed, lions with claws as sharp as Stanley knives. The petrol tank was punctured, presumably by a lion's jaw and the ammunition lay untouched. There was no sign at all of the American but there was a strange red cross on the ground which appeared to have been drawn in blood by the paw of a lion. Iqbal scratched his head then double checked the paperwork before making that awful telephone call to the relatives.

From then on, Iqbal decreed that all trips had to have accompanying armed guides to make sure that nothing could go wrong. It was working. Anyone even slightly put off by the American's experience was completely reassured by the new arrangements. Business was back on track until two Japanese businessmen arrived. They were not happy with the safari guides and insisted on taking their own. After much bargaining, the doubling of money and more paperwork, Iqbal acquiesced. The self-appointed team were fully responsible for double-checking the Jeep, guns and ammunition and they were duly waved off on their safari and last seen clutching their maps.

The entourage had not reappeared at the appointed time and a search party had been sent out to look for them. The businessmen had disappeared completely but their companions had been found untouched and in a deep sleep in the back of the Jeep. Iqbal shook his head in bewilderment and comforted himself that his own guides had never ever fallen asleep on duty. Iqbal decided that some lions were particularly selective. Or maybe they just preferred American and Japanese food. Either way, the business closed down.

Had Iqbal persevered, he might have discovered that there would be no more incidents, but the decision was made. He sold his share and decided to stick to trafficking live humans and dead animals. But even with this reduction in activities, David's businesses were taking up more and more of his time. He and David had set up at least two new hotels every year for the past few years and with each one, a new source of illicit cargo was created. Yes, he had local managers and couriers but there was no one to help him personally. David was no help at all; he had slowly been turning into something of a recluse which meant that even more stuff landed on Iqbal's shoulders. Now he was at breaking point. *Who can help me sort this?* he wailed to himself.

He first looked to his existing staff. Sunil. *That is a man who is a driver with no sense of direction or knowledge of car maintenance and who couldn't find a white line in the middle of a road,* he mused. *Maybe he can handle paperwork?*

But Sunil couldn't. Despite his cheery disposition, he was incapable of answering the phone, undertaking filing or even making arrangements of any kind. Before his week's trial period expired, he had even managed to book flights in the wrong year. His good nature soon became exceptionally irritating. He was always apologetic, always promising to do better. This was the sort of driving he was very good at; driving Iqbal mad.

Iqbal then decided to give Hari a try. Hari at least had been to school, but he was a suicide bomber and since you have to be stupid to want to blow yourself up... well you get the picture. When also tasked with booking flights, Hari didn't even get the right country. Initially, his mooching around looking miserable made a nice change from Sunil, but before long, Iqbal got heartily sick of him too. *Far better to let him have the solitary life of a driver,* he decided. To conclude the general mayhem, both of them, Iqbal noted, used an alphabet that nobody else in the whole world used, including each other which meant it took him longer to sort out

the filing than either of them had actually spent creating the chaos.

To be fair to Iqbal, it never occurred to him to get rid of either Hari or Sunil and not because he was stupid, but he had his own brand of loyalty. Both had their uses as drivers and Sunil, if you took the time and explained everything to him at least three times, was beginning to improve in this respect. Hari clearly had greater experience of driving so at the very least he had two completely loyal and trustworthy drivers and he put them to very good use. But it didn't solve his problem which was his urgent need for administrative assistance.

It was when he was scrolling through a rather rude website full of plump naked ladies that he began to dream. *Maybe I don't need a minder after all?* He speculated. *The only danger I am in these days is the danger of being flooded with this damned paperwork.* He lusted at a picture of a woman peeping out from behind a filing cabinet.

'Dammit. If only I could get such a woman who would also deal with my paperwork,' he said out loud. He had never remotely considered hiring a woman before; mainly because he didn't associate them generally with the sorts of things he got up to and most especially driving. Then he saw the next picture. A pouting woman posed, answering the phone while being discreetly covered by a strangely shaped desk lamp.

'How stupid you are, Iqbal,' he chided himself as he checked the next picture. There, a luscious Rubenesque lady posed sitting at a desk wearing nothing but a pair of glasses and a very suggestive smile. 'Dear Luigi can surely help me. I shall go to London.'

A couple of days later Iqbal arrived in London and checked in, naturally, at the London Wallows hotel. He breathed in the musty atmosphere and ran his finger across the dust on the reception desk before announcing himself.

'Iqbal Tahan. And I am your boss.' He smiled sweetly and

stared warningly.

The receptionist was ready for him. 'Honeymoon suite I believe?'

'Such good service. Bring me whisky on the rocks.'

As soon as got into the room and after taking a long gulp of his whisky, he began fumbling through his wallet to find the old business card Luigi had given him years before.

Luigi's Loyal List, he read. Perfect. Luigi will find me someone.

After taking a much-needed nap, Iqbal headed out from the hotel. He knew his way around London a bit but had never been to Luigi's premises before. After stopping several people to ask for directions he arrived at the location but had to double check the address on the card. It was right, he was at the office but it looked closed up, the place was deserted. After a few moments of loudly kicking the metal shutters, a security guard appeared from the back and walked up to him.

'Sorry, Guv,' he said. 'Business closed years ago. That Luigi bloke got topped they think. 'Orrible it was. Nobody ever found him. It was all over the papers. Didn't you see?' Iqbal shook his head, shocked by what he heard; he hadn't expected this. 'No one fancied taking these premises after that. Some reckon it's 'aunted by 'is ghost.' Iqbal shuddered.

'You looking for someone?' the guard asked. Iqbal nodded.

'Sort of.'

'Office staff?'

'Definitely.'

'Try Elle's Belles up the road. They say they're good.'

'Thank you, my friend.' Iqbal smiled but he didn't want *good* he wanted *special*, guaranteed, and especially *dodgy*.

Dolefully he trudged back to the hotel to think about it. How do you find someone without an agency? He thought to himself

and then just as he reached the hotel, he looked in the front window. That's it, he decided, I will place an advert. When he got back to his room, he wrote out a small notice then rang David to speak to him before he left for China, but David was distracted. He had something to do, he told him.

What David had to do was console Delilah who was very upset about his latest trip.

'You goin' away again David darlin'?' she'd asked. 'It gets kinda lonely out here.'

'Listen, my sweet,' David had replied, edging as far away from her as he could. 'I have explained this to you before. I will be undertaking some research, so important that it may save an endangered species from extinction forever. It's my calling, my love. It's what I have lived my whole life to do, it is my destiny...' What he didn't mention was that even if his appendage could have managed it, Delilah had let herself go a little and the overwhelming passion he had for her had all but gone.

Delilah had the same thought. She'd worried that he didn't find her attractive anymore. At first, she'd put it down to her blossoming figure all due, she constantly reminded him, to the lack of exercise since she had given up the Bare Bear Bar. Now at least she could comfort herself that it was all down to this good cause, whatever it was, and nothing to do with her. More importantly, she also knew that he would be away for such a long time she could, well, maybe renew her bedroom acquaintances. Since the accident David had no longer any interest in human skin as far as she could tell.

On their way to the airport, David continued to reassure Delilah, perhaps because he knew or at least had a pretty good idea that he would never be coming back again.

'I'll be looking in on our factory in China too,' he told her. 'I

promise we will have some wonderful new fabrics and lines in production very soon. You just keep those designs coming.'

Before David's plane had even taken off, Delilah was back home showing Billy Bob her new leopard skin bed throw. She worried a little at her deception, but she had needs and Billy Bob had availability and an ample supply. David's wedded to his research now, she reasoned. He's cheating on me with his first love, his love of animals, she concluded. He wouldn't mind if I get a little TLC. Had she really had any idea that she might never see him again, she would have cried her eyes out, just for a little while.

By the time Billy Bob had bogged off, David's flight had landed and he was already on his way from the airport straight to inspect the factory. First, he'd checked that all Delilah's latest designs were in production and then he had authorised two new ones, one using faux fur, the other, well let's not go there. He'd also checked out the main factory building and apart from a little shaking when the wind blew, it seemed not only fit for purpose, it also managed to fit in an extraordinary number of machinists. Well, they are small, David thought to himself as he waved at the children on his way out.

David had very much admired the efficiency of his Chinese managers and was especially taken by the vast volumes of stock which could be produced for the incredibly small pittances they had to pay the workers. Their families would have no money at all, he patted himself on the back, if it wasn't for my factory.

Attached to the factory was a small laboratory which was where the really interesting stuff was going on. David had brought in a team of scientists who were working on replicating various animal extractions. Imagine unlimited tiger bones, he'd enthused to Iqbal. Never-ending horns... After a quick nosey round the lab he headed back to his hotel. It had been a long day and he was looking forward to a little rest and relaxation.

The first time David had stayed there he had scared the

reception staff stiff. His appearance was bad enough but finding out he was their employer too was quite a shock. Now they were used to him and were ready and waiting for his arrival with well-practised smiles and bows. In his room, he unpacked his case and had a shower before going downstairs to decide what to eat.

Hearing a low hubbub coming from the lounge he wandered over, surprised to see that it was full. Curious, he saw that they were watching what sounded like a British programme but it was almost completely obscured by the heads of the small people crowded around watching. They were clearly not hotel residents and he wondered what was so interesting.

As he listened carefully, he recognised the voice but couldn't quite place it. He rudely walked in front of the audience to unintelligible shouts of protest and walked closer to the screen. What he saw nearly knocked him off his shaky legs; they were watching his old programme, *Animal Emergencies*.

'Bloody hell!' exclaimed David and he went to find the hotel manager.

'Yes, sir,' the manager nodded. 'People here really love that programme. It's shown over and over again; they know every episode. I hope you don't mind, sir. They're mainly from your factory up the road. They live in very small huts and don't see much television round here and what's on is usually about our glorious leaders, so it's really nice to see programmes about animals. And that presenter, what a fine handsome young man he is. He is very popular here.'

David, now completely unrecognisable from that handsome young man, still hurt under his scars. But if there was any scrap of that fine young man left in his soul, it was about to be completely extinguished. He rubbed his eye to remove the inexplicable moisture therein, then a wicked smile crept across his face. All his former self meant to him now was as a way to further his terrible intentions. Something he could exploit to give himself kudos and

integrity.

As David went back to his room his spine bent just a little more and he stood just a little shorter. He recalled the conversation he'd had with Iqbal and it made him think. Iqbal wasn't the only one who needed an assistant; David was now in dire need of one too. He picked up the phone and rang Iqbal, who had given way to despair and whisky and a rather nice plump lady he'd picked up the night before.

'Get me a number three,' David demanded. 'I need a Chinese speaker, translator and interpreter who is also a dogsbody. And send them out here ASAP.'

'Your wish is my command, my friend,' Iqbal replied, cursing Luigi under his breath.

'You know I have contacts everywhere,' he lied ever more convincingly.

When the conversation finished, Iqbal put the phone down and scratched his head as if somehow it would miraculously release some ideas into his brain. He sighed and said goodbye to his company from the previous night. If only she understood administration, he would happily have taken her on permanently. Sadly she didn't even notice he'd short changed her when he paid her off.

When she had gone, he sat on the unmade bed contemplating what to do. The obvious course of action, that he should first find his own assistant and then delegate, never even occurred to him. Instead, he went for a stroll to try to clear his mind and maybe give him some inspiration. Where on earth would he find a Chinese assistant?

His route took him right past the Chinese Embassy, the Chopsticks club, the Anglo Chinese Organisation for Networking, several Chinese restaurants and through Chinatown.

He began to despair.

'Where oh where can I find a nice Chinese person?' he wailed out loudly much to the bemusement of the passers-by. Then he promptly turned around with the aim of going back to his room but fate was to play another trick on him. Instead, with an extraordinary combination of both good and bad luck, he turned and walked straight into a rather beautifully decorated Chinese lamp post, hitting it with such force he rebounded and fell bottom down on the pavement right in front of a young Chinese man.

'Are you OK?' The young man, who spoke English with an American twang, bent down to help Iqbal to his feet. Iqbal looked up at him and beamed with delight. Here was a very obviously Chinese man, with a good grasp of English and clearly very intelligent, judging by the messenger bag slung over his shoulder.

'May Allah be praised,' Iqbal replied as charmingly as he could. 'Not only am I OK,' he accentuated, 'but you may just be the answer to my prayers.'

'The what?' The young man was completely taken aback, but also somewhat drawn to this strange smiley man.

'Please come with me,' Iqbal nodded his head and the curious young man followed Iqbal back to the hotel, gratefully accepting his offer of a cup of coffee in the cafe.

'My name is Iqbal,' he began. 'And I may have a proposition for you.'

'Ah Chu,' replied the student with a little nod.

'May Allah bless you,' Iqbal replied. 'What is your name?'

Ah Chu smiled tiredly and spoke slowly. 'My name is Ah Chu,' he articulated carefully.

'Ah. Ah,' Iqbal repeated a little unhelpfully. 'And what do you do, Ah?' he asked, overemphasising the Ah to demonstrate he understood.'

Ah sighed. 'Call me Jimmy. Most people do, I don't know why.'

'Ah, Jimmy.' Iqbal was now beyond confusion.

'I'm a graduate of international business studies,' Jimmy lied. 'And I'm in the market, looking for a job.'

'Ah!' said Iqbal, instantly regretting it and smacking himself on the side of his head. 'I am looking for an exceptional young man,' he began. 'Someone who will be the right hand, the very eyes and ears of the most important man in my organisation. Who knows...?' And he leaned close to Jimmy, 'He may one day be the most important man in the whole world.'

Jimmy was intrigued and a little star struck; it all sounded so wonderfully glamorous. All sorts of famous names begin to spin round his head.

'Anyone I know?' he asked eagerly.

'You will not know his name, my new young friend. But you may have stayed in one of his hotels.'

'Wow! Well, I've only stayed in cheap hotels being a student. Which one?'

Iqbal paused for a moment; Wallows hotels weren't exactly top of the range but they weren't quite the bottom. He decided to skip over it for now in case the young man was unimpressed. I'll tell him when he's on his way, he concluded.

'All in good time, my friend. How would you like to work with my organisation, Jimmy? In addition to an international chain of hotels, including several in China, we have factories where we make exotic clothing for people all over the world.' Iqbal paused to check Jimmy's reaction. Yes, poor Jimmy was well and truly on the hook.

'And to top even that,' he continued, 'our founder, the most secretive entrepreneur in the whole world is engaged on a top-secret mission there. He needs a personal assistant.'

Iqbal damned himself; he'd undersold the job and Jimmy's enthusiasm seemed to have waned.

'I'm not a PA,' Jimmy shook his head sadly. Actually, he had almost no skills at all.

He had been extremely loose with the term graduate, and all he had really done was to read a few business books. OK, the opening few pages of one business book. He hadn't even managed to enrol in college yet. Iqbal though, was so blinded by Jimmy's apparent suitability and his own desperation to recruit someone, he whispered something in his ear.

'But for that salary, I can try,' Jimmy smiled broadly. He couldn't believe his luck.

They shook hands and the deal was very nearly done. Since Iqbal himself had no legitimate qualifications of his own, it never occurred to him to check Jimmy's but it was important that David was happy with him, especially since they would be working very closely together. Iqbal took him up to his room and rang David who interrogated Jimmy as best he could in the circumstances. When the interview was over, he seemed satisfied.

David put a lot of trust in Iqbal and he had never let him down; except for the car in India and then there was the second bombing… No, he decided, this young man sounded just the man for the job.

Iqbal personally made the travel arrangements and checked them twice. Jimmy was then free to go home and sort himself out ready for his flight in two days' time. With that all sorted, Iqbal allowed himself a celebratory whisky, then he returned to look at the notice he had written out.

WANTED

RESPECTABLE LADY FOR IMPORTANT PERSONAL DUTIES.
YOU MUST BE WILLING TO TRAVEL TO FOREIGN COUNTRIES
AND YOU MUST BE ABLE TO FILE THINGS PROPERLY.

MATURE LADY PREFERRED

CONTACT   IQBAL TAHAN   WITHIN

In the glow of his whisky glass, it seemed perfect to him and he went downstairs feeling exceptionally pleased with himself. There, he not so carefully enough placed the notice in the corner of the front window at the bottom where it lasted just long enough for him to admire it before slipping out of view and onto the floor just below the window ledge.

Unfortunately, Iqbal was then summoned to sort out an emergency in Nigeria which took him several weeks to resolve. It was even longer before he remembered the notice and wondered why he had received no response at all, so he was destined to simply carry on as before but began to pay even more attention to mature plump ladies waiting around hotels.

Jimmy had been given a small advance on his salary which he used to buy himself a proper briefcase and a smart suit. Two days later, he was on his way out to meet David in Gansu; arguably the worst career move he would ever make in his life. He arrived safely at the Huanglong airport in China to an enthusiastic welcome from David.

'Hello Jimmy. Nice to meet you, I'm sure we will enjoy working together.'

'Thank you, Mr Swallow. Me too,' Jimmy replied, not entirely sure he liked the look of David with his wild blond comb-over and terrible lurching gait. But then he thought about his bank balance and he cheered up a little.

'When do we start?'

Delighted with his new assistant's enthusiasm, David led Jimmy to an awaiting taxi where they began the long journey up to the mountains.

'What has Iqbal told you of my work?' David asked.

'Absolutely nothing,' Jimmy began, 'Other than I will be your eyes and ears and that you are incredibly important.'

'That is all very true,' David agreed. 'I am working on something that will...' he hesitated. He knew he had to trust Jimmy but wasn't at all sure about the driver. He whispered in Jimmy's ear sending the young man's eyebrows shooting up so fast he nearly lost his baseball cap.

'Wow. That's awesome!' he exclaimed. 'I am deeply honoured to be working with you on this.' David put his finger to his lips to warn that they couldn't talk about it in the cab, and Jimmy smiled knowingly.

The journey passed amicably at first and Jimmy was content to look out of the cab window admiring the scenery.

'I've never been outside Hong Kong before,' he noted.

'But I thought Iqbal recruited you in London?' David responded a little surprised. Jimmy laughed nervously. 'I've been there too.' He didn't want to elaborate in case he was questioned on his academic achievements, but David continued.

'So you were born in Hong Kong then?' he suggested. 'Before it went back to China?'

'Yes, sir. My parents went to America with dad's bank before that happened.'

'So you've lived in America too?' David shook his head. Jimmy was not coming across as the brightest spark.

'Yes,' Jimmy replied, trying to avoid mentioning London. 'We had a fine life there.'

'For someone who's never been out of Hong Kong before, you've been to a lot of places. Have you been anywhere else?' David asked, now irritated.

'I've been all over Europe and Australia,' Jimmy replied, nodding his head vigorously in a way that David was beginning to find very annoying.

The rest of the journey continued in silence; Jimmy unsure

what he had said wrong, David wondering if he would ever be able to actually use this moron. It doesn't matter, he told himself eventually. As long as... David suddenly blanched in a way that gave finally meaning to the big Procul Harem hit... Then he shrieked.

'You do actually speak and write Mandarin, don't you?'

Jimmy nearly jumped out of his skin. 'Um... I speak it quite well. And my writing is not too bad...'

David smacked himself on the forehead but it was too late. Jimmy now knew enough of his master plan to cause trouble so it was either kill him or work with him, and he was keeping his options open. Besides, he'd had experience of accidentally losing people off mountains, and that could come in very handy indeed.

CHAPTER TWELVE

Crossing Paths and Elle's Monumental Management Meeting

Hari and Harry had communicated fairly regularly since their first meeting, but there were long intervals between each communication which worried Harry until she got accustomed to it. He had hinted that he was a long-distance driver so she assumed he was simply busy and she was right. Iqbal did give him many driving jobs all over the world so he was often absent for long periods of time.

Despite the passing years, Hari's determination to undertake a suicide mission had never diminished and as Iqbal's cargo became more and more illegitimate and competition increased, Hari sensed the time might be coming closer. Now was the time to confront this woman with whom he had become so close. One day after much thought he wrote: 'I would like to see your face, Harriet. Do you have a webcam yet?'

Harry had been expecting this and for a long time, she'd thought of almost nothing else. Hari had become her virtual lover and he now seemed ready for the next stage. In a move that shocked her mother far more than she could have anticipated, Harry asked her something very strange one day.

'Mom, I'd like to try a new hairstyle.' Still recovering from the

shock, the poor woman nearly fainted when it was followed up with, 'And some makeup.'

When she recovered, Harry's mother was thrilled and before you could say *plastered*, Harry was covered in the stuff. Her short hair was sexily quiffed, her eyebrows plucked, eyes mascaraed and shaded, the look all finished with elaborate earrings.

'My dear,' her mother gushed. 'I always knew there was a girl in there somewhere.'

When Hari saw Harry's face, his own dropped. What he saw was a pretty and kind genuine girl who was clearly in love with him and who could never be part of a suicide mission. She also looked a little like his beloved Anna, and this was too much for him to bear.

'I am sorry, Harriet,' he shook his head. 'I have something I must do and we must never talk again.'

'But Hari...' Harry replied.

'There can be nothing between us,' he insisted. 'My life is already accounted for. I have promised and my promise is my bond.'

'What? Hari!' Harry wailed. 'Please don't kill yourself! Not now we've almost met!'

It was too late. Hari broke the connection and Harry was left on her own. Refusing to cry, she grabbed tissues to wipe off the makeup, which as all women know, is no use whatsoever, especially the waterproof stuff. So instead, she ran to the bathroom and scrubbed and scrubbed at her face until all the makeup, and quite a large number of her eyelashes, had gone. Her mother, assuming it was heartbreak, wisely kept her distance but she felt her daughter's pain and wished she could take it away.

Elle was due to call soon so she had to pull herself together.

'Are you OK?' Elle asked the red-eyed Harry. Harry steeled herself and thought quickly.

'My hamster just died.'

'How sad,' Elle sympathised, but having better things to do than console Harry, she carried on, telling Harry that she still hadn't tracked the tenth trophy hunter. Disappointed yet again and now a little bored, Elle turned back to her work completely unaware of the human tornado who was about to appear in her life and shake it up.

Bessie Wainwright was sitting reading a copy of the *Financial Times*. It was going to be a cold night again so she welcomed the special supplement on renewable energy. She pondered, as she did every evening, on how a business could lose its wonderful reputation overnight. A possible murder, the disappearance of a businessman, yes. She could have lived that down, but an actual bombing was too much. Then when that was closely followed by an attempted one; well that took her too far down the road of no return. Bessie had found out after that how few friends she had. All her venomous comments were coming back to haunt her big time. She had no friends at all; she was poison.

Things had gone from bad to worse until she'd been forced to sell out to the Wallows group at a rock bottom price. She'd been sued to damnation and back by the murdered and injured victims at The Bestissimo in Azerbaijan; it wiped her out. She had nothing left, nothing at all. Now she'd even lost her usual spot thanks to an over jealous concierge she vaguely remembered from her old life. So she decided to go back to her old territory.

She coughed loudly before packing the supplement into her clothes and settling down for the night at the side of the Wallows Hotel using a half-full black bag of rubbish for a pillow.

Steven Holmes had been visiting the former Bestissimo hotel that night and had heard the cough. He peered round the side and saw the bag lady but as she turned her face to the light of a street lamp, he caught sight of her.

'That looks a bit like...' he said out loud, 'But it can't be. Surely not?' Confused, Steven went home to check his paperwork.

Chloe too, who out of habit now always glanced in the corners of windows, had been walking past the Wallows Hotel. This time though, her eyes were drawn to a movement in the window. She squinted and peered through the filthy glass, then sprang back. It was a mouse chewing on a piece of old card. Popping in and tutting loudly at the abysmal cleaning standards, she wrestled the card from the creature and retrieved Iqbal's notice – now covered thickly in dust and badly chewed.

Before she had a chance to look at it, she also heard a cough followed by some mutterings, then saw a man hurrying away. Concerned, she went to have a look and heard another cough followed by a *Bugger* and this time something hit her; it was an old paper cup but more importantly, there was something else. She would have known that accent anywhere; it sounded just like the voice that had so regularly featured in staff briefings. But it couldn't be. Surely not? Curiously, Chloe approached the woman, holding her nose as she got closer.

'Are you all right?' she asked.

As Bessie turned round, Chloe was shocked.

'No. It can't be. It's not is it?'

'Is it who? Spit it out, you silly woman,' came the reply.

'Is it Bessie?' she asked, 'Bessie Wainwright?'

'Mrs Wainwright to you,' the very dirty raggedy woman replied. 'Who's asking?'

'It's Chloe. I used to work for you here.'

'Did you now? Well, piss off. Nothing to see here.'

'No,' persisted Chloe. 'You don't understand. I'm going to help you like you helped me.'

And with that Chloe mustered all her incredible strength, grabbed Bessie by the arm and manhandled her, kicking and screaming all the way home to her apartment. She had a vice-like

grip for such a small frame but it was hard grabbing hold of Bessie without gagging. She pulled her up the stairs and into the bathroom.

'Now let me run you a nice hot bath,' Chloe said to the spiteful old witch as she turned on the taps. 'And I'll get you a nice glass of sherry.'

'No gin?' came the sneering reply.

'No, but I can get some,' Chloe replied. 'Just get in that bath and I'll sort it.'

Bessie began splashing around in the tub and began to enjoy it. Old good habits came back to her and she used Chloe's shampoo and bubble bath lavishly. Meanwhile, Chloe got straight on to the phone to Elle.

'You've got to...' began Chloe. Elle was shocked. Chloe was beginning to get very demanding, '...meet this woman. I just found her. Talk to her,' Chloe pressed. 'You need her, really you do.'

'Well...' Elle began, but above all other people, she trusted Chloe. Harry had turned out to be invaluable, so the least she could do was listen to what Chloe had to say.

'And bring gin,' Chloe commanded.

Thirty minutes later, a somewhat surprised Elle turned up at Chloe's door, gin bottle dutifully in hand.

'Well, who is it that I have to see, Chloe? I don't usually make house calls so I'm making an exception because...' Elle hesitated because there in front of her, emerging from the bathroom scrubbed up and just about in Chloe's dressing gown although she couldn't pull it together properly was a face she had seen many times before in business magazines.

In the flesh, Bessie looked almost regal as she glided to an armchair next to which a small table was laden with sandwiches. Elle's eyes widened as she recognised Bessie; Bessie's eyes lit up when she saw the gin.

'Well I never. Bessie Wainwright, as I live and breathe.'

'The very same.' Bessie snatched the bottle.

'What happened?' Elle asked rather foolishly. She had unleashed several years' worth of Bessie's story and once started, she didn't stop except to take large swigs from the bottle; these days she preferred it neat.

'That is quite a story,' Elle turned to Chloe, while Bessie took a very long and unpleasantly noisy toilet break. 'But I'm not sure she can help me. Her expertise is with hotels not staffing agencies.'

'But that's the point.' Chloe replied. 'There's something not right about the Wallows. Bestissimo hotels had the highest standards possible. I went into the London Wallows just today and I could have written my name in the dust.'

Elle gave Chloe her impatient look. 'And?'

'And I think there's a connection. What if the Wallows group were always wanting to take over the Bestissimo hotels?'

Elle sat up. 'So you think they could have had something to do with the bombings?'

'Yes,' Chloe confirmed, as Bessie came back into the room.

'I'd stake my miserable life on it,' Bessie agreed, already sounding more like the Bessie of old and less like a bag lady.

'Let me work for you, Elle. Chloe's told me a bit about you and I can see you're ambitious. I'll double your business in three months, and I'll work for board and lodgings until I have. After that, let me get my hotels back and more. Let me have the Wallows empire. It's what I deserve. I'll even give you a shareholding as a reward. You won't regret it.'

Elle had been unconvinced until Bessie spoke. She knew and understood Chloe's affection for the old hotel chain, but it wasn't enough of an incentive for her. How could that possibly help animals? But she looked at Bessie, past the gin and the fluffy stretched dressing gown, and saw Bessie's pride. She looked deep into Bessie's eyes and saw the fire still burning there; she still had *it* whatever *it* was, in spades. Elle wavered. Hotels around the

world would give her a base for her activities. Chloe watched Elle carefully and saw her moment.

'She can stay with me! I owe her for giving me the best start ever to my career.'

'All right then,' Elle caved in. 'We'll put it to the test. I'll send you some of my business plans and figures, and I'll get Harry to investigate Wallows. If there's something to fish for, we'll find it.'

Bessie beamed and sank back into the armchair with a big smile on her face. Seconds later she was snoring like a pig.

'Do you know what you've let yourself in for?' Elle asked Chloe.

'It'll be fine,' Chloe replied. 'She just needs to adjust a little.'

Later that night, Elle called Harry and explained what had happened.

'We think there's something dodgy about the Wallows hotels. Can you have a look-see?'

'I'm sure Chloe is right,' Harry replied. 'She has such a good nose for these things. I'm always digging around the Bestissimo bombings. It will be a pleasure to pick a bit more and if there's something dodgy there, I'll find it.'

The next evening, Chloe walked past the London Wallows and couldn't help looking at the spot where she had found Bessie. There were a couple of other people there, tramps she assumed, but as she approached she realised that one of them was not a tramp and he was asking questions.

'...The bag lady,' Chloe heard, and realised that this was the man she had seen the day before.

'Are you looking for someone?' She asked tentatively, brushing a hair from his jacket arm as she did.

'Yes. The woman who was here last night,' Steven replied. 'I was trying to find her. I know who she is. I wanted to talk to her.'

'You do?' Chloe's eyes widened. 'Are you a relative?'

'No, but I think I may know something that can help her. If it's

who I think it is.'

'And who do you think that she might be?' asked Chloe.

'Bessie. Bessie Wainwright.'

'And what do you think you might know?' she continued.

'I'm not sure I should tell you,' Steven answered furtively.

'I think you should,' Chloe gave him her kindest smile and put her vice-like grip on his arm. Steven shuddered a little as he remembered how he had arrived at this rather strange place.

Steven Holmes was mainly a kind young man, if a little incompetent and a tiny bit shady. He had however managed the organisation of his late aunt's funeral and given her a reasonable send-off once the confusion about her religion had been resolved. He was sure she wouldn't mind facing Mecca too much and the ceremony certainly made a change from the one his own parents had organised for themselves.

His was not a large family; Steven was the only one left that he knew about so he was pretty sure he would inherit everything of his aunt's but he still needed to try to find the will.

Almost immediately he'd come across a big brown envelope marked *Important*. And naturally thinking it was her will, was surprised to find instead her file of notes and cuttings on Mr Wildwald and Bessie Wainwright. Noting that it must have been important to Veronica he searched the rest of the flat, finally finding his aunt's will under the clock on the mantelpiece. He looked at it with eager anticipation. Veronica had signed it but it hadn't been witnessed and annoyingly she'd left all her worldly possessions to Battersea Dog's Home. So Steven very carefully ripped it up into tiny pieces, ate them and then made a small vow to his aunt.

'When I am rich, I will donate the same amount to the animals,' he spoke to the sky. 'I promise you, Aunt Veronica. But at the moment, I need somewhere to live and I'm pretty sure you

would approve.'

It took a while for the estate to be proved but Steven's assumption was right. As the sole survivor, he inherited the house and all its contents, except the television because that was rented. Then he thought about how he should best respect his aunt. First, he took down the box of Monopoly that he and she had often played in happier times.

'Be a businessman,' she'd told him. 'Make your fortune.' Then Steven looked again at the important papers she had put away and caught sight of the photograph of Bessie receiving her award.

'Best Business Newcomer Award,' he read out loud. It had a nice ring to it. 'Bessie Wainwright,' he added. 'I think I've found my vocation.'

And so, having explained his determination to carry out his aunt's investigation, leaving out the inheritance bit, he smiled back at the captivating young woman he had just met.

'You'd better come with me then,' Chloe beamed. 'I'm sure you'll want to talk to my boss.' She took him by the arm as she whipped out her lint remover and led him back to Elle's office cleaning his jacket as they went.

When they arrived at Elle's flat she was already online talking to Harry.

'It's nothing specific,' Harry was saying, 'But I have found something. Not what you thought, but something you might find interesting.'

'Go on,' Elle encouraged.

'Well, I may be adding two and two and getting three hundred and forty-six,' Harry added randomly, 'But it seems that everywhere a new animal is identified as being at risk from some sort of exploitation, a Wallows hotel opens up nearby.'

'That is very interesting indeed. Keep on it, Harry. Find out everything you can about Wallows.'

'I'll try. They're very strangely organised and there's not much

about them online, but you know me, Elle, if there's something to be found, I'll find it.'

'Thanks, Harry,' Elle signed off, and she knocked back the rest of her gin and tonic. Still deep in thought, she opened the door to Chloe and Steven.

'And you are?' Elle commanded Steven with such authority he was taken aback.

'Steven Holmes,' He replied. 'My late aunt was investigating the Bestissimo bombings. I think I have some information that might help Bessie.'

'Over there,' Elle pointed to a chair. 'Tell me what you know.' Elle listened carefully to what Steven had to say about the papers he had found and when he had finished, she said, 'I want you to come back tonight at seven and bring these papers with you.'

She turned to Chloe. 'I'm calling a very special meeting. Tell the others. Six forty-five.'

At the appointed time, Elle held court in her flat while Mel, Chloe, Penelope, Harry by video phone, and Bessie, listened carefully.

'Now I need to tell you why you are here,' Elle began. The others drew closer. 'As you all know, I have been committed to fighting for endangered animals for many years now, and we may just have stumbled upon a major perpetrator.'

Mel, as usual, looked a little disinterested, but just at that moment, there was a loud bang at the door which made them all jump. This was no ordinary bang on the door, most people used the bell. Penelope was the first to get up and she opened the door slowly, truncheon in hand. On the other side stood a wild-eyed mad woman in a pith helmet. She took the helmet off and hung it on Penelope's outstretched truncheon shouting.

'Elle! Elle, hurry, look at the time!'

Elle, like Pavlov's dogs but without the retching, reacted instantly. She had absolutely no idea that Pat was coming to see

her, and it was certainly well past gin o'clock there, but the critical thing was to get the gin into Pat before she exploded. She ran straight to her drinks cabinet and poured her a large gin, quickly popping in a slice of lemon and some ice from the fridge.

'Pat!' she exclaimed handing her the drink. 'Why didn't you tell me you were coming?'

Pat took a long gulp and turned to the open-mouthed Penelope. 'Get my bag will you please? It's just down the stairs.'

Penelope turned round and went out with a loud grunt.

'Happy fortieth birthday dear. Did you think I would forget that?'

Elle then did something she hadn't done for years; she laughed. 'You've come all this way for my birthday?'

'Don't be silly, Elle,' Pat scolded. 'I had an inkling that something was up and I just had to tell you something I remembered from ages ago.'

Chloe looked agog at this strange woman, but it reminded her that she too had something to tell Elle.

'Happy birthday, Elle. I had no idea. And I have something to tell you too,' she added, lest she forget in the confusion.

Pat looked around the room and her eyes fell on the pictures on the wall. She caught Elle's eye then looked back at them.

'You haven't...?' Elle nodded, and Pat went closer. She peered at the faces and noted the nine big red crosses.

'Yes, Pat. Just the one left and we're pulling out all the stops.'

'You clever girl!' Pat beamed. 'How did you...'

But just then there was another knock at the door.

'I'm not bloody well getting this one,' Penelope grumbled, having just heaved Pat's case upstairs still bearing the pith helmet on her truncheon.

'I'll go,' Chloe said, and got up, 'It will be Steven.'

And indeed it was. Steven came in and looked around and when he saw Bessie, all scrubbed up and presentable, he nearly

burst with excitement and admiration.

'Bessie Wainwright,' he gasped. 'I am Steven. I am your biggest fan!'

Bessie blushed, but it was the gin really. Bessie didn't do modesty.

Elle had been silent for a moment because she didn't really know where to start and there had been so much to take in, but her eyes came to rest on Steven and the file under his arm.

'Everybody. This is Steven Holmes, whose aunt was a detective,' she announced. There was an audible *Ahh* of appreciation from everybody except Pat who also considered herself to be a pretty good detective.

'Steven has been researching the Bestissimo group and has something to show us of great interest, I think. Steven?'

Steven began a little nervously in front of all these very forthright ladies, but he also somewhat relished the drama of the moment, and with a flourish, produced a large sheet of paper which he held out for the others to see. It was a blow up of the picture he had found in his aunt's papers; the Best Business Newcomer of the Year award photo.

Chloe gasped; this wasn't the photo she knew and loved, this was a photo of everyone at the event. Steven saw her surprise and continued.

'This,' he announced as dramatically as he could but without being able to point at the picture because he was holding it, 'I believe that this,' and he nodded his head and looked downwards, 'is the man responsible for blowing up the Bestissimo Hotels.'

Now the others were staring open-mouthed but not at Steven, at Pat, who was practically exploding in her chair.

'That's the man Sunil took to the tiger reserve,' she spluttered, dabbing her finger at David's image.

'What?' Elle asked. 'The same one?' Who is he?' and she turned to Steven.

'He was known as Sovan Wildwald, and very briefly, he was a representative of Delilah's Doo Dahs which is based somewhere in the Rockies...'

Elle gasped with shock. That was the make of the thong Harry had sent her. Mel nodded with appreciation.

Harry wriggled a little more in her chair. 'He was also once on the board of Wallows Hotels.'

Chloe was also itching, in an entirely non-thong related way to tell her news, but it didn't seem quite so important compared to Pat and Elle's revelations. Elle carried on.

'So our task now is to infiltrate the organisation. See what he's up to. Harry? What have you found out?'

'The man who runs the hotels is one Iqbal Tahan,' Harry began, and she showed them an image on the screen. 'He's currently in London and he regularly visits dating sites looking for plump middle-aged women with blonde hair.' At this point, Chloe and Bessie nearly hit the ceiling.

'And he's trying to recruit a bookkeeper!' Chloe got in first. 'Look at this!' And she retrieved the notice from her pocket and waved it about; not that anyone could read it even though it was in big print. 'He's trying to recruit an assistant.'

'And that's the rude Arab man I met at the awards ceremony!' Bessie yelled. 'Look here,' and she pointed at the photograph. 'There. That man there.'

While they all peered at the shadowy figure trying to make it out, Harry spoke. 'Bessie's right. I'm almost certain that is the man, the same man who also recruited the suicide bombers.'

Elle smiled with enormous satisfaction. Things certainly were coming together.

'And there's more,' Harry continued. 'I have picked up conversations with Iqbal Tahan about cargos to be shipped from Lagos very shortly.'

'So, in order to catch this man,' Elle began, We need to find

him a personal assistant.' She read from the advert. 'Mature, willing to travel and good at filing...'

'And preferably blonde, plump and middle-aged,' added Harry.

'And who do we have who ticks all of those boxes?' Elle looked around, 'At least nothing that a little peroxide can't fix?' She turned to Chloe. 'Someone who has just passed their admission test with style...' she added. There was, of course only one. A plumpish, stylish lady, who was also a badass bookkeeper.

'Beryl!' Chloe squealed in such a high pitch it rattled Pat's glass.

'Yes, Beryl,' Elle agreed. Now it really does feel like my birthday. All we have to do is get her on board.

CHAPTER THIRTEEN

What Happens in Lagos...

David hadn't thought about Lagos for several years now. He had become comfortable and happy where he was in China, besides, Iqbal was ably handling the other trade, he just took the money that rolled in. He had discovered that hiding away from the world was no bad thing and had become completely immersed in his research, and that was expensive. He certainly hadn't cared about Iqbal's trafficking side-line, there were much more important things to do now and things were beginning to go rather well.

Despite David's initial misgivings, he discovered early on that Jimmy was not quite such a liability after all. No, he hadn't changed his opinion, Jimmy was still an idiot, but David's plan was so perfect that it was entirely possible to dupe Jimmy too. In fact, the more he thought about it, the more he realised what an incredible asset Jimmy was. A completely and entirely innocent idiot on his team could only serve to increase his credibility. Once he'd achieved this realisation, he began to rather like Jimmy, tolerated his ineptitude and treated him kindly, a little like you would a pet. In return, Jimmy spoke with such enthusiasm, and even, let's say it, love, about his boss, his truth shone through like a guiding light and everybody believed every word he said without a hint of doubt. They were the perfect partners in crime.

While there was still much research to do in their first few

years together, David used Jimmy mainly as a gofer to help out here and there, acquiring ingredients or equipment and scanning the increasingly important internet for the research of others. At this, Jimmy turned out to be very useful.

Before too many years had passed, David began to make the breakthrough which would change his future forever; it was time to get the Chinese government on side. First, David taught Jimmy enough of the basics to sound credible, and more importantly taught him how to present which, naturally, he was an expert on. He also had Jimmy convert his old *Animal Emergencies* videos to disk so he could not only study presentation techniques but also incorporate snippets into his presentation. Jimmy was a fast learner and David could then stand by and watch with genuine admiration as Jimmy turned his proposition into something extraordinarily irresistible.

Like a salesman with his foot in every door, Jimmy worked his way up the ranks of the Chinese authorities, charming each one until he was finally introduced to the top man, Professor Wong himself. By then, this man had already heard so much about David from his underlings, all he really needed to do was sanction the project. He, like they had been, was a little star-struck with this once famous man whose memory was kept alive by frequent showings of his old programmes. Collectively, they were as keen to meet him as little girls at a boy band concert. Even more importantly, his research credentials were impeccable and they all wanted to work with him. The project he was suggesting was so important, money was no object. A date was immediately agreed for David to come and present his case.

On the day of the big presentation, David and Jimmy pulled up outside the forlorn featureless science institution to be greeted by a line of the top managers bowing in turn like a Busby Berkeley dance formation. They were led to a boardroom and while Jimmy set up the presentation equipment, Professor Wong shook David's

hand and introduced him to the audience to somewhat less than enthusiastic applause. It was obvious to all of them that he didn't look much like his old television persona and they were a little suspicious.

'Thank you so much,' David said to a light appreciative murmuring from the assembled scientists, there was no mistaking that silvery smooth voice. There was a uniform *Ahh*, which momentarily confused Jimmy but removed all the prior tension.

'We are very pleased to meet you, Mr David Swallow.' Wong stifled a girly giggle. 'And we are all great fans of yours.'

David bowed graciously to his audience, who to his now spectacled eyes all looked identical in their white coats. They stood as one and bowed back at him.

'Gentlemen,' David began, and then somebody gave quite a high-pitched cough.

'Ladies and gentlemen,' he corrected. 'I have come here to show you the remarkable results of my experimentation so far. But first, let me explain precisely who I am and how I got here.'

He nodded at Jimmy, who pressed the button for the first bit of the presentation. Unfortunately, instead of the prepared film coming up, the audience was treated to a short film comprising Jimmy wearing nothing but his underpants, staring out at them, saying *Testing testing*, several times. Because the audience knew of David's show business background and nothing could dampen their enthusiasm, they laughed heartily as if this was David's little joke. David, however, threw a very stabby look at Jimmy, who was now red with embarrassment.

A few clicks later and the titles of *Animal Emergencies* appeared with the young handsome David as its presenter. There was a spontaneous round of applause.

'Yes, dear friends. I was that young man in what seems a

lifetime ago now. And you may wonder what happened to me. Why I gave up my career.'

Well, it was very clear they did wonder. They had all heard stories; most of them thought he was dead, so they leaned forward intent on catching every word.

'I was trying to personally save an endangered bear,' David began. 'It was about to fall over a cliff. I knew I had to do everything I could to save it and I tried to catch it.'

There were gasps of admiration.

'The poor creature held on to me the only way it could, with its giant claws.'

The gasps turned to cries of 'No!'

'I struggled to hold it but its claws were pulling at me, tearing my flesh, I was in agony...'

Hands were held up to mouths, terrified.

'We teetered on the very brink of the cliff, back and forth, back and forth...' Someone in the back row fainted and for a moment David wondered if he should go back into television, but then he remembered his disfigurement.

'Finally, using every tiny bit of muscle I could find, I pulled the bear back onto the ledge.'

Big sighs of relief.

'He bounded off happily, turning back to smile his goodbye to me. But sadly, the damage had been done.' David paused for dramatic effect. 'I stood there bleeding, my colon ripped from my stomach, one of my eyes hanging on its stalk, my arm,' he raised the useless limb up, 'wrenched from my body. My colleagues managed to carry me down the mountain where after many hours, an ambulance was waiting to take me to hospital.'

There was stunned silence.

'They got me into the theatre where my life was hanging by a thread as fine as a baby bear's hair. I died not once, not twice, but three times on the operating table. And then, at last, thanks to

a wonderful doctor,' he paused to get the crowd roused, 'a Chinese doctor working in America, I pulled through.'

Now there was clapping. The audience were on their feet, some were even cheering. Professor Wong was puffed full of pride that an entirely invented Chinese surgeon had saved the day. When the noise had subsided, which took a good few minutes, David continued.

'Yes, they saved me, but I was scarred so horribly that the American television company no longer wanted me.' And with that, he pushed back his blond mop and tore open his shirt to reveal the scars of that fateful day to more gasps of astonishment – and not all to do with the scars – from the audience.

'I love animals too much to worry about a little scratch,' he carried on rather passionately. 'So I decided from that day on I would devote my life to saving endangered animals with every breath of my body.' David looked out at the audience; they were hooked, he had saved the best till last.

'But how could I devote the rest of my life, my studies, my research to that country, America, which values appearance over ability? Where ratings matter more than research?

'That is why my friends, my colleagues, that is why I decided that I would come here, to China, to devote all my learning to you and your people.'

This dramatic finale had the scientists up on their feet again, clapping and cheering loudly. Even Jimmy came round. David stood there, taking in the rapturous reception. He bowed and smiled at them, both inwardly and outwardly, but the inward smile was the more sincere.

Now David had them in his scaly palms, it didn't take much more than a bit of smoke and mirrors to convince them of his intentions. His abilities and the depth of his research was beyond question. The presentation continued with the more serious stuff and to be fair, it was totally legitimate; David was always a brilliant

scholar and knew his stuff inside out. So after a little more bowing and a great deal of talking amongst themselves, the scientists readily agreed to his proposition. Professor Wong spoke for them all.

'Thank you, Mr Swallow. Thank you for choosing to share your skill and knowledge with us. We are indebted to you already. There is a laboratory already set aside for you which we hope will suit your purposes. But it will be our pleasure to make any alterations that you need. Our beloved government is fully committed to this project and in this case, money is no object.'

David smiled broadly and bowed again, 'I am honoured to accept.' And he really, genuinely meant it.

It took many months to set up the laboratory the way David wanted it, but by the end of that time, it was so up to date, so well kitted out, so secret and well-guarded, he could not have wished for more. Except that being David, he did wish for more.

'Tell the workmen that I must have an identical laboratory built into the rocks behind the original,' he told Jimmy. 'I've surveyed the site; the rock will withstand the low-grade explosives needed to carve out a cavern. If anybody asks, it is for emergency backup and control purposes.'

Nobody did ask questions. David exuded such a tidal wave of goodwill and enthusiasm, his every whim was catered for. The even more secret laboratory was built to specification and nobody but nobody knew its location other than David and Jimmy. The builders who built it, all succumbed to a strange virus just after the lab was finished, and being simple workmen, nobody cared a jot.

And so it was that David, like a bizarre Pharaoh, had built himself a splendiferous temple in which to bring life to his evil plans. Everything seemed to be falling into place at last, yet unbeknown to him, Elle's team were beginning to be dispersed on their missions to track him down.

Only one person had noticed that Mel had not been quite so enthusiastic as the others at the meeting at Elle's flat, that is until Lagos was mentioned. No one else had been looking at Mel or Harry, but Harry had been looking at Mel. Elle never had much expectation of Mel's support when it came to animals, knowing she was more concerned about women's issues but she had never bothered to find out why. They got on well enough but their working hours clashed and to be honest, Elle wasn't really that interested in anything other than trying to save the tiger, elephant and rhino.

Harry's time zone, however, overlapped with Mel's quite well and she had begun to use Harry quite a bit for client investigative work. They never expected to become best friends as neither understood the first thing about the other's work, but that changed a little one night. Mel cancelled a new client after receiving Harry's feedback on him and Harry had checked up to see she was OK. She'd caught Mel at home, halfway through a bottle of whisky and feeling very vulnerable. Bit by bit, Mel's story had come out.

Born in a village in Nigeria, Amelia Morathi was the product of, well, if not quite rape, certainly deception. Her mother Maria had been a good but spirited child and one day had been roundly spanked by her own devout Christian grandmother Mary, for uttering blasphemies. All the girl had done was to utter 'Jesus Christ!' when she tripped over a tree stump; something that she'd heard her father say a million times but her grandmother had cut her no slack.

'You are the child of Satan!' Mary had shouted at Maria with each clout of her hand. 'I will beat him out of you.'

A rogue of a man who'd just travelled in from England, and who happened to be passing through the village in his Jeep had witnessed the punishment and become somewhat aroused by the

experience. He parked up and waited behind a tree until Maria's beating was over and she had been left on her own in floods of tears. The man put his shirt on back to front, pulled his black T-shirt over his head and, smiling ever so kindly, sat next to her trying to comfort her.

'My poor young lady,' he held her hand. 'It is a terrible thing to be filled with the devil.' Maria sobbed into his chest. 'I know a way that God can enter you to make your mother happy,' he continued. At these words, Maria stopped sobbing and looked up at him.

'You do?' she asked.

The man smiled and took her hand. 'I am a man of God and if you do what I say, you will be filled with the Holy Spirit.'

He was so nice and kind and persuasive, Maria acquiesced. She followed him right out of the village and into the bush where he found a secluded spot. Then, the poor innocent child was certainly filled with something but God had nothing to do with it.

When Amelia was born, Maria was all but outcast from the village and the poor baby was blamed for it. Amelia's pale dusky skin set her apart from the other girls and as she grew up, her life was never easy. She was accused of being a witch and blamed for everything that went wrong in the village.

One day a man with a smile as wide as a crocodile's came to the village and when he saw Amelia with her mother, he made straight for her.

'This child is no good,' he proclaimed. 'You give her to me, you find a man for yourself. I pay you well. I get her exorcised in England.'

Maria didn't care whether what he said was true or not; his promise of money and the thought of her freedom from the metaphorical shackles of this child was enough to persuade her.

So for a paltry few Nigerian Naira, Amelia was handed over to the smiling man. Minutes later she was literally shackled for the whole of the long voyage overseas.

At just ten years old, Amelia began her own adventure into an old cold grey world full of cold white men. Her inauguration in England was as a virgin for men burdened with money but bereft of morals.

As she began to grow into a woman, her body could no longer pass for a child's and she was relegated to the ordinary ranks of young meat. It was there that one day, having been bought and paid for by one of Smoky Joe's less favoured employees, she found herself in his back office.

Smoky Joe was making an unscheduled visit that night to retrieve a gun or some weapon of killing, when, hearing strange noises coming from within, he stopped short of opening the door to listen. When he heard Amelia's pitiful crying, he opened the door and was horrified at what he saw.

'I paid for her good and proper,' the employee whined. 'I'm just having a little fun.' The young and obviously naked Amelia wriggled from the man's grasp sensing that this older man was more important than the other and might pay more for her. She stood boldly in front of him.

'How old are you child?'

'I think I am twelve years old, sir.'

Smoky Joe took off his jacket and put it round Amelia's shoulders. 'Will you go outside for a minute? Wait for me on the big red chair.'

Amelia curtsied and stepped outside. Without saying a word, Smoky Joe went to the safe, opened it and took out the pistol, silencer already attached. The man stopped in his tracks and was getting nervous.

'What's wrong, boss? Is it the office? I'm sorry I should've thought. I won't do it in here again.'

'I just needed to come back for this,' Smoky Joe waved the gun around. 'Now tell me, by what divine right do you think you can rape a child of twelve?'

Well, whether there was an answer or not, the conversation was certainly terminated. Outside the door, Amelia heard a scream followed by a muffled thud. A moment later, Smoky Joe's smiling head appeared round the door.

'Just you stay there, little one. I won't be long.' Seconds later he was on the phone to one of his favourite madams. 'Shirley, I'm calling in a favour. I've got a girl who needs a mother here.'

So it was that Amelia found herself being brought up by one of the nicest brothel keepers it was possible to meet. Shirley, in true East End style, shortened her name and Amelia became Mel. She liked this; it felt a bit like a new beginning and Shirley took great care of her, bringing her up as best she could. It was impossible to get Mel into school for fear she'd be deported, but Shirley taught her to read and write.

Mel was a keen learner and in time could get by at least as well as the girls that worked there. It wasn't enough to escape a life of prostitution; her illegal status was too big a difficulty to overcome, but she learned how to deal with it. Shirley had taught her courteousness and subservience in dealing with clients so she developed the ability to switch off when she needed to.

As she grew taller and more beautiful, she became the elegant escort Amelia, but she wore that name like a badge of dishonour and swore that one day she would get her revenge on the man from Lagos who had purchased her like an animal. Suddenly in the most unexpected of circumstances, one mention of that place brought all her emotions, all that anger back to the surface.

In Harry's world, women could do anything they wanted, so she didn't understand much about trafficking and how women and men could be so badly treated. Mel's story was enlightening and she promised she would do whatever she could to help. Now it looked as if that help might just be coming a little closer.

'Tell me what you find out,' Mel had asked Harry later that evening. 'I must go back. I must kill that man.'

Harry had tried her best and had eventually managed to track down a very grainy image of a man with the same name as somebody Iqbal had contacted. She sent it to Mel.

'It's him,' Mel had confirmed.

'But you can't be completely sure,' Harry had replied.

'It's close enough,' Mel countered. 'I'm going out there and even if it isn't him, I will find him.'

'But you haven't got a passport. You told me that,' Harry said.

'What, you don't know about Penelope's side-line?' Mel sneered. 'She sorted that ages ago.'

'You've got to tell Elle what you're up to,' Harry insisted.

'I'll be back before she misses me,' Mel replied.

Elle, as usual, was completely tied up with her own mission and hadn't given Mel a thought. She had her own man to get; or rather woman, and now she was sitting right in front of her where Mel herself had once sat. Beryl was listening to Elle's proposition.

'What's the pay?' Beryl asked bluntly.

'I'll pay you the same as he pays you. Two wages, two roles.' Elle replied, 'Any extra expenses will be reimbursed, and think of the travel.'

'Lagos?' sneered Beryl. 'Not that hot on shoes and fashion, are they?'

'It's not just Lagos,' Elle said. 'It's all sorts of places.'

'Italy?' Beryl hazarded.

'Probably,' Elle lied.

'So what's the real game?' Beryl asked.

'We think this man is working for a master criminal. We need

insight into everything he does. The business, the people, the locations...'

'That's child's play. Anything really serious?'

Elle remembered Beryl's despatch of the man in the pork factory. 'Definitely,' she lied again but more enthusiastically, having absolutely no idea at all.

'How can you be sure I'll get the job then?' asked Beryl. 'It's a real job, isn't it? Not an agency job.'

'True. Let's just say he likes a certain type of lady.'

Beryl raised her eyebrows. 'Oh goody. They're my favourites,' she smiled. 'Now where do I go?'

Elle handed Beryl the card that Chloe had retrieved from the hotel window. 'It's all here. Go do your stuff. Oh, and you have to be blonde.'

Beryl, as we know, was very good at doing her stuff. She brazenly rang the hotel from Elle's office, while Elle watched, fascinated. She was put straight through to Iqbal. Just the sound of her simpering got him excited.

'Oh yes, my dear lady. Can you just confirm that you can manage finances?'

'I'm a properly qualified bookkeeper,' Beryl replied a little haughtily. 'I wouldn't have applied otherwise.'

'Of course, of course. And are you amenable to a great deal of travel?'

'That sounds very nice indeed.' Beryl was more pleasant this time. 'I like to see a bit of the world now and then.'

'What about...' Iqbal hesitated, 'family?'

Beryl held a pause just long enough to make an impact. 'It's complicated. My man and I...' she began to whimper just a tiny bit.

'My dear lady, I understand. And you think that some time apart might help?'

'Something like that.' Beryl breathed heavily as if to hold back tears. Iqbal felt his spirits and other things rising.

'Please come and see me in my apartment at...' He began enthusiastically.

'I'm sorry Mr Tahan. I'm not *that sort* of girl,' Beryl replied with perfected indignation.

'Oh goodness me. I didn't mean... Will you meet me in a hotel bar then?' Iqbal suggested.

'Well, that's a bit more usual,' Beryl agreed.

'And what is your name, dear lady?'

'It's Neryl,' Beryl replied, putting a bit more sauce back in her voice. 'Neryl Wilkins.'

'Then it would be my absolute pleasure to meet with you at ten o'clock, in the bar of the Wallows hotel in London tomorrow, if it would suit.'

'That will suit me well enough Mr Tahan. See you then.'

Elle sat smiling in appreciation. She was witnessing a bookkeeping grifter at the height of her prowess and she delighted in it. *If only I had skills like that*, she thought.

'Good luck Neryl, I mean Beryl. Not that you need it, I'm sure.'

'It's in the bag dear. I'll pop in tomorrow. Just to confirm it.'

Elle had a restless evening; the more she thought about Beryl's mission, the more she realised how important the role was and she was getting nervous. This wasn't a poxy fur farm; this was worldwide illegal criminal activity. Spending the evening with Pat didn't help. Pat had bought her cribbage set with her and insisted on playing it, all evening and every evening for money. Each round Pat won was met with a *Never mind eh?* and a big grin, and she won every time. By bedtime, Elle was down three hundred pounds and another bottle of gin.

Elle needn't have worried about Beryl; the next morning, she was confidently checking herself in the mirror before setting off to her interview. This was no time for dodgy buttons or glimpses of stocking tops; this time she was in it for the really long haul and she had to protect her assets for as long as possible. She was

smartly dressed and she knew very well that nothing would disguise her ample figure. When she sashayed into the bar, Iqbal was already sitting waiting for her and the closer she got the more his tongue hung out of his mouth.

'You're hired,' he said as soon as she sat down.

'But don't you want to know anything...'

'My very dearest lady. I trusted you the second we spoke on the telephone.'

A rather condescending Beryl reappeared in Elle's offices an hour or so later.

'As I said. All sorted. We fly to Lagos the day after tomorrow.'

Elle smiled. 'Right then. I'd better get the wire and camera organised.'

Neither Beryl nor Iqbal noticed Mel as she got on the plane behind them, mainly because she was in economy and Beryl had insisted on going business class. Beryl had prewarned Iqbal that she was not a good flier and would spend the journey with shades on, so he sat rather lonelily trying to watch the movie. He'd picked a classic, *Airport 1975*, and was now rather regretting it.

Beryl shuddered slightly under her shades as she felt Iqbal's fumbling attempt to put back her slipped blanket. She wasn't too concerned, she'd met all sorts, and Iqbal was a charmer, not a groper. She could handle him literally with her eyes closed.

Iqbal, on the other hand, wholeheartedly believed that, when Neryl's paramour was out of the picture, she would gradually fall for his charms. Until then, he would feast his eyes on her perfect English rose skin and pink cheeks with those oh so sexy wisps of blonde hair falling loose from her bun.

'Can I get you anything, sir?' was enough for Iqbal to guiltily jump and throw his champagne all over the poor air stewardess.

'That's all right, sir,' she mopped it up with a cloth and a plastic smile.

'Stupid fuck,' she said when she was out of earshot.

At the back of the plane, Mel had all sorts of terrible thoughts and memories running through her head. She hadn't returned to Lagos since she first came to England, always meaning to but never getting round to it. Now she had the smell of blood in her nostrils, she was determined to take her revenge on the man who had enslaved her. Harry had been clear enough; she couldn't promise that this was the right man, but the image of Iqbal's contact in Lagos had convinced Mel. She would never forget that face; that horrible wide smile for as long as she lived. Now all she had to do was keep out of sight, which was pretty easy since Iqbal clearly only had eyes for his new assistant Neryl. It never occurred to her, however, that she herself was being followed from the plane by someone.

After they had landed and cleared through the airport it was a very hot and clammy Beryl who wafted her hands in front of her face while Iqbal stared at her cleavage into which a small ball of sweat was gradually descending. Beryl, spotting his gaze, prodded him into action. Iqbal jumped to attention and grabbed a trolley balancing his very small case on top of two very large ones of Beryl's. He was just about able to push the load to the taxi rank, being far to mean to tip a porter to do it.

Stepping into the cab was a bit like getting into an oven. Beryl began to turn red.

'No air conditioning, I am sorry,' Iqbal told her. 'My official car has it though.'

'Gracious,' Beryl replied. 'I shall be staying in the hotel all the time. There is absolutely no need for me to go outside in this godforsaken place. The hotel has air conditioning doesn't it?' Iqbal nodded and was quite pleased to hear it. It suited him just fine for her to be in the hotel and not seeing what he was about to get up to.

Mel had also disembarked and was looking around. Since she'd never met either Iqbal or Beryl, she wasn't too worried about bumping into them, but she did tend to stand out in a crowd and really did not need the attention so she waited out of public view for a minute before getting into a taxi. When she did arrive at the hotel it was just in time to miss them going into the lift.

She approached the reception desk with some trepidation; Harry had promised to infiltrate the hotel booking system and prepay her room but if something had gone wrong... She needn't have worried, it seemed to have worked and she was delighted when she got into her room; it was very nice indeed. She called Harry straight away.

'OK. Give me a minute...' Harry said. 'Turn the TV on.' A few moments later, there was Harry talking to Mel through the hotel television.

'How the hell...?' began Mel.

'Trade secret,' Harry replied. 'Now, first of all, since Elle isn't here, I order you to have a good night's rest. Beryl will be staying in the hotel tomorrow to make sure all the cameras and wires are working and getting me into Iqbal's systems. I suggest you stay in tomorrow too and wait until I find out what Iqbal is up to today.'

Both of them knew that was not going to happen, but Harry had to at least try to dissuade her from doing anything too dangerous.

The next morning, while Beryl was tucking into full English, Iqbal was already on the road. His so-called official car was indeed air conditioned. It was loaned to him by an African chieftain for whom he had done several favours, mainly involving him dressing up as a witch doctor and poisoning a few people. Unbeknown to Iqbal however, Beryl had successfully hidden a camera in the fastening of his briefcase whilst he had been leching at the receptionist the day before. Harry's first task of the day was to fine tune the camera and decipher the images it relayed. The first shot

took her by surprise until she realised that Iqbal and his case were somewhere in a gent's toilet.

'Eew. Chloe would be horrified.' Harry couldn't bear to look. At least it's working, she decided.

After a while, the camera began to pick up more normal images. It had a fisheye lens giving Harry a huge width of vision, but things were a little distorted. Half an hour later Iqbal arrived at his destination somewhere in the bush and saw his contact waiting for him. As he got out of the car, Iqbal grabbed his case rather hurriedly and Harry crossed her fingers that the camera would stay attached. It seemed to but the image was of a man's legs. Harry strained to hear the conversation. It was very poor sound quality, not helped by the very heavy accent of Iqbal's contact but Harry concluded that a very large payment had been made in return for a consignment of Rhino horns and elephant tusks.

As the conversation drifted to other things, Harry was about to terminate the recording when she heard someone say, 'Our other business,' and then she strained so hard to listen she made an impression of her ear on the monitor.

'Other cargo?' she said out loud. The next sentence was unmistakable.

'The fresh meat is in the container,' she repeated, but more importantly, the camera was, at last, picking up a decent image. She saw the face of the dealer, and it was a face she recognised. She picked up her phone.

'Mel, yes, it's him. I'm sure. I have a location. Where are you?'

'I'm right behind them,' came Mel's reply. 'I followed him from the hotel.'

'What?' shouted Harry, but suddenly Mel's phone went dead. Harry clicked all the buttons she could find, ran all the programs she could think of but the connection was gone. All she could do now was to cross her fingers. As for Mel, she could do nothing.

Taken from behind and chloroformed, she was being bundled into a car boot.

CHAPTER FOURTEEN

Beryl's Bluff and Mel's Mission

Beryl was making very good use of her first day in Lagos, especially without her new boss. Within minutes, she had sussed his appalling accounts. All it needed was for her to 'top and tail' one of her readymade reports, adding a little mix of very obvious things that Iqbal would remember, and hey presto! A bespoke report. Most of it, naturally, was intended to be completely unintelligible to him anyway being so full of jargonese, it might as well have been Japanese. By contrast, the Executive Summary was printed in big letters in words of no more than two syllables and could have been understood by an idiot.

> There has been a MAJOR BREAKDOWN in record keeping. This not only makes it difficult to understand how much money the group is or isn't making, there is a severe risk of problems arising from dealings with all local TAX bodies. This could result in LARGE FINES. ACTION REQUIRED NOW. Estimate of time needed to correct is at least THIRTY WORKING DAYS.

Beryl sat and admired the printed report just for a moment, then she got back to the really major breakdown; the breaking down of cellulite in her thighs. She had turned her nose up at the appalling

facilities in the Wallows and transferred herself, at Iqbal's expense, to the pool area of the spa at the Regent's hotel.

Tablet in hand, Beryl ran some pre-prepared business reports on the Wallows accounts database which she sent straight to Bessie, who lapped them up voraciously. While Beryl was having her pedicure, she called up all the electronic banking information she could find and sent the details to Harry for investigation.

Look at the research and development payments from the subsidiary accounts, she typed. *Find out who the payments went to.* Beryl laughed when her tablet pinged to announce an email from Bessie.

I'm concerned that R&D is far too high for a group that size, it read. Does she think I'm an idiot? Beryl wondered. While her fingernails were being sanded ready for polishing, she dashed off a voice recognition email.

'That's the slush fund,' she explained. 'I've already got Harry on it.'

Finally, while her butt was being buffed, Beryl called Elle to check in her progress and pass on details of their trip.

'Wee're offf too Indiaa inn threee daysss,' Beryl vibrated. 'Thenn eeeither Aaazerbaijan or Rooostovv or bothh. Noo mention of Chinaa yet. That's all I have so far.'

'Right,' Elle was curious. 'Are you OK? You sound as if you're about to burst into tears.'

'No o o onsense,' warbled Beryl. 'It must be ro o o oad works or something.'

Elle frowned, 'Keep us posted of all movements. The camera's working fine but we may need another one actually on his body too.' There was a pause in the treatment.

'Is that it?' Beryl was dismissive. 'When do I bump him off?'

'When we've found the ringleader,' Elle retorted. 'Not a moment before.'

By the time Iqbal returned from his meeting, Beryl was sitting at the desk in his hotel room, wiping her brow and looking the very essence of an overworked bookkeeper.

'How is it going, my dear lady?' he enquired.

Raising a harassed looking face, Beryl replied, 'Mr Tahan. It is an absolute nightmare. I have no idea whether I can continue with this job. The working conditions are intolerable and your accounts are in such a state.' She handed him her report, which he started to leaf through with an almost entirely vacant expression, not managing to disguise the terror he felt when he saw the word TAX.

'I can see you have been busy,' he noted as he spotted a reference to the cock-ups with the plane tickets. 'But, my dear Neryl, Rome wasn't built in a day. Please bear with me. Finish now, and tomorrow I insist you rest. I will delay India for a day, and India you must visit, I promise you will love it.'

'It's true I'm not one to quit that easily,' Beryl pretended to ponder. 'Yes, a day off would be nice, I am very tired. And I shall call room service for my evening meal tonight. I need an early night and I am far too frazzled to eat in the restaurant.'

'Whatever you want,' a relieved Iqbal agreed. 'Let us talk again tomorrow evening to make our arrangements for our next port of call.'

Beryl got up, feigning exhaustion to perfection, and sighed deeply as she left Iqbal's room and made her way to her own. Once there, rejuvenated, she kicked off her shoes, rang room service and put on a George Clooney movie.

In London, Mel had at last been missed. When Chloe came into the office, Elle looked up expectantly. 'Ah, it's you. You haven't seen Mel, have you?'

'No, I haven't. Why? Is there a problem?'

Elle wasn't listening she was looking at her watch. 'Hang on,' she said before preparing three G&Ts from the cabinet behind her desk. Thirty seconds to five o' clock, Pat came in and took a glass.

'Chin chin!' she knocked back half of hers in one swallow. 'I'm a bit thirsty today. Missing home,' she added.

'Ah well,' began Elle. 'Our man is off to India soon...'

'Excellent,' Pat perked up. 'I know you will miss me terribly Elle, but I will find out who this dreadful person has been seeing and make sure he is locked up. That is my mission and I won't hear any arguments.'

Elle was silent but inside she was doing somersaults of happiness.

'I shall pack tonight,' Pat continued. 'This has to be done. Don't try to stop me. I'll find out what that savage has been doing to my precious tigers...'

Chloe looked suspiciously at Elle who was silently nodding along with Pat's speech.

She jumped in.

'No Pat, you can't go on your own. It could be dangerous. Someone should go with you. Isn't that right Elle? Maybe I should come too.'

'Stuff and nonsense,' Pat protested, and at that precise moment, Penelope stuck her head round the door. 'I'll take her with me,' Pat pointed at Penelope. 'Not being unkind, but she's far more useful than you, dear.'

While Pat left Penelope speechless yet again, Elle inwardly breathed a huge sigh of relief. Just for a second, she thought Pat had waivered and much as she loved her aunt, she was getting thoroughly sick of cribbage, and was losing far too much money and gin.

'No time to waste. Penelope? Go home and pack,' ordered Pat. 'Take a pistol and a rifle for each of us, oh, and body armour.

I'm a size ten.' Penelope's open mouth slammed shut and she turned to Elle who shrugged in an *I'm not going to argue with her,* sort of way.

Penelope turned round and left, slamming the door behind her.

'Manners!' shouted Pat, then she turned to Elle. 'Look dear, you book the flights. I'll arrange the cab. I know someone else who could be very useful if he's available.'

'On to it, Pat.'

Elle waited until Pat was out of the door and out of the office. 'Thank God for that.' She was speaking to Chloe, but Chloe was miles away.

'Earth to Chloe?' Elle stared at her. 'You know a bit about Azerbaijan. What could this man Iqbal possibly be doing there other than hotel business? And why would he go there after Nigeria? Or is it random?'

'That's just what I was wondering,' Chloe shook her head a little. 'I'll ring Ulka. She keeps an eye out for strange things.'

With a nod from Elle, Chloe picked up the phone and dialled.

'Ulka, hello, it's Chloe here.'

'Hello, Chichek. How are you? It must be important for you to ring.'

'It is, Ulka. We think there's another problem brewing. Not with the hotels this time, but endangered animals. Maybe from Africa.'

'I will ask Baghir, if I can reach that useless boy...' Chloe drifted into happy memories of Baghir as Ulka went into her usual rant about him. 'There was something about the leopard on the news. But I will know more when I talk to the little shit.'

'Thanks, Ulka,' Chloe gave a big sigh. The longer the separation, the more she missed Baghir although she never told anyone. 'I'll wait to hear from you then.'

When Chloe had gone, Elle's thoughts turned to Mel again. There was still no answer from her phone, so she called Harry. It wasn't so much that she cared, but part of the deal was Mel's safety.

'It's Mel. I can't get hold of her and I've had clients asking for her.'

'No idea,' lied Harry. 'She was due a holiday, wasn't she?'

Elle ummed thoughtfully. 'Maybe. She did say something but I didn't know that she'd sorted anything out.'

'Oh, she told me something about visiting relatives,' Harry lied again. Elle was reassured and got straight back to her main business.

'What about Delilah's Doo Dahs and Wallows Hotels?' Elle asked. 'Have you found any connection yet? What do we know about this Wildwald man?'

'I'm getting there,' Harry crossed her fingers as she spoke. She'd actually had a minor crisis. Some of the old links she had found ages ago seemed to have been deleted just after a strange young Chinese man's face had suddenly appeared on her screen one day. It was at the exact moment that she was hacking into some old Wallows company records. She had, however, retrieved some of her very old searches which she had very carefully saved and she had looked through them studiously. Without knowing why, she was hesitant to ask Elle something, but decided it was potentially too important to ignore.

'Elle, did you ever know a man called David Swallow?'

Elle sat back in her chair and reached for her gin. She took a large swig and it seemed like an eternity before she responded. Harry was perplexed at her reaction.

'That bastard? Do you mean the TV guy? I heard he died a long time ago after an accident. Why do you ask?'

'Dead? Yes, that makes sense, I suppose,' mused Harry, not

at all sure it did. 'I did some research and his name came up; he was big on endangered species wasn't he?'

'Is it important?' snapped Elle. Harry was taken aback; there was clearly another connection she wasn't quite getting.

'OK, I'll keep looking.'

Harry was actually getting much closer than she could possibly have realised. Nor was she wrong about things being deleted. This was one thing that the strange young Chinese man with a habit of appearing when he shouldn't, could do rather well. But her main concern was Mel and she resolved to try to contact her. She failed and she was right to be worried.

Somewhere in Lagos Mel was just coming round to find herself lying on a sofa in a sparsely furnished room.

'Here. Drink this,' a familiar voice said to her. She sat up and looked around.

'You!' she shouted. 'What the...' the Hitman smiled at her.

'Smoky Joe sent me. You were just about to walk into one helluva mess.'

'I can take care of myself,' Mel snapped. 'You have no idea...'

'But you're wrong,' the Hitman interrupted her. 'I know more than you do. That's my job. Your job is to look good.'

'Don't you dare...' Mel began, but he was smiling. She gave in. 'OK, you tell me then. And where the fuck am I?'

'Coffee?' the Hitman asked.

'Thanks,' Mel nodded and took the cup from his hand and listened to what he had to say.

'You were abducted by Buburu Oni, known as BO, when you were ten.'

Mel nodded. 'That's the bastard.'

'He's still trafficking for sure, but he's getting on a bit and he's moved into dabbling in rhino horns for the Ruskies. There's a route

through Azerbaijan.'

'Oh,' Mel was unimpressed. 'So you're not here to kill him then?'

'Shit yes,' the Hitman nodded. 'But we gotta do it right. There's a trailer full of what he calls meat.'

'More girls?' Mel shook her head. The Hitman nodded.

Mel smiled as the realisation hit her. 'And you said *we*.'

'Smoky Joe says I gotta let you have your shot. You up for that little girl?'

'You bet,' Mel grinned.

'We go tomorrow. When you're rested and trained up. You OK with that?'

'Yup,' Mel replied, the tiniest tremor in her voice.

'OK. There are two trailers going to the port, one with the horns and tusks, one with the girls. BO will be with one of them, probably the girls.'

'Can't we cover both? You take one, I take one?' asked Mel.

The Hitman roared with laughter. 'There will be goons everywhere. Armed to the hilt. We're getting backup, lady. Smoky Joe had friends everywhere. You and I will stick together, that's Smoky Joe's orders. Like glue.'

'So who are the backup, and where are they?'

Right on cue, the Hitman's radio crackled. 'OK,' he answered. 'We'll meet at the second junction. You got people on the trailers?' The Hitman turned to Mel. 'Come on, sugar, it's a day early. We're on.'

It was good, Mel decided as she sat in the front of the Hitman's Jeep, that she didn't have time to think about things. She had no idea who the backup were or where they came from, all she cared about was getting rid of BO once and for all and saving other girls from her fate. She was relishing the opportunity, she had never felt so alive in all her life.

When they arrived at the junction there were two trucks full

of camouflaged men waiting for them. One got out and approached the Jeep. The Hitman got out with a warning look to Mel to stay put, then he high fived the man.

'Saul, good to see you. What's the intel?'

'One trailer, east high road. Ventilated; since dead animal bits don't need no air, I'm guessing that's where the live cargo is. Who's the broad?'

'Mind your own. And the other?' the Hitman shot back.

'Coast road. Probably already at the port,' Saul replied.

'OK, we're going east. See you at the port later.'

Saul saluted and pointed at one of the truck drivers indicating he was to follow the Hitman. He climbed into the other truck and waved goodbye to the Hitman who was already back in the Jeep.

'You sure you wanna stay?' he asked Mel.

'You try and stop me,' she replied.

With that, the Hitman hit the gas and the Jeep pulled off down the dusty road followed by the truck. It was a bumpy ride and Mel was beginning to wish she'd worn thicker pants, but before too long, they approached a junction.

'There's BO,' the Hitman pointed to a large trailer. 'I can smell him already.'

'No guards?' Mel peered, incredulous.

'There'll be guards,' the Hitman confirmed. 'OK, we're going to head them off. Get your gun ready and hold on to your tits!'

The Jeep screeched into action and tore down the road towards the junction. They were much faster than the trailer, so it was easy to get in front of it, and turning round, Mel could see BO sitting next to the driver.

'He's there, the bastard,' she yelled. 'When can I shoot?'

'Hold on, Not till I say. We have to try to negotiate first.' Mel scowled but sat back in the seat.

The Jeep pulled out ahead of the trailer and within seconds armed men appeared from the top, but then the truck pulled round behind the trailer, and the camouflaged men stood up. BO got out of the cab as did the Hitman, hissing at Mel to duck down.

'We were expecting you,' he smiled that awful smile as he spoke. 'What's the offer?'

'Three mill,' the Hitman replied. 'But we gotta see them all first.' BO glanced round to check that each of his men had a gun trained on each of the Hitman's men.

Mel had her own ideas; too excited to stay put, she slid out of the Jeep and crept around the side to watch as BO went to the back of the trailer and opened the doors. Inside were about forty young girls, all trussed up, mouths covered with duct tape. Mel gasped – too loudly; BO turned round and she ducked down darting round the side before he could see her.

'What the fuck?' BO was clearly rattled. 'You got someone here?'

'No one,' the Hitman waved his arm behind his back to urge Mel back to the Jeep. BO calmed a little.

'Show me the money,' he demanded, not at all sounding like Tom Cruise.

'Get the girls out first,' The Hitman demanded. 'I wanna see them all walking.'

BO turned and shouted to them. 'Get up. Show the nice man how you stand.' He began to grab at them, pulling them clumsily to their feet which was hard since they were bound with rope.

'Here, you,' he pointed at one of his guards. 'Help.'

As the guard got down from the trailer, he just caught sight of Mel who ran ahead then dropped on all fours out of sight of the driver.

'Hey boss, one got away!'

'What you say?' BO was confused and now on high alert. 'You play any tricks man, this blows,' he shouted pointing inside the trailer. The Hitman stared; there was a mass of explosives all wired up around the walls of the trailer. He hadn't expected this; he was

panicking but not showing it.

'Where's the detonator?' he asked. 'We don't want no accidents.'

'Here!' BO waved his mobile in the air. 'You'll get it when the deal's done.' He turned to the guard. 'Now what you talking about?'

Mel had decided she was not taking any chances. There was only one thing she wanted to do and she was going to do it now while she had the chance. She crept further round the other side of the trailer until she could just see the outline of BO as he stood talking to the Hitman. Breathing deeply, she jumped out to face him, her gun pointing at his head.

'Hey, I remember you!' were BO's last words as a smiling Mel fired, shouting, 'I've got you, you bastard!' Seconds later she was dead; picked off by two guards on the roof. Mel's single bullet had not been so true. BO had a few moments left to live and he spent one looking at his phone. Quick as lightning the Hitman shot it from his hand, praying it would not set off the explosives. He too was instantly hit by a hail of bullets and he and BO fell towards each other, noses down in the dust.

'Fuck fuck FUCK!' the Hitman gasped his last words. 'Smoky Joe ain't gonna like this one bit.'

CHAPTER FIFTEEN

Pat's Poison

Harry tried over and over again to contact Mel but there was no answer from her phone or email and now she was seriously worried. She knew roughly where Mel was headed and began trying to pick up radio communications. It wasn't long before she picked up a great deal of activity on the port road. She couldn't understand most of the language used but from time to time she heard the odd English word and was pretty sure that she was on to the shipments. It sounded like something had gone badly wrong. When at last she picked up reports of a major incident involving captured females being transported, and that there were thirty casualties including one woman, she guessed that the worst had probably happened.

She'd surreptitiously gained access to Smoky Joe's phone a while back so she had a sneak peek and was shattered at what she saw.

Harry must have seen the photo of Mel's body at more or less the same time as Smoky Joe. Saul had suspected correctly that the rhino horn and elephant tusk consignment had already shipped, so he hadn't hesitated in rounding up his men and turning round to where BO had been going. He'd assumed that the Hitman would have had everything under control but it didn't hurt to check. He was too late. When he arrived at the scene even

he was shocked at the carnage. The girls had all survived and were huddled together well clear of the trailer, but almost all the guards on both sides were now dead, bodies oozing blood and covered with flies. There were police and paramedics swarming everywhere. Saul had followed protocol and rung Smoky Joe.

'Find the girl,' Smoky Joe had yelled at him. 'Just get her out!'

Saul, almost sure there was no hope, scanned the trailer then, with a bundle of notes in hand, just in case, went up to a policeman.

'Any western women?' he asked. He was nodded to a body bag about to be loaded into an ambulance. 'I need to see her.'

The ambulance man unzipped the bag to reveal Mel's smiling face. One of the rescued girls came running over, crying with shock, relief and sadness.

'She saved us. She is a true heroine.' Saul took a picture of Mel on his phone and sent it to Smoky Joe. When Smoky Joe saw that photo, tears started rolling down his grizzled face.

When the tears stopped, he was already on his way to Elle's office, and if the office door hadn't been open, he would have pulled it off its hinges.

'What the fuck did you do to my little girl?' he yelled.

'Mel?' Elle jumped. 'She's on holiday, isn't she? I haven't seen her in days.'

Smoky Joe grabbed Elle by the neck, lifted her up and shouted at her. 'You tell me why the fuck she was in Nigeria fighting traffickers and horn smugglers or I will make pasta out of your brains.'

Luckily for Elle, Chloe had just arrived and hearing the commotion, came into the office.

'Mr Joe,' she quietly and gently wiped the spittle from around his mouth. 'Sit down. Elle can't talk with her windpipe all crushed

like that.' At last, Smoky Joe calmed down enough to sit down.

'What happened to her?' Elle rasped. And Elle's face went from bright throttled red to Chloe clean white as Smoky Joe told her what had happened.

'But you knew she was there. You sent the Hitman. I had no idea. Why didn't you tell me?'

While Chloe wept silently into her J-cloth, Smoky Joe choked up again. He had to admit Elle had a point.

'So you really didn't tell her to go?' he asked.

'I swear it,' Elle declared.

'Then who did? My man only followed her, and together we worked out what was going on. Is this man you're chasing behind it all?'

'Probably.' Elle, now recovering, was sensing that the blame was being transferred.

'He seems to have fingers in pies everywhere. They're dealing in tiger parts too. I've got my aunt out there...'

'You're risking your own aunt?' Smoky Joe was incredulous. 'I gotta think about this.'

'You never met Pat, did you?' Elle pointed to the small framed photo on her desk that Pat had left there. He shook his head. 'She'd have cleaned out your casino in one hit,' Elle spoke with the tiniest hint of malice, remembering the cribbage games.

'I'd have liked to have met the dame who could do that,' Smoky Joe nodded. 'But she's still your aunt.'

'You needn't worry about Pat. She's a warrior and Penelope's with her too.'

'And you gotta learn to take care of your own,' Smoky Joe insisted. 'If you don't get this bastard, I will. And then I'm coming after you. You're in trouble here getting involved in things you don't understand and getting people killed.' Smoky Joe slammed the door behind him.

Chloe glared at Elle until she reacted.

'I'm going off him,' Elle commented.

'Pat!' Chloe nearly shouted. 'You sent Pat out to fight terrorists?'

'What?' Elle was taken aback. 'Yes, I mean, no. She and Penelope were only meant to stop the consignment. I had no idea there would be guns and explosives. Anyway, that was Africa, not India. I'd better call Harry.'

Elle made the call while Chloe shook her head sadly. If she had an aunt, she wouldn't have let her go, and she was beginning to get very fond of Pat. Pat, on the other hand, wouldn't have thought a jot about it.

'I've got some bad news,' Elle announced when Harry appeared on screen. Harry was prepared. Initially wracked with guilt, she'd thought things through and remembered Mel's determination. She had known all the risks and had done what she wanted to do and it was also clear from the photo that she'd died happy.

'I already know,' Harry replied. 'It's Mel, isn't it? I was just going to call you, I picked something up. It's terrible.'

Elle didn't dwell on it for a moment longer. 'What's the latest with Pat and Penelope?' she asked, as Chloe cringed beside her. Harry saw Chloe's look but she didn't want to dwell either. It would not help anyone to know that she had told Mel about the Lagos deal. The best thing she could do now was make sure that Penelope and Pat would be safe.

She steadied herself and spoke again.

'They're due in Delhi any minute. Pat has got hold of this driver. Sunil? He's waiting for them, I got him on the airport CCTV.'

'What do you know about him?' Elle asked anxiously.

'Not a lot,' Harry replied. 'But I'm working on it. It will help if your aunt remembers to fix the camera.'

'Penelope will do that,' Elle assured her. And indeed, almost as she spoke, over in Delhi Penelope was inserting the camera in

Sunil's car while he put their bags in the boot.

'It is very very nice to see you again, Madam Pat,' he smiled, as they drove off. 'And to meet your lovely friend Miss Penelope.' Penelope sneered a little, she didn't like idiots and this man clearly was a prime example of one. Pat was quick to take charge.

'Now then, Sunil, let's not beat around the bush. We are here to find the man who is smuggling contraband out of the tiger reserve.'

'Oh deary me. I thought it was tiger bones and skin.'

'Generic term,' snapped Pat, leaving Sunil none the wiser. She continued. 'Shortly, your boss Iqbal will arrive to meet with this man; we think he will be handing over payment in cash. The sooner we get back to my house, the sooner you can go and pick him up at the local airport. Then we will follow you. Is that clear?'

'Oh yes, Madam Pat. But I am having this feeling that Mr Iqbal will not be liking this.'

'Don't worry about him. He won't know anything; it's his contact we are after.'

'But he will be flying back with the cargo to Delhi,' Sunil added. 'From the local airport.'

'Then what happens?' Pat asked.

'That I do not know, madam,' Sunil replied.

Pat turned to Penelope. We may have to split. You must follow that cargo wherever it goes. I will deal with the trafficker.' Penelope nodded.

Pat turned to Sunil. 'And your boss will not know a thing about this, I promise.'

'That is very reassuring, madam. Very good. Very good indeed.'

Later that day when Pat and Penelope were home, Sunil rang to say that Iqbal was not coming for another day, so they had more

time.

'Good,' Pat said. 'We needed more time. We need a faster car. My old banger is no good.'

'Let me take a look.'

Penelope went to inspect the old heap of a rusting crock of a motor. A few hours later and well past gin time, she emerged, face blackened with oil, but smiling broadly.

'You almost look like a native!' Pat exclaimed. 'What have you done?'

'Well, I needed a few spares...' Penelope explained in far too much detail for Pat to take in but she understood the last few words. '...But I've turned her into a proper little racer.'

'Good show,' Pat was pleased. 'So all I have to do is catch the trafficker and take him to the police station while you go with the cargo?' Penelope nodded. 'Bath time for you, young lady then. I am having an early night. See you in the morning. Oh, and the uniforms are in the cupboard.'

Penelope got cleaned up as best she could, but even after following all Chloe's best tips, she could not get all the oil residue out of the bath; the enamel had cracked a bit and now all the cracks were highlighted in black. Remembering something she had seen in the garage she made her way out, spotting a hip flask on the kitchen worktop. 'Perfect,' she muttered before tipping out the contents and going outside to the garage. She emerged a few minutes later clutching the flask happily. With a small cloth and a tiny drop of the liquid she had found, she managed to remove all the marks around the bath. Pleased with her efforts, she curled up and went to sleep on Pat's sofa, and being one of those lucky people who can sleep anywhere, she slept very soundly.

The next morning while Penelope was still snoring on the sofa, Pat was already up, and dressed for action in her tiger reserve uniform.

'I just called Sunil. They won't be at the reserve until at least midday. Maybe not until two. I suggest a big hearty breakfast and then a game of cribbage?' Penelope nodded cheerily. She was good at card games.

Much later on, with Penelope three million rupees down, Pat got a call from Sunil.

'They will be at the reserve in thirty minutes.'

Pat was excited. 'We'd better get going.'

'How long does it normally take you? Thirty minutes?' Penelope suggested.

'That's what I said,' Pat snapped.

'It'll only take ten minutes now. Just time for me to win some money back.' Penelope grinned, something she was about to regret. When the tally hit five million, Penelope got up.

'Time to go,' she sulked.

When they went outside to the car Pat was unimpressed; it looked exactly the same as it had always done.

'It doesn't look any different,' she pouted.

'It is. I promise you. I'll drive.' Penelope rudely got into the driver's seat.

'But I'm sick if I don't drive myself,' Pat wailed.

'You'll be sick anyway the speed we have to go,' Penelope snarled, as she started the engine and the poor old jalopy sped off like a racing car.

They arrived at the entrance to the reserve just as Sunil drove Iqbal to the far north entrance. They followed behind as inconspicuously as they could, but as they got closer, it became apparent that they would have to hide.

'Quick, in there,' Pat pointed into the reserve. Penelope looked at her in horror.

'But there are tigers in there!' she exclaimed.

'It'll be fine. They sleep most of the day.'

Pat led the way and they slipped under the wire, crept through the reserve and crawled up a small hill to get a better look. Pat had her binoculars; Penelope lay on the ground peering until she felt the strangest sensation. She smelled a powerful smell and felt a warm furry presence behind her; it was licking her leg. She turned and nearly screamed; the largest tiger she had ever seen, in fact, the only tiger she had ever seen close up, was eying up her leg as if it were a juicy steak.

'Pat,' she whispered. 'PAT!' Pat, startled, turned round then smiled broadly.

'Hello, Snuggles.' Snuggles gave a growl of welcome while Pat tickled him under the chin. Penelope rationalised that if she ran, she would literally be dead meat, so she tried to pretend that none of it was happening and turned back to watch the scene down below.

'Pat,' she whispered. 'We're on.' And she pointed the camera, turned the microphone up to maximum and began to film.

Down below, Iqbal got out of the car to talk to the smuggler. Luckily, he did not notice Sunil smiling and waving at Pat and Penelope from inside the car.

'Idiot,' Penelope muttered. Snuggles purred and she shut up.

'Here is your money, dear friend,' Iqbal handed the smuggler a travel bag. He pointed to a white van. 'Is that the consignment?'

'Yes,' the man, who was very frugal with his words, replied.

'As we agreed.' The man nodded and checked the money while Iqbal checked out the van. Then he called Sunil over to move the contents into his car. When the car was full to bursting, and the van empty, Iqbal spoke to the man again.

'Thank you. I will be in touch about restocking shortly.'

While Pat and Penelope waited for Sunil and Iqbal to drive off, Pat realised something.

'Damn! I was meant to be down there. And you should have been in the car.' Penelope was speechless. She couldn't fault Pat's logic. 'Fucking amateurs,' she muttered under her breath.

'We'll have to catch up with that Iqbal instead,' Pat decided. 'We know what the trafficker looks like now, we've got him on film. Let's get going.'

Penelope had to agree. 'Yes, I can get on the plane, radio ahead and we can get the cargo impounded and Iqbal arrested in Delhi. You can take the car back and see the local police here.'

'Quick then. No time to waste.'

They went back to Pat's car but all was not well. However much Penelope fiddled with it and Pat kicked it, the poor old banger would not start. Penelope opened the bonnet and rummaged around for ages. Finally, after what seemed like years, the engine began to purr almost as loudly as a Bengal tiger. She jumped in the driver's seat; there was no time to argue.

'The plane will have taken off before we get there at this rate,' Pat moaned. 'Put your bloody foot down woman!'

Penelope didn't need telling twice, but fast as the car was, it couldn't compensate for Pat's poor directions and by the time they arrived at the airport, they could see the cargo already being loaded into the plane.

'Damnation,' Pat said. 'That Iqbal chap must already be on board. Look! It's Sunil.' Sunil was still waiting at the gates, once again waving at them very conspicuously.

Penelope parked up next to him. 'I do wish you wouldn't do that.' She scolded.

'It is too late, Madam Pat. It is all on board.'

'No,' Pat was defiant. 'There's still time. Penelope?' she ordered, 'Get on that plane now and do what you can.'

'And what will you do, Madam Pat?' Sunil asked.

'My goodness, is that the time?' Pat took her hip flask from its pouch and unscrewed the lid. Before Penelope had a chance to

say *caustic soda*, Pat had knocked back a large measure.

'Argh,' she gasped, before falling flat on the ground, writhing a bit.

Penelope looked down at Pat, then looked up at the plane. She had a microsecond to make a choice. She knew that Pat could not survive that fateful gulp and there was only one way to catch that cargo.

'Take care of her, Sunil,' she shouted, and like an Olympic runner well past their competing days, Penelope ran up to the private plane, charged up the landing steps and got inside the plane just before the steward closed the door. She began brandishing her pistol like a mad woman.

'To Delhi,' she ordered, pointing the pistol at the pilot's head. She looked around at all the frantic screaming passengers as the plane took off, but to her despair, there was no sign of Iqbal.

CHAPTER SIXTEEN

Iqbal Gets an Itch

Elle had been shaken not so much by Mel's death but by Smoky Joe's reaction to it. She felt too exposed at the office now, especially without Penelope around and began to spend more time in her flat. This was her true sanctuary and one evening, under cover of darkness, she transported everything she needed for her operations from her office back to her flat. Bessie had been making noises about needing more space, so this suited both of them.

Elle did shed a few tears for her aunt but resolved that the only way she could honour her properly was by finding that last remaining trophy hunter. She covered the walls of her flat with maps to plot the missions. Any remaining spaces were taken up with her old photos of endangered animals. The picture of the trophy hunter was given pride of place and Elle's determination to find him grew ever stronger.

While Bessie began to get stuck into the nuts and bolts of the business, Elle stayed holed up in her flat until Penelope made it home. When she did, Elle convened a meeting; the mood was not good.

'But at least Mel got rid of that terrible man and an important supply link,' Elle argued. No one spoke. 'She saved a lot of women too. It was what she wanted to do *most*. Kill that awful man. Even Smoky Joe had to agree with that.'

Penelope was silent but Chloe piped up.

'And what about Pat? How did that help?'

Elle sighed. 'She helped stop the consignment which is now in police hands. It wasn't a complete waste.'

'Never mind that, shouldn't you be out there?' Chloe retorted. 'Seeing to Pat's affairs? Arranging the funeral?'

Elle was quiet for a moment. 'I have to carry on from here. Pat would understand. I can't help her now,' she explained. 'Besides, I expect there will have to be a post-mortem so there's nothing we can do until then.'

'The local police still haven't caught the smuggler,' Penelope added glumly. 'I gave the footage to the Delhi police. I'm not sure they were interested.'

Elle tried to change the subject. 'That reminds me, Penelope, it was ingenious of you to hijack the plane like that.'

'For God's sake, it wasn't a hijack,' Penelope snapped. 'The police understood that... in the end.'

'How long were you in the cell?' Chloe asked politely. Penelope snarled at her. Elle spoke to break the tension.

'I'm going to ring Harry. Iqbal and Beryl must be on their way to Rostov soon. We should find out where the consignment is now.'

The others nodded; they too needed to be doing something to take their minds off things. Elle made the call but for the first time ever, Harry wasn't there. Now they all looked at each other shrugging their shoulders, Chloe especially concerned. None of them had any idea how to track Harry down; they needed Harry to track people down.

'We can't lose anyone else,' wailed Chloe. 'It's all too much. Don't you even care about people anymore, Elle?'

Elle didn't hear Chloe. Nobody did. In Chloe's head she was screaming it, but outside, nothing emerged. Already very upset about Mel and Pat, now she had Harry to worry about too.

'I have to go to Azerbaijan,' she announced, and this time it was out loud and everybody heard her. 'Nettie can cover for me,' she stated. 'Ulka maybe has a lead and Baghir's good on the internet. He'll find Harry.'

Elle glared at Chloe; it was becoming a habit for Chloe to speak her mind.

'We have to look after our own, Elle,' Chloe responded to Elle's stare. 'I still care.' And with that, she got up.

Elle was getting even more annoyed; was Chloe judging her?

'They were accidents, Chloe, it wasn't my fault. I'm not the monster here...' but Chloe, already at the door, left, slamming it behind her.

Elle shrugged it off; nothing that Chloe did was going to stop her from finding and destroying the villainous man behind all the animal carnage. She looked at Penelope for support and found none.

'I've got a local meeting to go to,' Penelope said and she too got up and left.

Elle had never felt more alone. Without Harry, she had no idea what Beryl, and therefore Iqbal too, were up to. But Elle was nothing if not resourceful.

As it happened, Iqbal had been up to quite a bit; not least taking advantage of the situation. He'd been plotting his pursuit of Neryl for several days and was sure he detected a mellowing. She hadn't even mentioned her beau recently, and he'd just been handed a treasure trove of aphrodisiacs.

When no one was looking, he'd grabbed some musk and acquisitioned a dried tiger penis. After seeing the rest of the cargo safely on the plane, he'd run to the nearest airport toilets. He'd read that it took a few hours to work, so he'd sat in a cubicle trying to chew his way through the dried phallic lump in the hope that when

Neryl fell for his wonderful sexy aroma, he would be able to satisfy her every need. Sadly, the only thing which came up was a great deal of vomit and so ill was he that at the exact time Penelope's pistol pointed at the pilot, Iqbal was kneeling with his head over the toilet hole.

Once he had sufficiently recovered to emerge, not only had the plane flown but Sunil and the car had also disappeared. He saw an ambulance drive off and ran after it for a little, waving his arms but it didn't stop. Now furious as well as stranded he looked up and down the road. He saw a big truck coming and he jumped out into the road to stop it. Luckily, he had enough rupees on him to entice the driver to take him to Delhi. Unluckily he found out after he had given the man all his money, that it was carrying a load of durian fruit. What was worse, there was no room to sit in the front so he was obliged to sit in the back which did nothing whatsoever for his fragile constitution. The driver's sense of humour didn't help either.

'Why don't flies eat durian?' he asked.

'Because it smells like shit!' Iqbal yelled through the window.

'No no no, that is not the answer. Shall I tell you the answer?' The driver was giggling. 'It is because even flies have their standards.' And he laughed almost all the way to Delhi.

By the time Iqbal arrived back at the hotel, he was actually relieved to find that Neryl had already taken herself off to bed. He was in no state to make love to her. Besides, she had left him a note explaining how complicated his expenses were and that he had possibly been over claiming, which was just enough to put even more wind up him. So Iqbal went into the bathroom and ran himself a hot bath pouring in the contents of every little plastic bottle he could find. His bloated stomach soon eased and enhanced the number of bubbles, if not quite the aroma. When he

emerged he had, at last, got rid of the smell of vomit, tiger secretions and that bloody awful stinking fruit. His better mood did not last long; he found an encrypted message on his phone which told him that the consignment had been delayed at the airport by officials.

'All that effort...' he sighed as he got into bed, 'for nothing. Please be a little more friendly tomorrow, Miss Neryl.'

Never mind friendly, Beryl had been extremely busy extracting even more supplier information for Harry to investigate. Back in Chicago, Harry had been sifting through copious lists of obscure payments made in local currency all around the world, almost all with no details of what the payments were for. There was one, however, which really stuck out; a reimbursement of the cost of car hire to a certain Hari Vlostok in Rostov. There surely can't be two, she thought. It's such an unusual name in Russia. Then she cross-checked his name against the database and found even more surprisingly, there was a Hari on the temporary payroll too. Tentatively she called up his data record, and there, staring out at her was a blanked-out silhouette of a head.

'Damn!' She called Beryl. 'Do you know anything about this Hari person?'

'Yes,' Beryl replied. He's the driver in Rostov. Iqbal's just sent him off to pick up a consignment coming in from Lagos.'

'Why didn't you tell me this before?' wailed Harry. Beryl, who was relaxing in a hot tub with manufactured, as opposed to manmade, bubbles, sent her eyeballs skyward and put on her most irritated voice.

'Do you ever actually check anything so old-fashioned as your emails, Harry?' and with that, she curtly cut off the connection.

Harry scrolled through her emails and there it was; the day before in fact.

'Check out Lagos consignment through Azerbaijan. Could be missed trailer. Driver called Hari; no pic.'

'I've got to find out,' Harry said to herself and in that instant, she decided that she was going to go to Rostov to find him. With a prolonged search for her passport and rushed announcement to her mother, Harry hared off to O'Hare airport from where she rang Chloe, who coincidentally had just arrived at Heathrow.

'I'm off to Baku to meet up with Ulka,' Chloe told her.

'OK, that's great. I'm going to Rostov. There's a consignment coming through the border from Azerbaijan. If you cover that end, I'll pick it up this end and maybe we can meet at the border?'

'Sounds good to me,' Chloe agreed, then added, 'Have you told Elle you're going out there? She's almost worried about you.'

'Not yet,' Harry replied. 'I may go off radar for a bit. I'm gonna meet up with Beryl first then check out some more info.' But what she really meant was, she was desperate to see if it was her Hari working for Iqbal. She had never forgotten him and was worried that he was mixed up in the smuggling, he might be in danger and she cared too much for him to let that happen.

Back in London, Elle wasn't so much worrying about people as feeling lonely and very sorry for herself. With Mel and Pat now gone for good, Chloe in Azerbaijan and Penelope in a deep sulk, there was no one to order around apart from Nettie, who was far too vicious to be good company. She was very frustrated at having to stay behind whilst everyone was out doing things and worst of all, she was now having to put up with Bessie. She poured herself yet another gin and sulked a little more. Then something of her spirit returned and she renewed her vows. 'I know what I must do now,' she said, 'I must confront Bessie.' But by morning she'd almost forgotten it.

Bessie Wainwright was now completely removed from the

broken down smelly disgusting wreck of a woman Chloe had discovered sleeping rough. Elle had been amazed at what the provision of a clean bed, washing facilities, good food and proper gin can do to a person. Like a phoenix from the flames, Bessie was banking on a triumphant return to the world of hotels. Elle's business was a tiny distraction to Bessie, a mere trifle. She was already well on her way to her target of doubling Elle's business and was beginning to reset her sights on the capturing of the entire Wallows hotel group. Nothing less would do. Also, she had a decent business associate in Beryl, who much as they disliked each other, she recognised as a very smart lady. Equally usefully, she now had a devoted friend, or should it be lapdog? Steven Holmes was proving himself to be invaluable and she had just taken him on as her personal assistant.

Steven's life had changed when he received his inheritance from his aunt. He had chucked in his miserable little office job in admin and it was probably because he'd played too much Monopoly with her, that he thought money was the key to everything. The business course he took was meant to set him up as a new entrepreneur, however his growing obsession with Bessie's Bestissimos was not helping.

The Bestissimo chain did not follow normal market rules, his tutor had explained. *A business which ends due to a terrorist attack is a very bad choice of subject matter.* But Steven was resolute and produced an essay which ignored the business aspects altogether and instead concentrated on his theories about sinister people sabotaging the hotels, and surprisingly, he wasn't too far from the truth.

'Steven, think carefully,' his now weary tutor had opined as he handed back the FAILED paper. 'Are you sure you wouldn't be happier in investigative work?'

'No,' Steven replied firmly. 'I've never heard of a fabulously rich policeman.'

Had Steven been a little more engaging, his tutor might have tried harder, but Steven was obsessed with all things Bessie and was exceedingly boring. When he re-sat the paper, he produced a long and tedious tribute to Bessie Wainwright, citing malicious creditors and complainants as being responsible for the demise of her business. It was meticulously presented with immaculately produced footnotes, external references and even article extracts; but it still failed and that meant he was off the course.

'I'm sorry, Steven,' began the tutor as sincerely as he could manage, while inwardly sipping champagne and dancing naked in the college hall. 'I'm not at all sure you're cut out for this. Have you ever considered a career in office administration?'

Steven had held himself together just long enough to leave the building, but as an act of outrageous defiance, he tore up the offending essay and put it safely in the rubbish bin outside the college. On his way home, he'd contemplated becoming a sleuth like his aunt. He even got as far as revisiting the site of the London Wallows hotel but when he thought he saw Bessie herself, he had second thoughts. She had looked incredibly smelly and bad tempered and he needed to be absolutely sure and anyway, there was no way he was going into that alley after dark.

Now, however, his dream had come true and when he'd met the newly renovated object of his worship, he was star struck. Bessie, in return, was delighted to have someone who adored her, there's always a first time for everything, she mused, so they became inseparable.

'You're like the companion dog I never had,' she told him, and he very nearly wagged his tail.

Because Steven did genuinely have some skills in administration, especially computer banking skills, he had become very useful to her as she began to start plotting her return to

business.

'Good morning,' Elle was welcomed into her own office by Bessie.

Elle had been so distracted of late, she hadn't seen that the inch she had given Bessie was now at least a mile and a half. Yes, she had agreed rather too quickly when Bessie asked if they could share her office but room enough for two did not stretch to three and Elle was stunned to see Steven too now installed.

'I don't remember...' she began, unable to stop her face falling into a profound glare that Bessie took absolutely no notice of.

'It was essential, my dear.' Bessie was both condescending and patronising. 'I do hope you've seen the latest results?' Elle shook her head and nodded at the same time. Business, rather like The Bestissimo hotels, was booming and suddenly she felt useless again. Any ideas she had about confronting the woman-who-had-become-a-mountain had disappeared.

'I'm going to be working only from home from now on,' she announced as if it had been her decision. 'I must concentrate on my main activities.'

'Very good, dear,' Bessie nodded, and at that moment, no one would have realised which one was the boss.

After she had gone, Bessie turned to Steven. 'Have you finalised the authorised facsimile signature list yet?' she asked.

'Yes, and I've set up all the banking authorities just as you requested,' Steven replied. Bessie began to smile. She wasn't stealing, she fully intended to pay back every penny, it was just that, well, she needed to speculate a little to accumulate a lot. And it was all going rather well.

Elle, apart from those very early days of being dumped, had never had such a crisis of confidence before; it had all begun when Smoky Joe had first grabbed her by the throat. Now she sat in her apartment sad, lonely and rather drunk yet again. Yes, they were busier than they'd ever been on all fronts, but her bank balance was rapidly falling and she couldn't understand it. How could she fund her international activities without the money? She couldn't put her finger on it, but she comforted herself, at least she had Bessie's business brain on side. So miserable was she that she very nearly wished she could be sharing the evening with Pat until she remembered the cribbage and the mounting supermarket bills for gin. Then, in a rare moment of sentimentality, she looked around for Pat's photo. 'Damn,' she said out loud, realising she had left it at the office.

Elle rummaged around in some drawers to see if she could find any other photos of Pat but all she found were photos of herself as a young woman. She stared at them one by one. Where had the beautiful baby-faced blonde gone? She caught her reflection in the television screen. Where had this hard-faced harridan come from?

Then her eyes fell upon Pat's tiger album, the one that had inspired her all those years ago. As she leafed through it, her resolution began to grow again. What would Pat do? She wouldn't wallow, she'd bloody well get up and fight. And as Elle remembered Pat, she also remembered her cousin and that she still hadn't even told him what had happened. She rang him straight away.

'Gee cuz. I wondered what happened to the old bat. Who's doing the arrangements?' Rob asked. 'She was your mother,' Elle retorted.

'Aww heck,' Rob conceded. 'I guess. Where is she?'

'I don't know. A hospital in India somewhere. Delhi way.'

'Thanks for nothing, cuz.'

'Just one more thing,' Elle remembered.

'You're going to help?' Rob was hopeful.

'No.' Elle was blunt. She had remembered her aunt's stirring words. 'Do you still have explosives?'

'Now you're talking,' he enthused. 'Enough to blow an

underground laboratory carved into the rock,' he continued with incredible prescience. 'Do you need any?'

'Probably. Good luck with finding Pat.'

Elle hung up and raised her empty glass to the ceiling in a toast to her aunt. 'I'm sorry Pat. I nearly lost my backbone again, but by God, I've got it back now.'

She rang Harry straight away, but once again there was no reply. Now she was getting angry. This was outrageous, she thought. What is a retainer for if not one hundred per cent attention?

Harry, of course, was un-contactable on the plane. She'd only ever flown once before when they'd emigrated and never on her own, but the further away from home she got, the more excited she became. Nowadays all her devices were portable so she wasn't tied to a desk, a house or even a country any more; she could rig up almost anything she needed wherever she was.

Once she had landed and was through the airport, with great confidence she found a taxi, which luckily took dollars, and she checked in to the Rostov Wallows hotel. There she made straight for the bar where she had arranged to meet Beryl.

'You really are a man,' Beryl was surprised. 'I thought...'

'I'm a woman,' Harry snapped. 'I just don't choose to look like a hooker.'

'Well!' declared Beryl.

Once the lines had been drawn, the serious discussions got underway and there was a great deal to talk about.

'Iqbal's just gone out somewhere,' Beryl told her. 'We haven't got long. He met up with that Hari chap earlier, gave him instructions to go pick up the consignment.'

'What was he like?' Harry asked. 'He was a complete idiot of a man,' Beryl replied.

'I meant, what did he look like.' Harry held up her tablet. 'Did he look like this?' she pointed at her screen saver.

'No idea,' Beryl peered at the image. 'I only saw the back of his head. Why? Who is that?'

'A friend of mine,' Harry replied as casually as she could with her mind racing.

She was piecing all the information together. Could she really have been friends with someone who was mixed up with Iqbal? He was surely too depressed to work but then again, he had mentioned he was a driver.

Beryl handed Harry all the paperwork she had copied. 'And don't forget to check your emails in future,' was her parting shot.

When Beryl had pranced off, Harry went to find her room and tried to concentrate on the business at hand. But as she remembered her on-line encounters with Hari, she also thought of the Chinese man and how he had appeared on her screen. She'd traced through her history files and discovered it was when she'd seen a Wallows data trail emanating somewhere from the Gansu region of China and leading to Delilah's Doo Dahs that he had actually appeared. Could this be Elle's link? What was very clear to her was that if she had seen him, he had almost certainly seen her.

Then there was the old stuff. Beryl's cutting remark about old technology emails had reminded Harry of the references she had found about David Swallow and how Elle had reacted to hearing his name.

'Swallow. Wallows. I wonder,' she speculated. 'It's a shot in the dark.'

After a brief moment of contemplation, mainly to work out a

convincing story, Harry rang Elle.

'Where the hell have you been, Harry?' shouted Elle, now sobering up and in full on temper. 'You've never been AWOL before.'

Harry didn't have time to waste on this. 'Elle, be honest with me. Tell me the last thing you know about David Swallow.'

'Why is this important?' Elle demanded.

'It just *is*,' Harry replied with such vehemence, Elle was taken aback.

'He ran off with a stripper in the Rockies. We were...' she could hardly bear to say it so she didn't. 'Friends. Ages ago. Then I heard he was killed.'

'It's like Steven said,' Harry continued. 'There's definitely a connection there and I've found a link to China now, from Delilah's Doo Dahs. Someone should go there.'

Elle thought for a minute. 'Are you telling me what to do Harry?'

'I think you should go,' Harry began slowly. 'You're the business head. Go and meet Delilah; the woman who runs the thong thing. I can't be sure but I think it could be very important.' Harry let that sink in while she rehearsed her rationale. 'And I'm difficult to track down for a reason. I've been rumbled. Don't call me again, I'll call you when it's safe.'

Harry ended the call, leaving Elle a little bemused and greatly put out. In fact, with the mention of David, she was dipping again.

What happened to you, David? You wouldn't recognise me now, she mused but only very briefly before that photograph flashed in front of her mind's eye.

'You bastard,' she spat with venom and went online to book plane tickets.

If David couldn't recognise Elle, there was no hope of her

recognising him. He had been talking to Jimmy and had smiled so evilly at him, only an idiot like Jimmy would not have seen it. The rest of his features were looking pretty damned evil too; some actual baldness was now catching up with his scalp damage, and his wild blond locks were turning white. All it needed was thick glasses and a white coat and he was as bad and mad a scientist who ever walked the screens of Hollywood.

David had smiled because he had finally found something that Jimmy was good at; he was a whizz on the internet. So impressed was he that he had given Jimmy a task that even an idiot couldn't get wrong. He had asked him to find and obliterate every single mention of David Swallow and Sovan Wildwald from the internet. Nobody, he thought can get deletion wrong and if he takes off too much, or the wrong stuff, what do I care?

Jimmy was perfectly adept at deletion; his weakness was his curious ability to accidentally turn on his webcam at inappropriate moments. It was precisely on one of those occasions that Jimmy had found himself momentarily staring into the eyes of a strange young American man. Panicking, he closed down the contact instantly then carried on making sure everything was now gone. He composed himself before speaking to his boss.

'It's all done sir,' he told David. 'Those rascally spammers will never find you again. No one else will either now.' Jimmy smiled back in his innocent admiration and reminded David that his visitor, Professor Wong, had arrived for his weekly meeting and was waiting for him in reception.

'Send him in,' David ordered, and Jimmy disappeared to reappear a few moments later with Wong. They all shook hands and bowed and shook hands again, then Jimmy left and they bowed and... 'Enough,' shouted David.

'So, how you getting on, Dr Swallow?' Wong asked.

'Cryogenic storage facilities operational,' David replied. 'Mitosis level 95%.'

'Excellent,' replied Wong, his eyebrows rising. 'When you start species testing?'

'Not until we reach 100%,' David replied. 'When we have attained perfection. Nothing less will do. Soon. I would expect a week, ten days at most.'

'Ah! We will implement full security measures now. Keep me in touch, Dr Swallow.'

David bowed just the once and escorted his guest out of the laboratory. Then he went to visit his real pride and joy; his secret lab. A hidden tunnel ran from behind his desk leading into the other place and David delighted in the skilfulness of it. The workmen had done a fantastic job under the circumstances, in fact, a couple of them were still there preserved in the concrete. David had been forced to chop out an extending hand, then make good with Polyfilla which sort of spoilt the patina of the concrete but improved the overall visuals dramatically.

The lab itself was carved wholly out of rock in an unconscious tribute to various James Bond villains. He'd watched the films over and over again in hospital and the wonderful rock formations in the Gansu had been impossible to resist. The *pièce de resistance*, the last thing the very last workman had completed, was the secret exit, so secret it had not even been broken right through and only the tiniest thickness of rock remained. A large hammer had been left for when the time came.

David gazed at the giant refrigerator and caressed it gently before looking around one more time, then returning to the main building. Already there were signs of the new security systems. Armed guards were at the entrance and posted all along the road to the lab; the only road that went into the mountains. David nodded to himself. *I am truly a genius*, he declared.

CHAPTER SEVENTEEN

Time Changes Everyone

Elle and David weren't alone in changing beyond all recognition. Delilah too was also looking at herself in the mirror with critical eyes. The blonde temptress's roots had grown out grey and straight. Her figure, instead of the ins and outs, now just had outs and even the saucy sparkle in her eye seemed to have been extinguished.

David hadn't come back from China for years, and now he rarely returned her calls or emails. Delilah's biological clock had ticked its last few tocks and had there been any eggs in her basket, there was nobody interested in paying her that sort of attention. Even Billy Bob had moved on.

Delilah sighed to herself as she went back to her office, realising that this was the beginning, the middle and the end of her life now. She still had some enthusiasm for the products despite the fact she could no longer wear them, but her sense of style endured and kept her interested. Most of the production took place abroad or was heavily automated so she rarely saw other people. The only time she ever had much human contact was from potential buyers. It was business but at least she had someone to talk to for a little while. It was hardly surprising that, when she received an email from a certain Angela Gold, she was seriously looking forward to meeting her.

Elle had finally found her mojo. It was about time, she decided, to get out there herself and see what was what. She'd written to Delilah as a prospective buyer for a new international chain of luxury clothes, which would be so exclusive that almost no one would ever have heard of them, other than the super-rich. Delilah knew that David relished these specialist requests and wondered if it was successful, would he maybe come and see her again? There was no doubt that she could supply whatever was required so she accepted the request for a meeting by return.

'I'll pick you up at the airport,' she wrote. 'Then we can go for a nice lunch in town before I show you the factory an' all.'

When Elle's plane landed, she picked up a taxi firm card, just in case, and almost walked past the woman holding up the sign saying 'Angela Gold.' When she stopped, Delilah was surprised to see this thin miserable looking woman. *If she's Gold, it was surely plated and all rubbed off*, she thought to herself.

'Are you OK, honey?' she asked. 'I'm Delilah. My wagon's parked just here. Let's have lunch. You look like you need it.'

It had been so long since Elle had met people outside her own circle, she was completely perplexed by both Delilah's reaction to her and her suggestion. I must look worse than even I think, she thought. But she really was hungry, so she duly followed Delilah to her car. She wasn't so impressed when she got to the restaurant. It was decorated throughout with stuffed bears dressed as waiters and mounted bear heads wearing bow ties.

'I'm a vegan,' she announced.

'Oh my!' Delilah exclaimed. 'You mean like Spock? I thought that was make believe!'

'No,' Elle smiled patiently. 'It means I don't eat meat. Or animal products.'

'Aw shucks,' Delilah looked despondent. 'I don't think anyone here doesn't eat meat. Heck, we'll just have to have a liquid lunch.'

Delilah led Elle to a table and they sat down, Elle grimacing

at the decor.

'Are you scared of bears, honey?' Delilah asked. 'They can't hurt you now.' Before Elle had a chance to answer, the waiter came over.

'Two bourbons on the rocks please and do you do Vulcan food at all?'

The waiter shook his head. 'We do pizza. I can tell them to take the steak chunks off if you like.'

'Can you take the cheese off too?' Elle suggested.

'Well it's kinda gooey but we'll try.'

'Thank you. I'm not sure about the bourbon though...'

'Hell, you have to drink the local stuff here,' Delilah insisted. 'You'll love it I know. The usual for me, Clint.'

Elle wasn't so sure, but then she remembered she hadn't liked gin much until... She snapped herself back into action and began the business discussion.

'I've come all this way because we have some very exclusive customers who want to buy your thongs.' Delilah saw straight through it and was not one to hold back.

'No you haven't, sugar. I know your game.' Elle stiffened apprehensively. 'You're just a lonely old buyer doing a crap job because you have to,' Delilah finished. Elle looked up, perplexed. 'And I'm still churning out stuff I can't even get round my ankle now because I don't know anything else.'

Their drinks arrived and Delilah knocked hers back in one. She looked at Elle challengingly. Elle stared at her glass then picked it up and did the same. The combination of fire and ice was exquisite. She smiled. In one swig she had become strangely mellow.

'You're right. So right you don't even know how right.'

Delilah shook her head; it was her turn to be perplexed, but before long they were eating their meal and chatting like old friends. When they had finished, Delilah asked 'Angela? How's

about you come back to mine instead of a lonely old hotel. Then we can wallow in each other's misery for a change.'

How could Elle resist? 'That sounds like a great idea,' she agreed, and a few minutes later they were parked outside Delilah's lodge and going in.

'This is, er interesting,' Elle opined, her mood somewhat relaxed by the bourbon as she took in the vast array of fur things all around Delilah's living room. She sat on the soft buckskin sofa and nearly bounced on it; it was so comfortable, but she steeled herself. This is the enemy she reminded herself. Plastic is just as good.

Delilah bought out a bottle of bourbon and glasses and they chatted at a rate of knots, or at least Delilah did. She was getting a little tiddly and was spilling out her life story.

Elle was beginning to get a little bored until Delilah brought out her photo album.

Then it got extremely boring until Delilah turned up a certain photo.

'And this is my poor darling departed daddy...' Elle sprang to life as she stared at the picture of a man standing by a lion's carcass.

'You said departed...'

'Yes,' Delilah said sadly.

'What happened?'

'He was killed by a bear.'

'Well, that's just perfect...' Elle exclaimed joyously having enough nous to add 'ly terrible.' She hadn't changed her tone, but Delilah was too woozy to notice.

'It was, honey. Same thing nearly happened to my man. I don't have any recent ones,' she said flicking through the album, 'But he wasn't always a weirdo. He used to be so handsome and fine. Why he was the best-looking man I ever slept with. Do you wanna see, honey?'

Elle nodded slowly, suddenly very apprehensive. She had caught sight of some of Delilah's early photos and was beginning to think she recognised her but couldn't remember where from. She tried to put it down to the research Harry had done on Delilah's Do Dahs but her stomach was beginning to churn and not just with scraps of melted cheese.

Now she was catching glances of older photos of Delilah when she was very blonde and glamorous. Before you could say, 'Shit. That's my guy!' Delilah had whipped out an old photo of her and David. But not just any old photo, it was *that* one; the one that was in the newspapers.

Elle couldn't hide her shocked reaction but luckily for her Delilah misread it.

'You remember him, don't ya?' she slurred as she finished another slug. 'He was on the TV.'

Now, and against orders, Elle's insides were doing all sorts of somersaults.

'I thought he...' she began.

'Died?' Delilah finished. 'No. That's just what they thought. He just wanted to get back into his animal research after the accident.'

'But where is he now?' asked Elle, incredulous. Delilah visibly sank into a deep drunken depression. She tipped the last of the bottle down her throat.

'He's in China. Trying to save the panda,' she said, before passing out on her rug.

China? Trying to save the panda?' Elle wondered. This did not make any sense to her at all, or did it? She hadn't quite recovered from the shock of seeing David's face again but she did know she had to get out of there. She wrote a very nice note thanking Delilah for her hospitality and that she'd be in touch, then she rang for a taxi and headed back to the airport. Once again she tried to reach

Harry, but this time the line was busy.

At another airport many miles away, Chloe had arrived to be greeted by a smiling Ulka.

'It is so lovely to see you, Chichek. You look well but very sad. Have you not heard from your strange boy girlfriend Harry then?'

Chloe smiled. 'Yes, I just have. She is heading to Rostov. Apparently, there is an illegal consignment of ivory and rhino tusks coming through here. It's going to be smuggled over the border to Russia. How is Baghir? Where is he? I'd love to see him again.'

'So it is not the leopards then?' Ulka was surprised. 'That is extraordinary,' she stopped, deep in thought for a moment. 'Baghir too is in Rostov. He is no longer the revolutionary student. Now he is the successful young man about town who is far too busy to ever talk to his mamma. But he might talk to you; he was very fond of you. He is now an importer of local produce from here to Russia.'

At first, Chloe had glowed inwardly at the thought that Baghir was fond of her, but then she worried about what he might be importing.

'You don't think...?' Chloe hesitated. She was sure her Baghir was not like that.

'My son is a good man, Chloe. You know that well. And he would never risk the wrath of his mother even when he sees her so little,' she smiled. 'But he may have an idea who is importing such revolting stuff. Let us go home and we will talk to him.'

As soon as they arrived at Ulka's house, Ulka rang Baghir and explained what was happening.

'Tell Chloe I have missed her,' he said and Chloe beamed when Ulka repeated it. 'I am not surprised,' he continued. 'All of us who trade respectfully and honestly get picked on all the time, but these wretched smugglers, they have the money and they pay the officials and whoosh, they sweep through the borders.'

'Will you help Chloe?' Ulka asked.

'Of course I will help Chloe,' he replied. Any day, any time. I owe her my life. But this will also help me if we stamp out these cheats. What information do you have on this consignment?'

Ulka put Chloe on the phone. She was trembling a little as she spoke.

'Hello Baghir, it's lovely to talk to you again. Are you still in touch with Harry? She may have got all the details now.'

'I have not really needed to use the internet like we did back then,' Baghir told her. 'But it would be good to speak to her again; I will call her now. Goodbye until we speak again.'

Baghir put the phone down and called Harry who answered straight away.

'Hi handsome,' she joked. 'How's it hanging?'

'It is hanging just as it should, young man,' Baghir responded which was just about as much of a joke as he could manage. 'Your friend Chloe is in Baku,' he began. 'But you know that.'

Harry smiled. 'Yes. She wants to help with stopping the consignment. I expect that she will be on one side of the border while you are on the other.'

'That is a good idea,' Baghir agreed. 'And you have the details?'

'Yes, siree,' Harry confirmed. About four-thirty local time.'

'Tell me.' And Harry explained the arrangements that she had discovered from Beryl.

A few minutes later, Baghir rang Ulka back and spoke to Chloe.

'It is settled. The consignment is due to come through the border tomorrow afternoon. I am happy to be on my side of the border, but there is a small complication,' he said.

'What?' asked Chloe.

Harry thinks she may know the driver of the consignment. He might be a friend of hers. She is anxious that we take care with

him as she thinks he is being exploited.'

'Oh no!' exclaimed Chloe, worried that her friend was worried. 'But we can be careful.'

While strategic arrangements were made to disrupt the arrangements that Iqbal had made between Baku and Rostov, Iqbal was on the final stages of his own strategy to ensnare the woman he knew as Neryl. He was tired but also now completely consumed with a mad passionate desire for her which he just had to quench before their trip came to an end. He was too worn out from all the shenanigans of the previous days to play games but he had enough energy to be himself. And when Iqbal wasn't playing games, he could be very charming indeed. You just had to get past his face, but that was pretty easy when he actually smiled.

'Good evening Neryl. May I join you?'

Beryl, as I'm sure you've guessed, had her own agenda and had just reached the point in her research where she was on the cusp of a very different climax from the one that Iqbal was seeking. She had thoroughly investigated his personal affairs and was a few keystrokes away from divesting him of a large proportion of his wealth.

'Yes, Mr Tahan,' she replied gently.

'Have you ordered yet?' he asked

'Not yet,' Beryl simpered.

'Then may I recommend the stroganoff? It is particularly superb here, especially when washed down with a nice French merlot.'

'You know wine?' Beryl was a little surprised.

'What can I say?' Iqbal beamed. 'I was brought up in a Catholic school in India,' he lied.

'How interesting,' Beryl responded, 'You must tell me all about it.'

'May I order?' Iqbal enquired and Beryl nodded.

Their conversation ranged from the trivial to the banal and being lightweight and effortless, it suited them both very well that evening. Beryl could almost see something good in Iqbal; he certainly wasn't the worst man she had ever fleeced. When the meal was finished, she invited him back to her hotel room for coffee. Iqbal understood instantly.

'It would be a pleasure to spend a little more time in your company,' he spouted.

Actually, Beryl called room service and ordered two very large Irish Horlicks. This was one of the most useful tools in her vast repertoire. The unsuspecting man's tongue would invariably loosen with whiskey, then the Horlicks would kick in and sleep would take over before he could become too much of a nuisance. And so it was with Iqbal. Beryl sat on the bed and patted the space next to her. Iqbal didn't need telling twice.

'So tell me about the big boss,' Beryl asked, just relaxing her shoulders enough to make her bosom wobble a little.

'Ah. David. I mean Sovan,' Iqbal replied. 'He's in China now. That is my final destination but he has not yet confirmed if you can come too.'

'And why shouldn't I?' asked Beryl, turning to him and bending forward a little.

'I will have to persuade him.' Iqbal was now talking to the bosom, his head nodding and slowly lowering into it.

'Promise you will,' came a disembodied voice. 'I've always wanted to go to China.'

'It is a promise,' said Iqbal, his head falling straight onto the pillow Beryl had grabbed from behind her back. Letting him doze for an instant, she couldn't quite decide what to do. Could she pull the big one? No. Not yet.

'Naughty boy,' she scolded him. 'I'd better get you back to your own bed.'

As we know, Beryl was surprisingly strong and had no trouble at all manhandling Iqbal back to his room. He didn't even wake until the next morning and cursed himself for being so tired the night before. He was absolutely convinced that had he been able to stay awake, it would have been to sleep in Neryl's bed that night. He was wrong of course, but the thought of it was enough to make him beg David the next morning to let him bring Neryl with him to China. David agreed and Iqbal began to plot his next attempt at seduction.

In Azerbaijan, the teams tracking the consignment had advanced. Ulka and Chloe were making good progress and were getting closer to the border from their side. From the other side, Harry had a satellite fix on the lorry which now put it ten miles behind them. She and Baghir were both due to reach the border at three-thirty local time. The agreed plan was to let Hari get past the border before approaching him. The layout was more conducive on the Russian side, and Ulka's contacts could get her and Chloe through the border on foot far more easily than they could get Harry through the other way by car.

At three-thirty precisely, Harry got out of her taxi and walked over to a car she was certain was Baghir's. He recognised her straight away and they shook hands.

'It is very good to meet you finally,' Baghir was sincere. 'I owe you a great deal from my former life.'

'Shucks, it was nothing,' Harry blushed a little. 'I was a zillion miles away on a computer. You were doing the serious shit.'

Baghir smiled. 'But without you, we might have died. And today you are here where the shit is very serious.'

Harry nodded. 'Exciting isn't it?'

Baghir's smile widened. 'I still miss the adrenaline rush every day.' He nodded.

'Now come; we must get into position.'

Harry listened carefully. 'The driver will come through there,' Baghir pointed to a junction. 'We will have to stop him before he gets any further. I will place my car by that tree,' he pointed again, 'to stop him. Then we will have to reason with him. If he is indeed your friend, then he will be willing to talk.'

Harry nodded. Now wasn't the time to talk about Hari's suicidal tendencies. 'And what will your mother and Chloe be doing? They don't have transport,' she asked.

'They will take charge of the cargo and get it back over the border. My mother is very good at arranging papers; it will just be this consignment going back temporarily for a technical issue.'

'Excellent,' Harry enthused. Then she saw two people coming towards them.

'They're here!'

Harry ran towards Chloe and Ulka. 'Gee Chloe, you don't look a day older,' Harry enthused.

'And you don't look a jot more feminine,' Chloe made a rare joke.

The women hugged and kissed each other, then parted remembering that they had company. While Chloe hugged Baghir, Harry shook hands with Ulka.

'We don't have much time,' Baghir reminded them, and this was true because they turned to see that Hari was already at the border talking to the official.

Hari handed over the bung and smiled to himself, pleased that it had been so easy. He drove on having no idea what was on the other side to meet him. When he reached the junction blocked by Baghir's car, he frowned and stopped, looking around nervously. Harry was watching his every move.

'It's him. I'm sure it is!' she exclaimed, and began to walk towards the lorry.

'Be careful,' Baghir shouted, but she carried on regardless. Chloe grabbed his arm.

'That's my bomber; the one that got away, I'm sure it is,' Baghir watched now on full alert; he too recognised the man.

Hari, seeing Harry, got out of his cab and stood by the lorry, unsure what to do.

'What is the problem?' he asked.

'Hari? Is it you? It's Harry. From Chicago. We used to talk online. Do you remember?' It was only then Harry realised what she'd done. When Hari had seen her on screen, she'd been made up and looking feminine. She looked down realising that to the untrained eye she looked like a man. 'Damn!' she said out loud.

Now all sorts of things were flashing through Hari's mind. Could this man really be the woman he chatted to? It sounded like her. But what sort of trick was it that she now looked like a man. Then he remembered that she had seen his video and he patted himself down to remind himself he was still wired up. In fact, he never left the house without his explosive suit these days.

Baghir, watching intently, saw the patting down gesture and instantly he sprang into action. 'Harry!' he shouted, 'Come back now please.'

Harry turned back to look at him. 'I need to talk to him,' she insisted.

All Harry saw was a sad and troubled man; she did not recognise the panic in Hari's eyes. All Hari saw was a threat; someone who wasn't who they should be, someone trying to trick him.

'Hari! It's me, Harriet!' Harry shouted. The faintest hint of recognition seemed to flash across Hari's face.

'But you are not Harriet. You are a man.' He was stunned and his hand reached to grab the photo of Harriet he always kept in his breast pocket. Baghir saw the movement.

'Harry!' He shouted. 'He's going for his gun!'

He ran towards Harry and threw her out of the way. Hari immediately recognised Baghir as the man who had beaten him up in Azerbaijan.

'So it's you,' Hari looked at Baghir as he approached. They stood face to face. 'I won't fail this time,' Hari said and reached inside his vest as Baghir's eyes reflected the terror and understanding of what was about to happen. In the time it took for him to blink, Hari and the lorry exploded in a massive fireball. Baghir was sucked into it and was consumed in seconds. Harry, still reeling on the ground, couldn't even turn around to look, the heat was so intense. Only Chloe and Ulka saw.

Ulka screamed. 'Baghir!' but it was too late. It was far too late.

As the stench and smoke engulfed the others, all they could do was stand and watch, horrified, until the border officials came out from their huts carrying guns and fire extinguishers. Ten minutes seemed like an eternity to all of them and Ulka went into shock unable to speak or move. Chloe, on autopilot, took charge. First, she ran back to speak to Ulka's friends at the border who agreed to call the proper authorities to take charge of what was left of the illegal consignment. Dealing with Baghir's body was another matter but they summoned an ambulance from the Azerbaijan side. Chloe ran back to Ulka.

'Ulka, we must go back home,' she spoke slowly and carefully. 'To your home. There is nothing you can do for him now. Your friends over there will make sure he is sent back to you.'

Harry was beyond shocked, and now wracked with guilt too. How could she have been so stupid to turn up looking like she did? After weeks of speculation, she had finally seen the only man she had ever had feelings for, then watched him die before she had a chance to enjoy her imagined wonderful reunion. As she trudged over to Chloe, she had no idea that Chloe too was mourning a man she had secretly adored for years.

'I have to go with Ulka,' Chloe told her.

'Yes,' Harry agreed. 'I have to go back to Rostov. To see Beryl.'

'Yes,' Chloe said, and the two friends parted silently until Harry shouted back.

'We must tell Elle,' but Chloe didn't answer. Instead, she took Ulka by the arm and walked away.

Harry took Baghir's car and drove back to Rostov but it was a while before she called Elle again and when she did it was brief and to the point. 'Baghir's been killed,' she said; there was no point mentioning Hari.

'But what about the shipment?' Elle asked. 'Did you stop it?'

'Yes,' Harry replied wearily. 'Most of it is destroyed, but what's left is with the authorities now.'

'That's great. We're getting closer. I can't talk now, I have to catch a flight.'

'Where to?' asked Harry.

'Gansu. China,' Elle replied. 'You were right. It's all beginning to come together. Collect yourself, Harry, I'll need you over there. There's no one else now.'

China? Harry mused. *The Chinese man?* and she went back to the hotel room to think about her next move.

And far away in another continent, someone else was about to make a move. A very disturbing move indeed.

CHAPTER EIGHTEEN

You Can't Keep a Good Pat Down

While poor Mel and now Baghir were very definitely dead, in the mortuary of a hospital in rural India, Avinash Mavani, was about to get the shock of his life. The assistant had just pulled the body of an unidentified Caucasian woman from the refrigerator and Avinash was gloved up and ready to begin the post-mortem. He turned round for a second to note the time and in that exact second, the corpse let out an almighty, 'What in the name of all that is British is the meaning of this?' Although to be fair, all poor Avinash heard was a load moan because Pat's vocal cords were still a bit cold. But the moan was enough; Avinash fainted on the spot. He was not out for long, however. He came round to find a mad old Englishwoman dressed in a hospital gown wafting a monogrammed hanky over his face. He took one look at her and passed out again. It was the icy cold water swooshing over his face which really brought him rudely to his senses.

'Are you all right, young man?' croaked the mad woman. 'I need to know where I am. Actually, I need to know who I am too. Can you help me?' Avinash sat up, closed his eyes and counted to ten. It was no good, when he opened his eyes again, she was still there standing over him staring at him.

He sat up. 'My name is Avinash Mavani,' he began. 'I am the mortician at the Pravan Hospital. You,' he paused, being quite a

sensitive soul, 'You madam, are recently deceased and as yet unidentified.'

Pat thought for a moment, then sat down on a chair. 'I always wondered what it would be like,' she mused, 'But never did I think it would be like this. It all looks so ordinary.'

'No, madam. I need to clarify,' Avinash said. 'I do not now think you are actually deceased. But I did think you were. Just until now. Unless I am myself dead, and then heaven knows what hell we are in.'

'Now you are really cheering me up,' Pat grimaced.

'I can still make a cup of tea if you like?' Avinash offered. 'My old kettle is over there.'

'Tea?' Pat pondered. She looked at the clock. It was five to five and something stirred in her. 'Do you have any gin?' she asked.

'Oh no, dear madam, this is a mortuary. I only have a bottle for personal consumption. But it is Indian gin. A nice Englishwoman like you would surely prefer Gordon's.'

Pat pricked up her ears. 'Yes, you're right. I can't drink Indian gin. It does terrible things to my nervous system. Good show. I'm getting my memory back, Avinash. Well done. Keep going.'

After about half an hour, Avinash and Pat were chatting like old friends. Some more of Pat's memory came back.

'I remember drinking from my hip flask,' she began. 'But I always put Gordon's in that. I do remember that Indian gin is particularly good at getting out certain stains, so I always keep some in an empty can of caustic soda.'

'Well it couldn't have been caustic soda,' Avinash speculated. 'Or you would very definitely have been lying here dead and completely unable to talk because your vocal cords would have been burnt out.'

'Maybe someone put it in my flask?' Pat wondered.

Between the two of them, they were pretty sure that Pat had suffered a particularly severe allergic reaction to the gin which had

put her in a trance-like state similar to death. In short, a very rare condition and far too complicated to explain here. However, they still had no idea who she was or how she came to be at the hospital in the first place. Poor Sunil, assuming she was dead, had simply driven off as soon as the ambulance arrived.

'What was I wearing?' asked Pat. 'Was there any ID?'

'I do not know, madam,' Avinash shook his head. 'You were brought in five days ago. All your clothes would probably have been incinerated by now.'

'Too bad,' Pat thought for a moment. 'What will you do with me then? Kill me to keep the records straight?'

'Oh my very goodness, dear lady, no,' gushed Avinash, until he saw the glint in her eye. 'I will have to speak to the hospital administrator. He will know what to do.'

Actually, the poor man didn't have a clue what to do; it was, in the end, Pat's suggestion which they took up. The very next day an article with the intriguing headline: 'Unidentified dead Englishwoman no longer dead after all,' was published right across the Indian Press although it is fair to say she didn't get anywhere near a front page in any of them.

Someone who did see the article, but to whom it meant nothing at all, was Jimmy. Reading papers was almost as close as he ever got to real life these days and he was getting very fed up. David had not talked to him for days, the main reason being that he was almost paralysed by fear. The last results were at 99.9% but it had to be 100%. Even David didn't dare risk what might happen to the entire ecological system of the planet if he got this wrong.

Yes; it was that important. He had locked himself away from everyone.

Jimmy, however, was a very sociable sort of chap and was beginning to regret taking on this job. He liked company; he didn't

care much if it was tangible or virtual so long as it was some sort of communication and he wasn't getting any nowadays. Dismissed by the scientists as irrelevant, he was very lonely. Even when he made the trip to the Wallows hotel, it was always full of children, never adults.

Today, having read all the papers online for something to do, he was so desperate for company that his thoughts turned to the last human face he had seen; the pretty faced young man who he'd seen on the net. A fellow surfer, he was sure, Jimmy wanted to know more about him. After a lot of very complicated fiddling around, he finally found a link which he thought might work and made an opening remark.

'Hello. I am Jimmy. I saw you wandering around the other day. Are you like me? I did that too. Can we be friends?'

Harry was still in shock, sitting in her hotel room but when Jimmy's message popped up, she just stared at her screen completely unsure what to do. After losing poor Hari she really didn't feel like doing anything at all, but after a while, she recognised Jimmy's face and she began to change her mind. *If he is connected in some way, I might be able to find out who the mastermind is*, she decided. And with heart-thumping bravery, she prepared to take that leap into the unknown. She had to think very carefully about her opening move.

Hi. I'm Harry, she typed. *I was researching endangered animals. Were you? Is that why we crossed links?*

Harry held her breath. It made sense to her; an innocent searching on the internet. She could always shut the connection down. Jimmy, however, was so delighted to get a response, all the pent-up frustration of not being able to talk to anyone came tumbling out.

That is so cool, he wrote back. *I work for someone who is*

looking at ways to save an entire species.

Harry sat back, pleasantly surprised. Had she got it all horribly wrong? Had she picked up on someone also trying to stop the trade instead of the perpetrator?

Who is it? she asked. *Anyone I'd know?*

Jimmy should have pulled back a little, but he was too proud of his boss, and hey, the world would know what he was doing soon. He jumped in with both feet.

I work for Professor David Swallow, he replied, adding the title for good measure. *He used to be a big TV presenter in the old days. He's very modest though and I'm not supposed to tell anyone he's here.*

WOW! this hit Harry like a bolt of lightning. Were they on completely the wrong trail? Was he a good guy after all? She had to try to find out.

I don't believe you, she typed. *Show me a picture.*

Now it was Jimmy's turn to sit back; but not with shock, it was more like indignation that she didn't believe him. I'll show her, he thought, and began rifling through his images. David had always been extremely camera shy, but just once, Jimmy had caught a reflection of him in the window. It was very fuzzy but just good enough to make David out. He loaded it right up.

Here's what he looks like now. He was attacked by a bear.

Harry frowned as she studied the picture. She'd seen this man before, and it took a few seconds before she remembered. Suddenly, it came to her. The man in the photograph with Bessie Wainwright.

I have to go now, she typed abruptly. *Nice talking. Chat again soon?*

I see you are at the Rostov Wallows. I am in China. Near the Gansu Wallows. Can we meet up? Jimmy asked.

Harry didn't reply straight away. It didn't take her long to figure it all out but there was still a missing piece. Yes, she could link David to a fur trade of sorts, but Delilah's Doo Dahs was legitimate; she'd checked and double checked that. Jimmy had said David was saving an animal species. Why then would he be involved in shipping illegal animal parts? Maybe that was nothing to do with him; maybe that was just Iqbal. Did they already have their villain?

I must talk to Beryl, she decided, feeling much happier again. The thought of a genuinely nice man helping animal species was very enticing and she knew that Elle would be thrilled. Maybe they could even work together? Old friends reunited. When she did manage to get through to Beryl, she was too busy to speak for long.

'But he must have mentioned his boss's name?' Harry asked.

'No,' she'd replied. 'He only ever refers to him as the boss. But I did hear him say something like Sovak once? Or something like that.'

'Sovan?' Harry remembered that name from somewhere. Suddenly something began to whirl around her head. 'Thanks, Beryl.'

Harry finished the call and went to look for a piece of paper. Luckily, even Wallows hotels had their own little notepad. Harry could hardly remember how to use a pencil, but she managed to print out SOVAN WILDWALD. That's it!

Harry immediately messaged Elle. She had a question for her and it all hung on an anagram. Harry paced and paced until she finally got a text back from Elle.

Yes, his middle name was Nathanial. Harry whooped with joy, but strangely it wasn't Elle she first spoke to. She called Chloe on the webcam. It was late and Chloe had just arrived back home in England and despite the fact that Bessie had kept her apartment almost as spotless as Chloe would have done, she was in no mood for Harry's enthusiasm.

'Don't you realise what happened? So many people have been killed. Even Elle's disappeared now.'

Harry was momentarily chastened. 'Sorry. But you do want to get the man behind all this, don't you?'

Chloe nodded her agreement. 'Go on then,' and she listened very carefully to Harry's update.

'...and now she's gone to China,' Harry finished. 'I'm going there too. I've found out something important and....' she hesitated, 'I've got a date.'

'That's lovely,' said Chloe but it also saddened her, reminding her of her own love life which never even got off first base. Still, practical as ever, Chloe knuckled down to it and turned her mind to home; Nettie and the other staff at Elle's Belles wouldn't run themselves. And there was Bessie; even Chloe was beginning to regret bringing her in.

'Good luck Harry. I'd better keep a watch on things back here then. Before Bessie takes over completely. I'll go first thing tomorrow.'

The next morning when she got to work, the first person Chloe saw was not Bessie, but a fuming Smoky Joe sitting in the reception area waiting for her.

'Where's Elle?' he yelled. 'Dontya know I gotta get this guy already?'

Chloe translated this in her head and when she understood it, she led him into Elle's office where Bessie was fully ensconced.

'Can we go somewhere else?' she asked him. Smoky Joe nodded. 'Back to mine.'

Chloe was horrified when she got to the casino; in daylight, the sun was still strong enough to pick out walls of dust through the grimy windows.

'It's about time we got you a decent cleaner,' Chloe was not one to take any nonsense from anybody, Smoky Joe included.

'I'll deal with it. But first I gotta deal with the guy that got my

Mel killed.'

'Hasn't there been enough killing?' Chloe asked him straight out.

'Chloe, I like you,' Smoky Joe replied. 'You're straight as a die, but I still like you. But I have to do this, you understand, don't you? For Mel. They don't call me Smoky Joe for nothin'.'

Chloe nodded sadly knowing she would not be able to stop him.

'Why do they call you Smoky Joe?' she asked. Smoky Joe laughed.

'Well, I can't deny I like you, Chloe, since I just told you that and I never go back on my word. But I won't tell you, I'll show you.' And Chloe sat open-mouthed as he did just that. Luckily she had her phone with her and made a little video, just in case, she told herself.

'Where's your cleaning cupboard?' she asked him. 'I think better when I clean.'

Smoky Joe didn't argue and led her to the cupboard where she picked out a few things and began to dust, hoover and polish. It took her a long time, but she needed a long time to think about things. When she had done all that she could, she sat down, mop in hand and thought about the team. Elle was in China, Harry was in Rostov but had talked about going to China, Smoky Joe was now on his way, but what had happened to Penelope? She rang her.

'I'm on my way to China,' Penelope yelled at Chloe. 'Elle's orders. You'd better stay there and watch the shop,' she added. Chloe held on to her mop handle. She had even more things to think about now.

Elle had not only ordered Penelope to come out there, she had also got hold of Rob and put them in touch with each other. 'I have

a feeling we're going to need those explosives.' she'd told him. With Penelope's general experience and Rob's dynamite, she was sure she could pull off something really big if she needed to. Whatever David was up to in China, that was definitely where Iqbal was heading and she needed to be prepared.

The Wallows hotel in Gansu was beginning to look a little like an Agatha Christie backdrop. One by one the characters appeared at reception, but naturally, not all of them knew who the others were.

First to arrive was Iqbal, with Beryl right behind him. Iqbal was still digesting the information he'd received about the African consignment and poor Hari's demise. It helped that David was so obsessed with his research; he had been showing almost no interest in the animal trade these days, other than the money it provided him. Iqbal, however, was cursing his lost cut on the deal. As for BO's demise in Nigeria, Iqbal was completely unmoved. He'd only really been the agent for the sex trafficking side of things, so now this gave him a neat way out of it forever. About Hari though, Iqbal had mixed feelings. He knew Hari was expendable, always fated to blow up one way or another but he was a little sorry. At least he almost got his heart's desire, in the end, Iqbal mused, and if he'd wanted to deliver it to Anna as promised, it was impossible; even if he could have got there, it would have been blasted all over the place.

A glance back soon cleared his mind; he had bigger fish to fry now and there were none bigger than Neryl. That foxy woman had outwitted him enough, he knew she was about to yield.

'Would you like a drink, my dear?' he asked when they had checked in.'

'That would be delightful,' Beryl was impressed with the scenery, if not the hotel.

Elle made her entrance while Iqbal and Beryl were having nice 'get in the mood' cocktails in the lounge. Iqbal knew nothing of Elle and Elle pretended not to see Beryl but did see her wink as she walked past. As Elle checked in, she held up three then two fingers to let Beryl know her room number then glancing round she saw Beryl reply with two V signs, which Elle hoped meant fifty-five. Elle went to sit in a different part of the lounge to wait for Penelope who lumbered in loudly about half an hour later.

Penelope had almost nothing to hide so after making a quick call behind a pillar, went straight to join Elle sitting in the lounge. The two of them then went up to their room and were noticed by Iqbal.

'I wonder which one's the guy?' He whispered to Beryl, who laughed a little too loudly in reply.

When the women were safely out of sight, Beryl turned to Iqbal.

'Now, Iqbal dear, I must go to my room and freshen up,' she looked at him seductively.

'Do you want company?' he asked eagerly.

'Not yet, Iqbal. There are some things a woman has to do in private,' she winked, then left him watching her as she flounced up to the lift bank swaying her butt as she went.

The second she was through the lift door and out of sight, she gave a big sigh of relief. Just one more night to outwit him and then, she smiled to herself, then, if all went well, she would be rid of him and everybody else for that matter. And she would be a great deal richer but until she reached that monumental position, she had to play along with everybody just in case it all went wrong. In order to play along with Elle, her first call was room thirty-two where Elle and Penelope were waiting for her.

'Good afternoon, ladies,' Beryl beamed.

'Well?' replied Elle, impatient as ever.

'They're sending a driver to pick us up in the morning,' Beryl

replied. 'It's some sort of laboratory where the boss guy is. There are lots of guards all along the route but they're put up here in the cheap rooms. Iqbal negotiated a lucrative contract with the Chinese government. I'm guessing they're in the staff quarters but you'll need to check.'

'Good work, Beryl,' Elle looked over to Penelope quizzically.

'No problem,' Penelope confirmed. 'Harry's on her way. She and I will get the guards sorted. We've got the explosives here too, or at least Rob is here already with his climbing gear. Harry's given him a plan of the laboratory.'

Beryl was listening to all this with increasing anxiety. Explosives sounded a tad too dangerous to her. You couldn't control *them* at all.

'Whatever this bastard is doing,' Elle stated, 'we will blast him to hell forever.' This was too much for Beryl.

'My job ends when we get there,' she spoke sternly. 'I'll not get into explosives, thank you very much.'

Elle nodded. She hadn't thought through Beryl's role past this point, but she didn't see how she could be used now.

'Fair enough. You've done very well and given us excellent intel. Thank you, Beryl. I'll be in touch back in London to finalise your payments.'

Beryl didn't actually give a stuff about her paltry payments; if plan A worked, she would be living the rest of her life in luxury, but since Elle had no idea what she was up to, Beryl smiled and nodded, looking as grateful as she could, then left them to it. She popped into her room just long enough to dab some scent behind her ears, then she commandeered a cleaner outside Iqbal's room and went inside to do something dastardly. By the time she got back to him, Iqbal was almost bursting with anticipation and excitement.

'My dear lady, I can wait no longer. I must know you now, carnally, right this minute.' Beryl blushed on cue and allowed him

to lead her to his hotel room while she followed behind coyly.

CHAPTER NINETEEN

The End is Nigh

Somewhere in another hotel room was Smoky Joe. He had been on the same flight as Penelope but had travelled business class so had arrived just before her. For a loud and conspicuous looking man, he could be very discreet when he wanted; it was a skill he'd learned over his very dangerous life when he'd had to deal with everybody from princes to mass murderers. So he'd snuck into reception and checked in without being noticed by anybody. This was something he had to do, to sort out once and for all.

He sat back for a moment and tried to remember all the people he'd killed over the years. All of them had it coming. There were no innocents in there; at least he'd tried to convince himself of that. They'd all deserved it. And now he was doing it personally. Gotta be a first for everything, he'd mused. He'd never taken to Elle; she was a freak as far as he was concerned so he'd had her tailed many a time and knew far more about what was going on than Elle could possibly realise. Harry? Smoky Joe scoffed; she was just a beginner when compared to the people he had on the case. They knew nothing. All Smoky Joe wanted was to get the real mastermind; the guy they called Sovan.

Downstairs in the far corner of the bar, a nervous Jimmy sat expectantly. It was years since he'd last had a proper date with anyone and he couldn't wait to meet the new man in his life, so much so he was two hours early, but anywhere where there were people was good enough for him to wait. Harry sure looked cute on screen, and was clearly as clever a geek as he was; probably cleverer.

Harry clocked Jimmy as she walked past. With flawless makeup, wig and dressed up to the nines, she was the epitome of glamour and Jimmy's was the only head that wasn't turned although if the other men had looked below her bust they might have been suspicious of her sneakers. Harry was almost beginning to like this attention, but she knew she had to get the job done, and that was to distract the guards who were on duty at David's lab the next morning. Beryl had confirmed all she needed to know.

'They're all being put up in the staff quarters,' she'd said. 'Penelope says the more we can take out before tomorrow, the easier it will be.'

It was Beryl who had suggested she dress up. 'That way you can be two birds with one stone. I'll sort out some gear.'

Luckily for Harry's feet, Beryl's killer heels were too small for her but although her clothes were too big, Harry was still a whiz with a needle and cotton. She spotted the guards instantly; it wasn't difficult, they were the ones dressed in khaki, drooling at the bar. She smiled coquettishly at them and called one over with a sideways nod of her head. As he came bounding up to her she whispered in his ear and while he followed her upstairs, she winked at another one and mouthed, 'You're next,' which was a bit pointless as he didn't speak English, but he seemed to get the message anyway.

Upstairs in the corridor, Harry opened the door to her room and hid behind it, beckoning with one finger to the unsuspecting idiot. As soon as he stepped inside, Penelope knocked him out and tied him up. Harry did this five more times and strangely, not one of the guards wondered where each predecessor had disappeared to. Finally, the last one was dispatched and Harry was

free to shower and change, reverting to the real Harry again.

This was the really hard bit, she thought, taking a deep breath as she went downstairs.

She walked tentatively up to Jimmy. 'Jimmy? It's Harry here.'

'Harry?' Jimmy got up and bowed. 'Delighted to meet you at last. Waiter!' he called. 'A bottle of your finest champagne.'

'Gee!' Harry enthused. 'You sure get paid well.'

'Ah no,' clarified Jimmy. 'I get paid well enough, but I never have anyone to spend my money on, so tonight I buy champagne.'

Harry wasn't going to argue and Jimmy hardly needed any encouragement to talk. So full was he of pent-up secrets with nobody to tell them to, he sang like a canary. No, like two canaries. In fact, an aria in an aviary, and Harry listened intently to all of it, with increasing concern. After Jimmy passed out on the sofa, Harry went to find Elle but no clearer in her original dilemma. Should she tell Elle that David was the same man as this Sovan character?

She couldn't make quite make sense of everything Jimmy had said either. It didn't sound that bad, in fact, you could argue it was spectacularly good. But then why all the animal exploitation? And what on earth were the clones for?

For her part, Elle was also confused. Delilah's David was in China, so was this Sovan man. Why the fuck did it matter if David's middle name began with an N? Pat would have known; she did the Times crossword every day, but as far as Elle knew, Pat was long gone.

Harry knocked on Elle's hotel door and was ushered in. Harry whispered what she had found out to a shocked Elle and Penelope. Shocked because they were now as confused as she was. Elle held her hands up for attention.

'So, Iqbal works for Sovan, and Jimmy works for David and they're both here in China but one is trying to save species, the other is killing them all. It doesn't make any kind of sense.'

'Unless they're the same person,' Penelope ventured.

'Remember the photo?'

'Why the endangered animal research then?' finished Elle. 'There must be more to it. We'll just have to go and confront him or them. But who is it? Is it Sovan or David or both?'

Back in Iqbal's room, things were still not quite going to plan. Beryl had added her own special *Je ne sais quoi* to one of the bottles in the minibar, and so far, Iqbal had not touched it. It was getting tiresome avoiding his attention. Finally, taking courage in both hands, she made the next move.

'Have you tried whisky, vodka and pineapple juice?' she asked. Iqbal shook his head. 'It is a powerful aphrodisiac,' Beryl nodded wisely. 'Enough to get a dead man rising.'

'But I don't need it,' Iqbal protested, he was already raring to go.

'But it will be so much better,' Beryl urged, now beginning to worry. 'You naughty, naughty boy.'

Beryl mixed the cocktail she nicknamed Beryl's Peril and pushed the glass towards him. Iqbal shook his head. Then in a rare moment of extreme bravery, Beryl took a very large mouthful and beckoned him over. Now he was willing. He began to kiss her and she skilfully pushed all the liquid into his mouth with her tongue. Fearing he might choke, he swallowed it down hard.

'I see what you mean,' he muttered, and fell face down flat on the bedroom floor.

Within an instant, Iqbal had been frisked and relieved of anything and everything which might have been useful to Beryl. Credit cards, pin numbers, anything she might have missed when she'd cleaned out his bank accounts that morning.

'Now comes the hard part,' she said to herself, as she looked out at the wonderful view through the window with a sheer drop down the side of the mountain.

Over at the laboratory, David's results had finally reached the magical 100%. It was on; now he had to talk to Professor Wong and then he could sneak off to his secret laboratory to finalise things. He wondered how he would react when he handed over fifty perfect panda embryos ready for implanting. He would be ecstatic, and then David could withdraw from his research and begin to carry out his real plan. Genuine panda skin thongs, bikinis, teddy bears. He could barely contain himself; his order book had grown exponentially; who'd have thought that so many millionaires would want something so exclusive? All he needed was the order book which Iqbal had been keeping safe for him; something he'd never dared commit to computer. He trusted Iqbal completely; he had been a true and loyal servant all these years.

Besides, he too would make a fortune on the deal.

That morning, he should have spotted something was up when the line of guards was less than half what it should be, but he was far too fired up to notice mere details like that.

When Beryl's car pulled up outside the lab, there was no one there to either greet or challenge her and to be fair, few people would be brave enough anyway. Beryl had to admire Penelope's skills at managing the guards. She only hung around long enough to make sure that Elle and Penelope were still following behind. Then in perfect Mandarin, she shouted at the driver.

'Gansu airport and make it snappy!' As she relaxed in the back seat, she was just beginning to feel happy. She had very nearly pulled it off. In a few minutes time, she would be a multi-millionairess. Iqbal had been her biggest haul ever. She'd had no idea that his despicable pickings from Sovan's trade could be so amazing. It was when she heard her mobile ping she got really

excited; she had been expecting to receive a text telling her that the funds had been transferred to her account. But her joy soon turned to apprehension when she looked at her phone. It was a text **from Bessie saying,** *Ring me.*

On a day that was to be full of surprises, nobody had expected Delilah. Elle was just about to get in the car with Penelope, who had confirmed that Rob had completed his work and the explosives were all in place, when she appeared.

'And to think I trusted you, you bitch,' Delilah drawled. 'Why are you after my man?' Elle stopped in her tracks; it was as if the scales had begun to fall from her eyes. All those years of suppressed pain and hurt came bubbling up through her body and out of her mouth.

'I loved him first, he was my man!' Elle shouted. Now it was Delilah's turn to stop still. 'He dumped me for you, YOU TROLLOPE!' Elle shouted louder this time. 'We were so good together...' she sniffed, the tears beginning to flow.'

'You mean that ol' bastard cheated on you? I'm going to give him hell.'

'You are?' Elle sniffed and wiped her eyes. 'Then come with me.' Delilah jumped into Elle's cab and they followed Beryl all the way to the laboratory.

Smoky Joe, on the other hand, never did anything in a hurry. His philosophy was always to take his time. He did nothing until he had read the papers from top to bottom. And that morning, he was reading the international news. As usual, he slipped straight to the back page, bottom left corner where there was always something interesting to look at. Today was no exception; there in the Indian section was a tiny photograph of a woman who had been found

alive after all in India. He held the picture up to his eyes. 'Why, I recognise you.'

David paced, waiting for his visitor to arrive. He was expecting Professor Wong at any minute and was already practising his withdrawal speech. As he patted himself on the back, he heard the door open and Jimmy called out, 'Visitor for you, Dr Swallow.' Visitor? David mused. Not Professor Wong? David wasn't expecting that, or was he? He never usually had visitors, especially unexpected ones. A few seconds later, Elle stood in front of him.

'And who are you?' David screeched.

Elle stood and looked at him in amazement. She'd heard the announcement and the name Swallow was just sinking in. He stood staring back; this hunchbacked, balding, painfully thin wreck of a man with wild white hair waving in the breeze of the open window before her very eyes was the most horrible human specimen she had ever seen in her entire life. But there was something about him. Just the faintest whisper of the man to whom she had promised her life, her soul, her future, and everything. She didn't want to believe it at first, but she looked deep into his blue eyes and she recognised him; there was no disguising those eyes. 'David?' she peered at him.

David looked at Elle at first dismissively. Then he stared at the razor-thin, shrew faced wrinkled woman who was Elle. There was something about her. He walked up to her and like an animal recognises the scent of another, something in his olfactory senses started up a chain reaction. Delilah, hiding out of sight could only stand and watch.

'Angel?' he asked. 'Is it really you? What happened. You used to be so beautiful.'

'You can talk, David,' Elle exclaimed. 'What the hell happened to you?'

'I met someone,' David spoke strangely as if he was recounting a dream. 'I'm sorry, Angel.'

Delilah, now furious and unable to stay quiet a second longer stepped forward forgetting how long it had been since David had last seen her.

'Delilah? When did you get so big? Did I really leave her for you?' he looked again at Elle and saw there wasn't much in it.

'You bastard,' Elle and Delilah exclaimed in unison.

Just at that moment Professor Wong arrived, horrified at the lack of security and all the strangers milling around.

'Dr Swallow,' he asked as authoritatively as he could, 'Who are these people?' David had no answer. What could he say?

'These are fellow scientists,' he lied. 'I have hit a tiny problem with the mitosis and I needed to consult. I'm very sorry.'

'Ah,' Professor Wong nodded. It didn't take him long to realise that neither woman looked remotely like a scientist and sensing that there was some sort of love triangle going on he decided discreetly to remove himself.

'Dr Swallow, please call me when you are ready. In the meantime, I will check on the security situation. I cannot imagine what has happened.'

David bowed and Professor Wong retreated.

'Now, where were we?' David asked, adopting a brace position over a table, but he was thrown off yet again, this time by a man. Smoky Joe emerged from the shadows.

'Wildwald? I hold you responsible for the killing of somebody very important to me and I will have my revenge.'

Elle looked around angrily. 'Not now Smoky Joe, please. Delilah and I have to sort out something first.' She paused 'You said Wildwald!' While they exchanged glares, stares, and surprised looks, David took advantage of the situation, slipped into his office

and locked the door. Seconds later when Smoky Joe knocked the door down, he was nowhere to be seen.

But there had been yet another interloper; someone used to undercover operations and getting much better at being quiet, having had years of experience. Nobody, including David, had seen Penelope sneak in, but she had seen everything. She had crept into David's office just before he did and saw where he pressed the button to the secret laboratory.

'He's through here,' she yelled. 'There's another lab back here.' Elle looked at Smoky Joe, then at Delilah and Penelope, then back at Smoky Joe.

'OK, Smoky Joe. You and me need to sort this out. No need for anyone else to get harmed.'

Smoky Joe nodded, 'I gotta agree.'

'Delilah, Penelope? You wait here.' Delilah and Penelope sulked but they did what they were told, at least for now. The big boys and girl needed to hammer it out.

Pouting, Penelope opened the secret door and Smoky Joe and Elle walked into the passage to find David. David wasn't stupid. He guessed that they would find him but he'd needed to prepare. When he heard them coming down the corridor, he was waiting for them and they walked into a big room where David sat at a small table in front of them. Elle couldn't contain herself any longer.

'What happened to you, David? How could you do it? Don't tell me you're just breeding pandas to make thongs? That would be beyond despicable.'

'And you are still a sweet innocent flower, are you?' David sneered. 'How many people have you killed, Elle?' Elle sat back in shock. How the hell... 'As for you, Joe Mansi.'

David continued, 'Methinks you doth protest too much. I know why you're here and it has nothing to do with that poor woman does it?'

'Well, I...' Smoky Joe began, while Elle turned to stare at him.

David caught the look. 'Elle. It seems like I need to introduce you to Mr Mansi. The single biggest importer of tiger skin products in England, and master trafficker of girls from Africa.' Elle's mouth dropped open but David continued.

'And did you find out if she was your niece? Did your poxy duplicitous brother identify the mother before you bumped her off?'

'It wasn't like that,' Smoky Joe started to say to Elle but David cut in.

'You came here to meet your supplier Sovan Wildwald did you not?' Smoky Joe nodded sheepishly. 'And you were going to take over my order book, weren't you?'

'No, I...' Smoky Joe began.

'I should kill you now,' David mused. 'But I think we can do a deal.'

'What about the broad?' Smoky Joe looked at Elle.

'I think that even she will be interested in what I have to say.'

'No way,' Elle protested but she was outnumbered and she knew it.

David was in full and gloriously mad flow. He stood up and was the very best mad scientist in the whole world. Yes, even madder than him.

'You must understand,' he began, 'this is the culmination of years and years of research. I have grown fifty panda embryos already. Perfect specimens which I could, if I wanted, lawfully hand over to the Chinese scientists. Enough to help save the panda population with a promise of more whenever they are needed.'

Smoky Joe looked at Elle in a, *This ain't so bad* kind of way.

'You said you could if you wanted,' Elle snarled. David took a crystal phial from under the table. He smiled one of those mad

sickening sorts of smiles which makes you want to slap the person smiling.

'I have them here,' David held up the phial, cold vapours circling around it. 'They are in here. I can grow them artificially, then I can harvest their skin to make the most exclusive garments in the world. They will feel no pain and they can make me millions. Billions.'

Smoky Joe was impressed and also relieved he was still alive. Elle glowered.

'What were you going to tell the Chinese government?' she asked. 'I know about the clones, David.' David looked at her for a moment; she couldn't read his face. Mind you, there wasn't ever much of it showing. He flung his head back and roared with laughter.

'So you know about the clones, do you? That was the sop for the Chinese. Enough clones to satisfy their needs but genetically engineered to be sterile. Do you think I would be mad enough to repopulate the planet with pandas? Why? Then anybody could have one.' Elle shook her head. 'In a strange way, I need both of you,' David said. He turned first to Smoky Joe.

'I don't like you, Joe Mansi, but you have contacts. I know you wanted to take all the orders, I even know about the fake names you supplied.' He paused while Smoky Joe gulped, 'But if you work legitimately for me, as my, shall I say, dealer? Then you will earn more money for less trouble than you have ever known in your life.' Smoky Joe smiled and sat back in his chair while David turned to Elle.

'Elle, you have been a thorn in my side for too long. From this, I could give you enough money to hire an army to protect your poxy elephants, rhinos and tigers. And to breed other species in captivity. Just think of the kudos you'll get. Elle Scarlett; the heroine of the world, saviour of animal-kind.'

By now, Smoky Joe was positively drooling. 'Are you getting

this?' he dug Elle in the ribs. 'All your shitty animal problems solved,' Smoky Joe slapped the table. 'I'm in.'

Even Elle was now wondering and the more she wondered the more sense it made.

Saviour of animal-kind had such a ring to it. 'OK let's talk.'

So the talking began and the tea lady came round and handed them all a nice cup of tea with a plate of chocolate biscuits and suddenly they all realised how thirsty and hungry they had been. After about half an hour of amicable discussion, David asked the big question; there was now no argument about *whether* it was all *when* and *how much*?

'So we have a deal,' David confirmed, as he wrenched at his collar; it had been getting very hot in the room. Elle scraped her hair back and looked at Smoky Joe who was sweating profusely. They both looked at David.

'It's the air conditioning,' he said lamely. 'I never did get it sorted.'

When the tea lady reappeared and handed out three glasses of chilled water, they were so thirsty, they all drank them down in one. Well, it looked like water. Elle was the first to react.

'I'm feeling a little strange,' Elle said.

'Now you come to mention it,' said Smoky Joe.

'It's the water!' David gasped.

'But it's not the water is it?' a strangely familiar voice spoke. 'In fact, it's not water at all.' The tea lady turned to face them all.

'Chloe!' shrieked Elle and Smoky Joe together. 'What the hell are you doing here?'

Chloe sat down at the table and smiled a little.

'Look at you all. You are all monsters.' The three of them stared right back at her. 'You Elle? You want to help animals, and maybe you still do but you don't care about people anymore. What about poor Mel? She helped you start your business. You would have been nothing without her.' Elle looked back at her blankly.

'You didn't even bother to bring her body back, did you? What about Baghir? You never met him but I loved him.' Elle still looked blank. Chloe continued. 'And worst of all there was your own aunt. The woman who you told me made a woman of you. You couldn't even be bothered to arrange her funeral.'

Smoky Joe's eyes flashed at that but he didn't speak. 'And now he...' Chloe looked towards David, 'Fills your head with thoughts of fame and fortune and suddenly all the wretched things he's done over the years are forgotten and you're going to let him do this terrible thing?'

Chloe turned to Smoky Joe. 'You, Smoky Joe, yes, maybe you cared about Mel, but what about all the other girls you trafficked. How could you look her in the face, Smoky Joe? Did you realise how close she was to finding out about you? Is that why you had her shot? It was never an ambush, was it? It was a handover and you wanted to be rid of that vile BO man so that Mel would never find out the truth.'

David sat unmoved, waiting for his turn. 'And as for you David; you were such a brilliant man you could have done anything you wanted. You could have saved species, protected animals; that was the original plan wasn't it? Were you so swayed by a pretty face and bitterness for the poor creature that ruined your good looks that you chose to use your brain to exploit that species for the uncaring rich?'

None of them could disagree with anything Chloe said; they couldn't even move their heads.

Chloe continued. 'And all I can say is how lucky you had good people working for you. Yes, you found out about Elle, David, but Jimmy found out about you and told Harry. At least there are some decent people left in the world.'

'Penelope,' she called, and Penelope came in looking as miserable as it was possible to look, followed by Delilah.

'You bastard,' Delilah yelled at David. But it wasn't until Chloe

picked up the phial from the desk that David gasped; the last noise he would ever make.

'Take this to Professor Wong,' Chloe instructed Penelope.

'I told him it would be worth his while to wait a bit longer. And take Delilah with you too. I've got some things to sort out here; I'll see you on the other side.' Penelope nodded but couldn't resist a last dig.

'I trusted you to do the right thing, Elle. But you let us down, you let us all down,' and with that, she and Delilah left back through the tunnel, slamming the doors behind them.

'I listened,' Chloe continued. 'I listened to all of you. I wanted to give you a chance to do the right thing. For Elle to give up violence and work peacefully to save animals. For Smoky Joe to stop trafficking and free the girls and for you, David, to help make the planet better. I soon saw you were beyond help David, and I guessed you too Smoky Joe, but for a minute Elle, just for a minute I thought you might hold firm. But you all failed in the end.' Chloe shook her head sadly. 'I'd prepared a potion for you all, just in case. It was a recipe I got from our dear Beryl; I must thank her for that one day. I had to tweak it a little to make sure it was permanent. You drank it about, hmm, five minutes ago. There's just a few minutes left and all you can do is think about what evil people you all are. And the world will be a better place without all of you.'

Elle, Smoky Joe, and David sat in stunned silence. Mainly because they were all now completely paralysed, but even if they hadn't been, they would still have been gobsmacked. Chloe carried on.

'Rob is waiting for my signal before detonating the explosives. The poison will take full effect before they go off.' She looked at Elle who looked back in unseeable terror. 'I'll tell Rob something about you trying to save the phial, Elle. Just so your family can think well of you. And yes, Pat did make it, not that you care. She's alive and well in India and I'm going to go and see her as soon as this

is over. Don't worry, I won't tell her what a despicable evil creature you became.'

She turned to David whose eyes were bursting with unseeable indignation. 'Don't you worry about me being trapped,' she smiled. 'Jimmy sang like a bird to Harry. I know all about your secret tunnel. We opened it early this morning, while Rob was doing the explosives.'

Finally, Chloe turned to Smoky Joe. 'And you, Smoky Joe. I kind of liked you too. I even thought that thing you did was funny. Elle, this is my last present to you; how Smoky Joe got his name.'

The last thing that Elle ever saw in her life was Chloe's film of Smoky Joe, dropping his trousers, inserting a cigar into his anus and blowing smoke rings. Oh how she would have smiled if she could.

'It's time,' Chloe announced, and without so much of a look back, she left the three of them sitting like statues around the table alone together, tormented with their thoughts about their end and how it would feel when it happened. Chloe ran through a small tunnel closed with a thin wall of snow. She kicked it through and walked down the mountain track counting to thirty as she went. She took her mobile and pressed a button, then she began to run as fast as she could.

Behind her there began a rumbling which grew louder and louder. Then the ground started to shake and the noise became deafening. If she'd been able to look behind her, she'd have seen the whole mountainside seem to fall apart just before it exploded into ice, snow, rock, and dust.

Even Beryl heard the explosion as she sat musing in the car on the way to the airport.

Bessie had never been anybody's fool but Beryl was kicking herself that she hadn't sussed her. The difference was that Bessie had Steven, who was especially good with electronic banking. Harry had sent more than enough information about Iqbal's bank accounts for Steven and Bessie to get on to it and what they couldn't find, they had let Beryl have a go. It was Steven who waited for Beryl to make that final transfer then, with the flick of a metaphorical switch, he'd diverted the funds.

So who would finally outwit who? Bessie held the best hand; she was home safe in England with Steven, whereas Beryl was out in heaven knows where, exposed to heaven knows what. Beryl, with a sinking heart, rang Bessie to be told what she had been dreading.

'Beryl dear,' Bessie began. 'It's about Iqbal's bank accounts...'

Bessie hadn't got to where she had been, fallen down and climbed up again by being unappreciative of other people's skills. She recognised Beryl's talents and she also realised that Beryl, back in Blighty, might well find a way to get her own back. So having let the bad news sink in, she then played her ace.

'I could do with a decent financial director,' Bessie ventured. Beryl sighed. She'd guessed it might be too good to be true, and like a true grifter, she also recognised Bessie's superior hand.

'OK, so long as I get 100 days holiday every year and a phone number salary, I'm yours.' Beryl negotiated. After all, she thought to herself, she who signs then tears it up, lives to earn another buck.

And somewhere, half frozen and hanging off a mountain face was an Arab gentleman, thanking whichever God he thought of first, that his nether regions were protected from the bitter cold by a little black book containing the names and addresses of some very rich people if he could ever reach it.

The End

Is it really?
We'll have to see...

EPILOGUE

Professor Wong happily took charge of the panda embryos and went on to help maintain the species. The legitimate bits of David's research were carefully preserved and documented and pandas are now doing well. Of course, other people soon moved in on David's other animal ventures but more organisations are growing all the time to fight these nefarious people so we must be optimistic.

Sunil had not forgotten Pat and was delighted when he too saw her photo in the paper. He got to her about the same time as Chloe and Rob did and all of them listened soberly to Chloe's tale about how Elle had been tripped up at the last minute and had sacrificed her life to the cause. Rob naturally wasn't quite convinced having been the architect of the destruction but he wasn't hanging around now he didn't have a funeral to arrange. Pat still needed a little help and Sunil had nowhere else to go, so he became Pat's carer and handyman in return for board and lodgings and the pair got on famously until she taught him how to play cribbage.

Jimmy and Harry's relationship blossomed until the fateful day that they tried to have sex. Inevitably Jimmy discovered Harry's secret and was traumatised by the experience. None the less, after another bottle of champagne, they decided not to give up on each other and as far as I know, they are still together now.

Ulka, in memory of her son Baghir, devoted the rest of her life to fighting corruption wherever she found it. She kept in close

touch with Chloe and even visited London a few times where Chloe shared some of her most useful anti-terrorist and cleaning tips.

Poor Penelope was so despondent after Elle's demise she gave up almost everything except her animal activities, working as a mechanic on the side to keep the money coming in.

She never quite forgave Chloe for what happened but Chloe had no need of Penelope's skills so the pair simply drifted apart.

Beryl and Bessie, despite never really liking each other, were a business match made in heaven. With Steven's help, they took over all the Wallows hotels and ran an extremely successful hotel chain, naturally rebranded as Bessie's and considerably expanded.

So what about Chloe? Chloe the kind caring cleaner? Absolute power corrupts absolutely. You can't bump off people, even bad ones and come out completely unscathed, but she did try. She looked deep inside herself and cleaned up her own act. She took over Elle's Belles and renamed it Chloe's Cleaners. The escorts were persuaded to either leave or learn how to clean and every single member of staff became legitimate in one way or another.

Once Nettie had achieved UK citizen status, she became Chloe's second in command. Then Chloe set her sights on a whole new mission as she looked towards Westminster and decided it would be the perfect place to benefit from a little cleaning. As for Iqbal, well that is another story altogether.

Jane was obsessed with horror, adventure, and humorous literature from an early age thanks mainly to her grandmother's book collection. By the age of twelve, she was writing funny genre-busting stories about vampires and gangsters while still wanting to be both a vet and an artist.

Flunked A-level exams closed doors. But inspired by men who advised her against accountancy as a career, she took it on and made a success of it. She emerged with the unpronounceable letters FCCA after her name and financial stability. In the blink of an eye, she transformed from boss behind a desk to art student drawing naked men.

An art degree later, she found herself in her dream-cum-nightmare house which needed major building work and landscaping. Finances dictated she return to paid employment and for several years she alternated between interim contracts and managing the land – especially planting hedges and trees. When the trees refused to talk back to her, she discovered Social Media. It wasn't long before she was murdering people online.

Inspired into mass murder for the Create 50 book *Twisted 50 Volume 2*, her story *The Violin Case* was selected for publication. She has since brought out her own volume of little horrors, *The Shockalot Box*.

With *Sinister Sisterhood*, Jane wanted to pull together her passion for writing, her love of animals and the belief that women can be just as capable and as horrible as men. So pleased is she to be an author with Bad Press ink, she hasn't even thought about murdering any of them. Yet. In the meantime she would like to thank them all for putting this book together.

Jane was put off living up mountains when she nearly gave birth at the top of one. She also avoids rivers and canals after badly injuring herself and nearly drowning in the Norfolk Broads. Her offspring having left the nest, she lives with her husband in a nice flat field in East Anglia surrounded by rabbits, deer, squirrels, foxes, badgers, horses and two cats.

BAD PRESS iNK,
publishers of niche, alternative and cult fiction

Visit

www.BADPRESS.iNK

for details of all our books, and sign up to
be notified of future releases and offers

YOUR INDEPENDENT BOOKSHOP NEEDS YOU!

Help us support local independent bookshops, visit:

www.BADPRESS.iNK/bookshops

to find your local bookshop.